Olivia Brophie

and the

Sky Island

Olivia Brophie

and the

Sky Island

BOOK TWO OF THE OLIVIA BROPHIE SERIES

Christopher Tozier

Pineapple Press, Inc.
Sarasota, Florida

Inquiries should be addressed to:
Pineapple Press, Inc.
P.O. Box 3889
Sarasota, Florida 34230

www.pineapplepress.com

Library of Congress Cataloging-in-Publication Data

Tozier, Christopher.
    Olivia Brophie and the Sky Island / by Christopher Tozier.
        pages cm. — (Olivia Brophie series ; book 2)
        Summary: "Olivia has accidentally frozen all of the world's water. Worse, her aunt and uncle have been kidnapped by the nefarious Wardenclyffe thugs. With the help of Doug and Gnat, Olivia must fight the forces of evil to save the entire world" — Provided by publisher.
        ISBN 978-1-56164-680-7 (pbk.)
    [1. Adventure and adventurers—Fiction. 2. Animals—Fiction. 3. Magic—Fiction. 4. Kidnapping—Fiction. 5. Florida—Fiction.] I. Title.
        PZ7.T673Ols 2014
        [Fic]—dc23
                                                    2013039115

First Edition
10 9 8 7 6 5 4 3 2 1

Design by Shé Hicks
Illustrations by Steve Weaver
Printed in the U.S.A.

Contents

To Melissa for never-ending love.
To Buttercup, Cheeto's favorite girl.
To my mother for always believing in me.
To all the children on adventures
with bears of their own.

1

The Cheeto Thief

Chuck Abernathy of Five Corners, Texas, had been playing Garage Door Smash all morning. In fact, he was on the verge of setting the all-time world record: thirty-eight in a row.

There are only three rules for Garage Door Smash. First, you need a driveway that slopes down toward the garage, the steeper the better. You have to make sure the garage door is open and the safety switch is disabled. Second, lie down on a skateboard at the top of the driveway, push the garage door remote button, then launch yourself headlong toward the closing door. Third, you pray.

The trick is to time your descent just right so the heavy door slams shut just as your feet whisk through the crack. Most Garage Door Smashers ride their skateboards feet-first because going head-first is just too scary. But feet-first leaves your head in the most vulnerable position to be smashed by the door. Feet-firsters almost always chicken out at the last second and veer off onto the lawn. In fact, no feet-firster has ever topped seven. Chuck was clearly the best Smasher in the neighborhood, probably the world. He is a head-firster.

Once, several months ago, Chuck had his left leg trapped beneath the garage door. He had to go to the hospital for X-rays (they were negative.) He felt justified in continuing his reign as the champion Smasher because his mother never *explicitly* told him *not* to play it anymore. She had said, "That should teach you a lesson" and "One day, you'll really be sorry." But she never actually said, "No."

Chuck was on the brink of greatness, the world record thirty-eight successful trips. His only regret was that Willy and John weren't there to see it. But that was all right. He would know even if no one else believed him. He hitched up his shorts and tossed the skateboard between his hands until he found the proper balance. He ran one hand through his big shrubby hair. Unlike the other boys, Chuck didn't lie down on the skateboard before pushing the remote. He always waited until the garage door started dropping before launching his whole body into the air and landing on the board already going full speed. The kids who push off are never sure how quickly they can get to full speed. Chuck was consistent. And crazy. That was the secret to his success.

Number Thirty Eight's launch was perfect. He could feel it. The air rushed past his face–slight adjustment for a rock, then flatten out—here it comes! The door opening had narrowed to the thinnest of cracks, barely enough to slip under. Just then, out of the corner of his eye, he saw some-thing large and dark emerge from the woods next to the driveway. He turned his head. Clawed feet? *Is that a bear? Is that a girl? Bear!* Chuck hurtled beneath the closing door, headlong into the lawn mower and a gi-ant mesh sack of soccer balls and orange cones. The garage door slammed shut, plunging him into darkness.

He could hear the girl talking outside. "Hurry. Hurry!"

Chuck leaped to his feet searching frantically for the garage remote. It had flown out of his hands on impact. *There—by the toolbox.* It fumbled in his hands. The door started slowly opening. When the door closes, it seems to slam down with frightening speed. But just try to get it to open quickly. It was excruciating. He lay down on the ground and peeked out the slowly opening crack. Four enormous furry feet took off running toward the woods followed by two worn-out blue sneakers. Chuck shimmied out as soon as the door opened enough. The girl and the bear were gone along with a full bag of Cheetos, two peanut butter sandwiches, a grape soda that he'd only drunk one-third of, and his favorite hooded sweatshirt. He stared at the dark wall of vegetation. He glanced down at the empty lunch plate on the ground and back to the woods. It looked the same as it ever did. Just a bunch of boring plants. But now, it seemed so much more.

Chuck Abernathy forgot all about the Garage Door Smash record.

***

Two hours later, Chuck settled himself onto his bed with a homemade strawberry shake and the game control for his video games. His tongue constantly slid along the newly jagged edge of his front-left incisor. He could hear his mother arguing with the insurance company over emergency dental coverage.

"Porcelain or gold, Sweetie?" she yelled to him from the other room.

"Huh?" He did not have the slightest idea what she was yammering about.

"We would prefer porcelain," she said back into the phone. "Yes. Uh huh. I see. How much do you say? Well, it was an accident. Yes sir. He . . . uh . . . he slipped on the driveway. I suppose his tooth is still out there. Yes, well you know how boys are. Oh, excellent. That is great to hear. Yes, we will. Thank you very much."

Chuck tuned her out but he did hear enough to catch his own mother in a lie. He hadn't slipped on the driveway. Actually, he skateboarded full-speed and headlong into the lawn mower. It was epic. Now, his skateboard was locked up inside the car trunk. Chuck couldn't imagine how he was ever going to play Garage Door Smash again.

What his mother *didn't* know, however, was *that* story was also a lie. The truth was that Chuck ran so fast to get inside after seeing the bear that he slipped and cracked his tooth on the flowerpot by the front door. When he ran inside yelling "Bear! Bear! Bear!" his mother only saw the blood streaming down his chin. She assumed he had finally injured himself by doing stupid things on his skateboard. At that point, she figured Chuck was delusional with pain, and Chuck figured his Mom was oblivious to anything having to do with reality on this planet. She was too dumb to understand it anyway. So he stopped talking about the whole thing.

Besides, he was beginning to wonder if he imagined it. The bear was probably a big Labrador retriever. It could have been Barney again. He loved to dig out underneath the fence in his yard down the street and go sniffing out squirrels around the neighborhood. Chuck had only seen a quick glimpse of the intruders before the garage door closed. Who's to say what happened? All he really knew is somebody stole his lunch and sweatshirt. Geez, it was probably Willy's older brother Drew. He was always stealing things.

Nothing exciting ever happened in Five Corners either, except that one time the president visited to give a speech on cattle subsidies and Mayor Danforth demanded everyone wear red T-shirts with "God Bless the President" written across the front. By the end of the speech, half of the angry crowd had taken their shirts off and thrown them on the ground. That was how Five Corners made the evening news. Three hundred angry, shirtless Texans, one embarrassed mayor, and one shocked president.

All thoughts about dogs and T-shirts erased from Chuck's brain when he looked out the window. He could see the dark, jagged line of trees outlined against the evening sky. There, at the top of a sycamore tree, fireflies were arranging themselves in the branches. More and more fireflies gathered in the sycamore. Chuck sat up. Unlike most fireflies, they didn't flash. Instead, they held their light constant. Slowly, their light started to form familiar shapes until their message was unmistakable. Thousands of fireflies spelled the words "HELP ME" with thick, bright letters. A breeze blew, sending the glowing insects tumbling through the air. One by one, they returned to the sycamore and built the message again.

Chuck jumped out of bed and ran to the window. There, at the very back of the yard between the old rabbit pen and the woods, stood a brown-haired girl wearing worn-out blue sneakers and *his* favorite hooded sweatshirt.

***

Exactly fifteen seconds later, Chuck stood in the backyard facing the woods with his back to the rabbit pen and house.

"Hello? Who's there?" he shouted as he glanced over his shoulder at the house. He could see the bluish flicker of a television casting a glow onto the ground. *Mom and her game shows.* He turned around.

"Hi. I need your help." The girl stood right in front of him. A small stick hung from her tangled hair.

"Who . . . who are you?" he stammered, a little shocked that she just appeared out of thin air.

"Listen, do you have a phone?" Her eyes darted back and forth along the wooded edge.

"Why don'tcha use your own phone?" Chuck answered.

"Because," she sighed, "I don't have a phone." She lifted her arms up to indicate that she really didn't have much of anything.

"Why should I, on account of you chipping my tooth, and that is my sweatshirt you are wearing. Why shouldn't I call the cops right now?"

Just then, his Mom swung open the back screen door and peered out into the yard. Olivia slipped back into the shadows. "Chuckie? You aren't peeing out there again are you?" Mom called out.

"Shut up, Ma. No!"

"Well, it's past your bedtime, Sweetie." She closed the door and walked back to her game show.

Olivia smirked and stepped back onto the lawn.

"What are you laughing at?" Chuck's face turned bright red.

"Listen, bring me a phone and I'll let you touch Hoolie."

"Hoolie?"

"The bear. You know, the one that made you cry and go running into your house and busting your tooth."

Chuck's eyes narrowed. He thought about it for what seemed like an eternity. "All right," he responded. "Meet me right here at eight in the morning. My Mom goes to Pilates at eight and she won't be back for a couple of hours."

"OK. Thank you. My name is Olivia," she said, relieved.

"And don't forget the bear," Chuck demanded.

"Deal."

"Oh, and how did you . . . with the fireflies? . . ." But it was too late. Olivia was gone.

Chuck wandered back toward the house, his mind racing. He was positive that his bag of Cheetos was long gone, but Olivia still had his sweatshirt. He would never be allowed to play Garage Door Smash again. And his chipped tooth was still her fault. But that was all right.

Chuck Abernathy had a plan.

2

The Study Room

Over the last several weeks, Hoolie had taught Olivia how to stand perfectly still, just beyond the edge of plain sight, and by doing so, remain unnoticed by humans. It struck Olivia as odd that she could hide so completely but not actually be completely hidden. "It must be that humans just don't pay much attention," she thought. Olivia shook her head when she thought like that though. It sounded too much like the Bobwhite Witch hissing her hatred for the Dark Eyes through her teeth. But in the end it was true. If you hide too far back in the woods, you are probably overreacting to the situation and more likely to shift your weight and accidentally snap a twig. By hiding half in sight and half out of sight, a balance is achieved, a calmness that cannot be sensed by others. Bears have always known this to be true.

Usually, Olivia used the hiding trick when a car surprised her on a remote road or a local dog caught a faint sniff of something unusual in its yard. But sometimes she used it to sneak up on people. She did it yesterday when she stole Chuck's lunch. And she was doing it now as Chuck's mother opened the front door of their house on her way to Pilates. She calmly watched as Chuck ran out after her, looking around nervously.

"Um . . . are you going anywhere after your class?" she could hear Chuck asking.

"Oh dear, you are going to miss me! I'll come home right after, don't you worry." She consoled him roughing up his hair.

"I love you, Mommy," Chuck's words dripped with syrup. But inside, he was rolling his eyes. He wished she would stay out all day but he really needed to know his mother's schedule for his plan to work.

"I love you too, Sugarcheeks," she said kissing him on his forehead and ducking into her small gray car. A quick snort rang out from the bushes. Chuck and his mother looked toward the woods for a few seconds. "Now go ahead and make yourself a snack. I'll be home before you know it!"

Olivia had all she could do to not burst out laughing. Who did he think he was fooling? As the car pulled out into the road she started to giggle. Chuck glanced over toward the woods. He couldn't see her, but he could certainly hear her. He didn't stop waving at his mom until the car was out of sight.

"All right, do you want my help or not?" he called out.

Olivia stepped out of the woods, disturbingly closer than he had anticipated. "Of course I want your help or I wouldn't be here."

"Well come on then. You only have a couple of hours."

Olivia started walking toward the front door.

"Aren't you forgetting something?" Chuck asked.

"No, I don't think so," she replied.

"Hoopie? You said I could pet him." He was more than a little irritated.

"Hoolie, you mean. I wouldn't be calling a bear by something other than his name if I were you," Olivia warned. "All right then. Hoolie!" she called to him with more of a whisper than a holler. She said his name so quietly that Chuck could barely hear.

"How is he going to hear that?" he sneered. But as soon as he finished his question, the large bear stepped out onto the edge of the lawn. Hoolie wasn't exactly thrilled with the idea of letting a human child touch him. He was no dog. But he had learned to trust Olivia. He knew the sincerity of her heart. The only thing that really mattered to him was Olivia's approval. Besides, he was a legend among bears now. The personal companion of the Guardian! How could he fret about a little inconvenience?

"Well, go on then, Sugarcheeks," Olivia mocked.

"What? I just . . . just walk up to him?" Chuck was more than a little surprised at how large Hoolie was. He could feel the hot breath blowing out his enormous nostrils. His feet pressed into the lawn like heavy barbells.

"Of course. He isn't going to roll over at your feet."

Chuck took a few steps forward. He held out his hand. "Here you go. . . . Don't be afraid. . . . I . . . I won't hurt you," he said slowly.

"I don't think Hoolie is worried about you hurting him," Olivia laughed. "But you are smart to move slowly."

His hand shaking uncontrollably, Chuck reached out and touched Hoolie's shoulder. His thick fur felt like a whisk brush. Hoolie stared directly into Chuck's eyes. "Extreme," he said under his breath. Willy and Drew would *never* believe this. "How many people has he killed?" he asked.

"Kill? Bears are animals of peace, not war." Olivia spoke with such authority and confidence that it startled Chuck.

"P . .p . . peace?"

"Of course. You think because they are big and have sharp claws that they are only interested in violence?" Olivia never gave it a second's thought that bears were anything but peaceful—despite the battle with the mammoth skeletons and the Wardenclyffe thugs. "What you call violence is really just them protecting themselves."

Chuck nodded. "All right. A deal's a deal." He turned back toward the house. When he looked back, Hoolie had already returned to the woods. "Come on in."

Olivia pushed past Chuck with a wild strength and smoothness that was almost feline. She practically flew into the kitchen. Glasses and plates rattled onto the counter as she poured orange juice. After gulping down the glass, she poured some milk. Then Coke. Somehow between all of that drinking, she had made a gigantic ham and turkey sandwich piled high with cheese, lettuce, mustard, and more cheese.

"You didn't say anything about taking food," Chuck protested.

Silently, Olivia's eyes shot over his head like bullets. With a mouthful of sandwich, she pushed past him again carrying a pound of cheese, a bag of iced oatmeal cookies, and a box of strawberry popsicles. She opened the front door, stepped onto the porch and launched the food into the woods.

"What are you doing?" Chuck screeched. But the crashing in the bushes answered him. The food was for Hoolie. After throwing him a giant can of mixed nuts, a full tub of moose track ice cream, and a jar of peanut butter, Olivia started making another sandwich for herself.

"What a pig." Chuck squirmed. Then he looked Olivia in the eye. "And you smell like one too."

Olivia stopped chewing for a second and sniffed her arm. "I need a shower."

"You sure do."

Olivia's eyes scanned the house. Finding the stairs, she was halfway up before Chuck could say anything. This was also not part of his plan.

Olivia yelled down to Chuck, "Bring me some clean clothes and leave them by the door." She locked the bathroom door and let out a gigantic breath. For a moment, at least, she could relax. She walked over to the sink and sank her hands into the clean, flowing water. She washed under her eyes with the water, letting it run down her face and onto her shirt. She looked up and stopped in shock. In the mirror above the sink, she didn't even recognize her reflection. The girl in the mirror was gaunt to the point of skeletal. Her eyes darted quickly, like a bird's. For some reason, her eyes were pale blue, like a chicory bloom. They had changed color somewhere between Florida and Texas. Her face was covered with dirt from five states. The necklace of coral snake beads and a single green beetle shone in the light. Olivia pressed her lips together. This is not what she had expected when she had decided to run away from the Corcoran house. She had expected an adventure to be sure. But this was long and grueling. She took off her backpack and reached into the front pocket. Her fingers felt around until they curled around a chalky, shivering lump.

"Squeak!" Squirt's voice was exhausted and weak. Olivia filled the sink halfway with water and dropped him in. She had run out of water for him awhile ago. Even when she had extra water, she had to be very careful. Her accident with the Pearl back in Junonia had raised the freezing temperature of water. If Squirt's water dropped below sixty-eight degrees, he would be trapped in a block of ice. He might even die. After a few minutes of soaking, Squirt perked up. He slid around the sink like a race car. Olivia threw a cookie and leftover crust from her sandwiches into the water. She didn't know how much food he needed to survive, but she did know that he never turned it down. For such a tiny thing, he was insatiable. Squirt pounced on the food, sloshing the water over the edge of the sink.

Olivia peeled the dirty clothes from her skin. The hot shower felt better than she had hoped. Rivers of mud and grime swirled down the plug hole. Her hair suddenly felt free and light. She never used to really pay attention to her Dad when he stood outside the bathroom yelling instructions, "Soap behind your ears," and "Don't forget your feet." But this shower was different. Dad's old advice was brilliant now. The soap felt beautiful. She couldn't stop rubbing it between her toes and along the top of her back. She washed her face several times before the hot water started to run out. Reluctantly, she put down the thin stub of soap, turned off the shower, and started to dry off.

Slowly cracking the bathroom door, Olivia glanced down the hallway. Sure enough, next to the door sat a pile of clean clothes. She regretted wearing the clothes of a brat, but she had purposely picked him for his height. She was positive his clothes would fit. She slipped into the jeans and a white T-shirt with green sleeves. Clean socks felt so soft against her sore feet. After tying her blue sneakers, she stepped back into the hallway.

Chuck sat in the middle of the hall, cross-legged. He stood up when she came out. "Are you done? You better not have used all the hot water."

"Can I have another shirt or two?"

"No way. That wasn't part of the deal."

"Chuck. Please. I don't have anything."

"No. I said no. Those are already my best skateboarding clothes."

"You can make this easy or you can make this difficult," Olivia threatened. She had heard those words on a TV show.

"No."

Olivia shoved past Chuck. Even though they were the same height, Olivia was far stronger than he was. Weeks of running in the wild had made her lithe and tough. She started opening doors until she found his room.

"Transformers?"

"Shut up."

"Transformer curtains? And bed covers?" Olivia could barely keep herself from bursting out laughing.

"It's my Mom's idea."

"Sure it is."

"It is." Chuck's face reddened with rage.

Olivia threw open the closet doors and shoved several more T-shirts and a pair of jeans into her backpack.

"Hey, that's enough. I thought you wanted a phone anyways. My Mom is going to be home soon and you better be outta here. The phone is in the study room." Chuck's eyes narrowed. He was nervous, but this was finally the start of his plan. He actually didn't care how many shirts she took. He was about to get it all back.

"All right, where is it?"

"Down here," he bounded down the hallway and opened a door. The study room was completely empty except for a small desk and chair. A dark green carpet covered the floor. There were no curtains or pictures on the walls. A single light glowed in the ceiling. Chuck had placed a phone on the desk.

"Here you go. Like I said, make it quick."

Olivia entered the room and sat down at the desk. She grabbed the phone and dialed her dad in Sun Prairie. The obnoxious, out-of-service tone blasted through the earpiece. *When is he going to pay his bill?* She took a slow, deep breath.

Olivia dialed another number.

"Hello?" a familiar voice picked up.

"Doug, is that you?"

"Olivia! Where are you?"

"Keep it down. Is your Mom around?"

"She's in the garage. Where are you?"

"I . . . I'm not sure. I'm in Texas somewhere. How's Gnat?"

"Who knows what he thinks? He's playing video games."

"Of course."

"Do you want to talk to him?"

"In a minute. What's happening?"

"You are all over the news. Not just Orlando news either. National news. Sometimes, they show video of you and Hoolie running from a helicopter in Mississippi."

"I remember that. I thought they were going to catch us."

"Everyone is looking for you. People keep coming here and asking questions."

"What kind of people?"

"Police. Firemen. *60 Minutes.*"

"*60 Minutes?* That TV show?" Olivia remembered her dad liked to watch *60 Minutes* when he made Sunday brats and kraut. She couldn't stand watching it though. It was a real snooze-fest.

"Yeah."

"Did my dad call yet?"

"I don't think so. The cops even said they tried to find him. Everyone in class is talking about you."

"Are the moron twins leaving you alone for once?"

Doug didn't answer.

"They're bothering you again. I can tell. I'll take care of them when I get back."

"Just . . . just don't. Everything's fine."

"It's not fine."

"Everyone is moving south," he was almost shouting trying to change the subject, "to be where the water isn't frozen. They can melt water on the stove up in the north, but it isn't enough. It isn't raining. Almost all of the atmospheric vapor has precipitated out. The crops won't grow. Some towns the army had to take over because people were fighting at the stores." Olivia couldn't believe her ears. "Oh, and I found out what sky island is."

"What? Where is it?" All of this time, she didn't have a clue where they were going. Hoolie always seemed to know where to run, like he had a GPS system inside his brain.

"It's in Arizona."

"Arizona? That's like half a world away." Her hands almost dropped the phone. "There's no way I can go that far. Are you sure there isn't a sky island closer? Like maybe in Texas?"

"That's what the Internet says. It's the name for a mountain isolated from other mountains by the desert. I don't know how you are going to find the right one. There are lots."

Olivia was so intent on the phone that she hadn't noticed the study room door slowly closing behind her. Finally, with a click, the door locked. She was trapped. "I have to go. I'll call you later." Olivia leaped out of the chair and started pulling on the door knob. It wouldn't budge. She scrambled to the window. The locks on the window had been bolted shut.

"Chuck! Chuck, let me out!" she screamed.

"No way!" Chuck yelled triumphantly. "I know who you are!"

"Chuck, you don't know what you are doing. Let me out!" She fought against the unforgiving door.

"There is no escape. Haw yeee, I did it. I really did it," Chuck taunted. He knew there was no escape because the study room was built specifically to keep him from escaping. The locks on the windows were disabled and even if he broke through the glass, it would be a two-story fall to the patio. The door itself only locked from the outside. Every evening, his mother would lock him inside the study room with his homework for one hour. This room is a study prison. Months ago, he had torn up a corner of the carpet and hid a portable video game under there. It gave him something productive to do while the nightly sixty minutes of incarceration ticked by. Thankfully, Mom never actually checked to see if he completed his homework. Regardless, there was no escape from the study room, at least from the inside.

"I know who you are," Chuck taunted again. "Everyone is looking for you. The Bear Girl is what they call you on the news. The police, the FBI, probably even the KGB are looking for you. I'm going to be famous."

"Chuck, you don't understand. Let me out. Please. Before it's too late."

"Never. I'll bet there is a reward for catching the Bear Girl."

"No!"

"How much is the reward? Tell me and I might let you out," Chuck lied.

Olivia's fists wheeled against the door. Slamming and pounding. The house shook. An enormous crash reverberated from downstairs. Olivia squealed, "Let me out now!"

Her cries were drowned out by what sounded like a series of explosions on the first floor. Sofas, tables, lamps flew against the walls. Doors splintered and folded in. Fabric ripped with long, tearing shears. TVs launched like boulders. Glass blew into a billion shards. Even the old upright piano thundered onto the floor.

"Hoolie, no!" Olivia called out. But Hoolie's rage only intensified when he heard her voice. Every piece of furniture was smashed and thrown as the frantic bear searched for her. Finally he saw the stairs and in two smooth leaps, he reached the upper hallway. Chuck's eyes flared open as he stumbled backwards. There was nowhere for him to run. He was at the end of the hallway and the study room was the last door.

"Hoolie, stop it!" Olivia screamed.

Hoolie rumbled down the hallway like a runaway dump truck, bouncing against the walls, knocking the pictures off their nails. Chuck curled up in the corner, whimpering. With a gigantic blast, the study door flew across the room, breaking through the bolted window. He rushed up to Olivia, sniffing her all over and rubbing his large head against her side.

"Hoolie, what have you done?" she scolded. She couldn't be too mad at him for protecting her though. "We have to get out of here." Olivia grabbed her backpack and Squirt from the bathroom and led Hoolie down the hallway and stairs.

"You can get up now, Chuck. Can't say I didn't warn you," she called up to him. All she could hear was a faint, wavering wail.

The first floor was a complete disaster. Every room lay in shambles. Splintered wood crunched underfoot. Carpeting curled up in large piles. A thin smoke of pulverized drywall hung in the air. Olivia stuffed her backpack full with as much food as she could fit, grabbed a six-pack of Coke, and handed Hoolie a bag of bagels. She filled a large Tupperware bowl and Doug's thermos with water. Part of her felt bad for Chuck as she stepped through the jagged opening of what was once the front door. But she knew they had to run as far away from Five Corners, Texas, as possible.

3

Aji el Diablo

Days passed while Olivia and Hoolie snuck through the scattered suburbs of Wheeler County. Once in a while she heard helicopters crisscrossing the sky above them and police cars roaring down the rural roads. But for the most part, it was business as usual. Unless absolutely necessary, they traveled at night and slept during the day. Olivia assumed that Hoolie had never been to Texas, yet he navigated the secret bear highways with the confidence of a local. Sometimes, Olivia walked behind Hoolie. Sometimes she climbed on top of his back and fell asleep. The gentle hydraulic rocking of his large shoulders always made her drowsy.

Resting for the day in a thick stand of mesquite and cottonwood, she thought about all of the places they have travelled through. Lyonia, Florida, seemed a lifetime away. There had been frantic races across bridges that spanned miles of open water. There was the time she first learned how to calmly enter a small grocery store and walk out with enough stolen food to keep them going for another day. There had been countless close calls with capture. There had been a wildfire rushing up behind and chasing them across the countryside.

There were more wildfires than Olivia could ever imagine. She knew it was because of the drought that she caused. She smelled smoke everywhere they went. Several times, they had to cross large patches of charred earth, the black dust kicking up behind them as they ran. The soil had turned to dust. Even the dry air was hard to breathe.

Olivia slid the Pearl out of her backpack. The gentle blue glow rose up underneath the cottonwood leaves. Cicadas began to chirr in unison high in the treetops. In the weeks since leaving Lyonia, she had improved her ability to use the Pearl. Little things were starting to make sense. Once she discovered something, she could replicate those results over and over. She just needed to find the switches that controlled water. She pulled out the Tupperware container with frozen water in it. The temperature was in the low sixties, so the water sat there like a chunk of vinyl. Frozen, but not cold. Her fingers trickled across the Pearl like hungry spiders. The Pearl unlatched and opened in five sections like a sliced orange. Olivia contemplated her next move. Every chance she got, she tried a different combination of switches. If the water stayed frozen, then she immediately changed back the switches to try something new. Eventually, she figured, she would discover the right switch for returning the thirty-two-degree transitional temperature of water. Thin arcs of green electricity spun off the surface of the Pearl, intensifying as she turned a conundrum dial. She had found the dial days ago and it was strangely relaxing to watch the green energy bolts zip in jagged paths into the air.

"Hoolie, should I try the wood switch?"

Hoolie stared at Olivia and chomped his jaws with a loud huff.

"Boy, I wish you could talk sometimes." Olivia furrowed her brow and stared straight into his eyes. "Come on. Talk. I know you can. I know you can understand me. Now, say something."

Hoolie stared back, then dropped his massive head to the ground. He was tired. Very tired. He understood what she was asking. Bears and humans speak the same language. They just do it in different ways. A sensitive observer can communicate very well with a bear. But bears can't actually talk, of course. Hoolie looked up at Olivia.

"OK OK. You can't talk. But you can understand me and sometimes I just need to talk. All right, let's try the wood . . . switch!" With a quick twist, she flipped the control and waited a second. The water in the Tupperware stayed frozen. The cicadas went silent in the trees. They started dropping like hailstones to the ground around her. By the thousands they fell, paralyzed in the brown leaves. Every beetle, every mosquito, fly, grasshopper, tree cricket, lacewing, dragonfly, thrip, moth, plant hopper, and caterpillar in the trees fell as if they all died in the same instant. Olivia quickly flipped the switch back to its original position. One by one, the insects stretched their legs and righted themselves, dazed from the fall. Olivia was surprised by the great variety and colors of the insects around her. Bright green mantids, midnight blue beetles, tiny golden flies all began to wake up. Olivia loved insects because she had learned to control their behavior with the Pearl. It was how she had signaled Chuck with the fireflies in his backyard. Her fingers moved to another segment. After a blur of fingers and switches, she paused and slowly turned a dial.

The cicadas started to chirr in rhythm. Katydids buzzed the counter notes. After a few beats, the crickets chimed into a soft melody. The locusts sawed their sharp violins. Hundreds of tiny yellow moths twirled into the air, dancing in the leafy light. In their midst, tiny green moths hovered in a heart shape.

"Ready, Hoolie? One . . . two . . . THREE!" And with another switch and whoosh, every insect launched itself into the air with a flurry of wings. Olivia laughed. "Whooo hoo!" The insects soared like a small tornado up into the sky, then settled back down to their simple lives.

"Did I ever tell you about Thunder, your father?" Olivia asked and fell down into the grass. "He was a hero just like you. Except he scared me at first," she said and rubbed Hoolie's cinnamon tuft. "But you never scared me, did you, boy?" Hoolie liked it when she dug her fingernails in his ears. He turned his head to the side and groaned. His hind leg started to kick, sending a pluming landslide of dirt roiling up into the air.

Olivia laughed. Her whole body was sore and tired. She felt like a walking bruise. Always hungry. Always tired and afraid. She wondered if running away was the best thing to do. Sometimes, she wanted to just shove the Pearl down the nearest sinkhole and pretend none of this had ever happened. She remembered that night in Aunt and Uncle's house. Uncle screamed "Sky Island. Sky Island," as the Wardenclyffe thugs beat him. Olivia had no idea how they were going to make it all the way to Arizona. She couldn't remember what states they had to go through to get there. There were no maps to follow. There was no plan. There were no decisions to be made. Nights passed in a blur of rushing vegetation and swamp. Days passed in sweaty languor. She dreamed of giant red kickballs rolling down a snowy mountain, bouncing over boulders and trees, unstoppable until reaching the river far below. She dreamed of blue light, sparkling in the dark and toothless mouths swallowing her whole. They only way to sleep was to crash from exhaustion. She could only hope they would find Sky Island soon.

The distinct whoomp whoomp of a helicopter echoed in the distance, waking her from her dreaming.

"Hoolie, here it comes." She relaxed her muscles and froze in place. Carefully, she breathed in and out through her nose. Hoolie tucked beneath a bush and waited. The helicopter passed just over the treetops but it kept going. She grinned. Chuck's destroyed house must have really caused a stir.

"That was close." She had no idea which helicopters were police and which were Wardenclyffe agents. But she knew if anyone found her, the whole area would be covered with gun-toting men. Hoolie would be in big trouble. He would be blamed for the demolished house, not Chuck. And she would probably be sent to some remote island prison to live out her days etching messages onto the damp walls. The Pearl would be in enemy hands.

Evening came and Hoolie decided that it was safe to move on. They emerged from the cottonwoods and started walking across the great flat plains of Texas. There was no moon and the night was too dark for Olivia to see, so she followed directly behind Hoolie. Once in a while, they had to shimmy beneath barb wire fences or scurry across a road. Olivia could hear cattle lowing nearby.

"Let's not step in any cow pies, Hoolie," she ordered. He had no idea what she was asking. Her foot splashed into a mushy pie. "Arrgh! Hoolie!" She had no choice but to keep walking. She limped for a while as if the cow pie had twisted her ankle. After several hours, she climbed up on Hoolie's back and fell fast asleep. Despite the sting of humility a human on his back caused, Hoolie preferred this time of night. He could run across the landscape unhindered by the slow, plodding child. He broke into a fast gallop. Grasses and cactus opened before him as if on command. Stars struck like sparks in the sky. A great and green meteor tore up the valley, bathing the vast landscape in a brief, eerie light. These were the moments Hoolie loved. He was fulfilling his destiny. He was alone to run through the world, free and fast. The miles sped past.

As morning cracked on the horizon, Olivia awoke and rolled off Hoolie's back with a thud. Their long shadows stretched out across the flat land. She spun around. Flat, dry dirt spread out in every direction. Not a single tree. No shelter. They were sitting ducks out here.

"Where are we going to rest for the day? I don't see anywhere. Let's keep moving." She didn't know where they would hide but she knew they couldn't wait around. Soon, the helicopters would haunt the sky above them, peering into every opening for a glimpse of a bear or a lonely girl. She could feel their eyes already scouring the world around them. She started to walk quickly to the west, almost jogging. Hoolie kept pace.

"Maybe this is the end, Hoolie. There has got to be somewhe . . ." Her voice trailed off. In the distance, the curving top of a large circus tent appeared. The thick blue stripes of the canvas were unmistakable. "Look at that. If we go, someone might find us. But it looks like the only place. We have to find cover." Hunkering down, they made their way closer. There were several smaller tents circled around the blue and white tent. A line of twenty semi-trucks were parked on the side of the main thorough-fare. A few men scurried about, focused on their morning chores. The sickly smell of burning sugar blurred the air. Off in the distance, a long line of cars was slowly making its way across the plain.

"We have to find a place to hide, fast!" Olivia blurted. "Quick, over there."

A pile of tarps lay against the rear wheels of a semi-truck. They skirted under the truck and leaned their backs up against the tarps. There was enough room that Olivia didn't even need to hunker down. They waited as the crowds of people swarmed the area. Olivia peeked out from behind the tarps. She read aloud the banner strung across the midway.

"Chili Pepper Fest—2014." Olivia scrunched her nose. Chili peppers? "Well, maybe we can get some food. It sure smells good. I'm thirsty too." Thankfully, the day was heating up and the water should thaw out so they could drink by mid-morning.

A large speaker attached to a telephone pole clicked on overhead. "Ladies and gentlemen! Booger eaters and curtain climbers! Despite this historic drought, I am pleased to announce the start of Chili Pepper Fest, 2014!" The speaker paused while the crowd cheered. "Although the harvest has not been as strong as years past, we have one cause to celebrate."

"What is it, Jake?" a single voice rose from the crowd.

"We have cause to celebrate . . . because we still have cotton candy. And funnel cakes. And fried Twinkees. Probably the last year for those." The crowd groaned. "And . . ." Jake paused, "the peppers this year are the *hottest* they have ever been!" The crowd roared. "So let Chili Pepper Fest begin!"

With that, the rickety carnival rides lit up and began to spin. The crowd dispersed into the field of rides.

"Be right back. Don't move."

Olivia slipped out from underneath the truck and disappeared into the crowd. She was counting on the distractions of the carnival to keep people from recognizing her. She also figured that any pictures they might be showing on the news would be from when she was younger. Or at least when she wasn't so skinny and wild. Besides all that, she didn't have a bear at her side. That would have been a sure tip-off.

Olivia had learned to steal food weeks ago. The key was to behave like everyone else. Act like a thief and everyone noticed. Act like a shopper, or carnival fan, and no one would see a thing. No jerking movements.

No looking behind to see if anyone was watching. Just keep walking and calmly reach out . . . there. A caramel apple covered with sprinkles and chopped peanuts disappeared from a counter and into her hand. She eased it in front so the apple vendor couldn't see it. She circled around back toward the semi-trucks and rolled it behind the tarps. She heard a satisfying crunch as she walked on.

"Fried Twinkees. I have to try one of those." She loped along. On the ground she picked up a string of raffle tickets that someone had dropped. It made her look more authentic. Besides, she might want to ride the Spider Swirl later. It looked crazy. She spotted the Twinkee vendor in the next row. She wandered past, pretending to work her way toward another stand. Moments later, the deep fried Twinkee crushed in her mouth. Powdered sugar covered her lips.

"Not bad," she mused. Two lemonades later, she found an old milk jug filled with water next to the livestock stables. The day was hot. She snuck back underneath the truck. Hoolie was panting. Cupping her hand, she poured him some water. His long tongue eagerly slurped up the water as fast as she could pour it.

"Hey! Leave me a sip." She lifted the jug to her lips and finished the rest of the water. "Here, I brought you two funnel cakes."

With a gulp, both cakes disappeared into Hoolie's mouth. If a bear could smile, he would be grinning from ear to ear.

"Pretty good huh?"

"Ladies and gentlemen, let me direct you to the main tent. The chili pepper eating contest will begin in thirty minutes. Please make your way. Ah . . . ahh . . . choo!" Jake's sneeze rung out across the fairgrounds. The speakers buzzed and screeched.

"Gesundtheit," a boy in the crowd shouted out to his laughing audience.

"Uh . . . excuse me," Jake announced with a loud sniff. "Seating is limited, so get your spot early."

"This I have got to see," Olivia announced, leaving Hoolie to nap the afternoon away.

Jake was a stout man. His legs were too long for his body and his chest stuck out like a shelf. He struck a pose onstage, twirling a microphone in circles before tossing it upward as high as he could. In a long curving arc, it descended until Jake whipped around and caught the microphone behind his back. The crowd clapped appreciatively. It was his signature move. Back in 2007, he had tried a different opening. He tried to do splits. That stunt hadn't ended well. So he stuck with what worked. A big grin came across his face. He swatted a swirl of flies away from his head. Behind him, a long table was covered with red, white, and blue ruffles. Eleven serious-looking men and one woman sat in chairs facing the crowd.

"Last year, our longstanding champion, Carlos Sabatine, lost to the young upstart Spicy John Bachmann in a frenzy of habanero and cay . . . enne," Jake growled dramatically into the mike. "This year, Carlos has returned to regain his crown." Jake turned and raised his hand toward Carlos. A large man wearing an intricately designed hat stood up and saluted the crowd.

"Will Spicy John allow the legend back in the winner's circle?" Spicy John stood up shaking his head and swinging his arms like a baseball umpire signaling safe.

"Or will one of our other ten contestants surprise us all?"

The crowd cheered again. "Come on, Suzy!" a man in back yelled louder than the others. "You can take all comers."

"This year, the rules have changed. No longer will our contestants be measured on how many habaneros and cayennes they eat in five minutes. Instead, this year is all about heeeeeeat. Each contestant will have nine peppers to eat, each one hotter than the last. First, they will consume a jalapeno. The crowd cheered. Then, a serrano, followed by a NuMex green, a cayenne, a Thai bird pepper, a scotch bonnet, a habanero, and finally a rare jolokia." Jake held a representative pepper above his head as he spoke its name. The crowd noise increased as each pepper was named. "Each contestant is required to chew each pepper ten times before swallowing. A judge will stand behind and count so there can be no cheating. There will be no drinking between peppers. There will be no eating of dairy products."

From behind the stage, a line of twelve young women emerged, each carrying a package covered with black cloth and a fizzing sparkler sticking out of the top. A package was placed in front of each contestant. Spicy John lifted a corner of cloth to peek inside.

Jack grabbed a pair of long silver tongs, clasping a dark wrinkled pepper. "Finally, if they survive, our lucky contestants will have to chew this beauty twenty times." He thrust the tongs high into the air. "Does anyone know what this is?"

A little girl raised her hand. "Yes, young lady. What do you think?"

"Aji el diablo," she whispered.

"That is correct! Aji el diablo. The most drastic, diabolical, devious, dreaded, dastardly, heart-pounding, fire-breathing pepper ever invented." Jake yelled into the microphone, pumping his hands. "Aji el diablo. Aji el diablo!" The young women pulled the black cloth off each package, revealing glass-covered platters containing a single aji el diablo pepper.

Aji el diablos were the specialty of Wheeler County. They grew in the caves outside of Five Corners, protected and fertilized by the vast flocks of bats that lived there. Like some kind of mushroom, they didn't require sunlight to grow. In fact, it was surmised, the darkness and bat guano made the peppers hotter. Aji el diablos were the pride and joy of Wheeler County.

"No one has ever been known to eat an entire aji el diablo. Those that have tried suffered the following fate: vomiting, temporary blindness, convulsions, foaming at the mouth, hallucinations, paranoia, dietary distress, and permanent memory loss."

The crowd grew silent in awe. A few of the contestants glanced at each other nervously.

"So let's get this show on the road," Jake screamed. "Is everybody ready?"

"Yes!" the crowd responded.

"I said, is everybody ready?" Jake cupped his hand behind his ear.

"YES!"

"In five . . . four . . . three . . . two . . . Begin!"

The crowd pressed in closer to the stage as each contestant started furiously chewing on their jalapenos. Spicy John finished his first and the judge behind him held up a small green flag to indicate that he could move on to the serrano pepper. Each contestant soon followed. Tiny beads of sweat started appearing like stars on their foreheads as they moved on to the next peppers. No one showed any signs of quitting.

"Halfway to the aji el diablo," Jake announced. The crowd stepped closer, sweating in the heat. The contestants' faces turned bright red. Three of them gave up.

Olivia moved toward the side of the crowd hoping for a breeze.

"That's her," a voice said behind her. "That's her," louder. Olivia kept edging her way through the throng.

"Mom, that's her. The Bear Girl." This time it was loud enough for Olivia to recognize the voice. She turned her head. Chuck was pulling on his mother's arm and pointing frantically at her. "That's her! She's the one that destroyed our house. That's her! That's her! The Bear Girl!"

The people around her stepped back, forming a circle around her. Hundreds of eyes watched her every move. Two policemen and an off-duty fireman started pushing through the crowd toward Olivia, curious about the fuss. She lunged forward onto the stage as the crowd gasped. "She's wearing my clothes!" Chuck was jumping up and down. "She's wearing my best skating clothes!"

"Well, it looks like we have another contestant," Jake boomed trying to keep the contest on track. One of the policemen jogged up the steps on the side of the stage. Olivia stumbled, slammed into the table. Hot peppers flew in every direction. The fancy platters clattered to the floor. The contestants jumped from their chairs. Several men in the crowd stepped forward to help corral her.

"That's the Bear Girl from TV," Chuck kept screaming. "I found her, I found her. The reward is mine. You are all my witnesses."

Olivia spotted a flap in the tent and bolted for escape. The stage erupted into chaos. As she slid out the small opening, no one noticed that of the original twelve aji el diablo peppers, only eleven remained.

Olivia sprinted through the fairgrounds. Most of the spectators opened up before her in a giant wave. Sometimes, a young man would stand his ground, arms held outward like a wrestler. But weeks of running had made Olivia fast and she easily scooted around him. She could hear the rumble of footsteps behind her as the crowd gave chase. She looked over her shoulder and saw a huge cloud of dust making its way in her direction.

"Hoolie!" she yelled as their hiding place grew near. "Wake up!"

The bear stepped out from behind the pile of tarps, shaking the dirt from his fur. Olivia ran past him grabbing her backpack. With a sudden, wheeling spin, she tripped on the pile of tarps and cracked her shoulder into the sharp edge of the truck frame. Her shirt ripped. A spurt of blood hung from the metal. Her shoulder felt heavy, but she didn't feel the pain yet. She didn't have time to be in pain. The crowd was running around the truck.

"Let's go. Run!" Olivia yelled to Hoolie. He turned on his heels as she landed with a thump on his back. Within seconds, they were running full speed through the Texas creosote brush with a thick cloud of dust following.

Behind her, a man in a suit stood on the hood of a car watching them run. He spoke quietly into his cell phone.

4

Vampire Hunters

Gnat ran full speed and slid along the gravel parking lot behind a pile of fill dirt. In the darkness, he could barely make out the shapes of the vampire hunters jumping from shadow to shadow. Helicopters circled the sky, searchlights scouring the city for any signs of movement. A bus was slowly making its way around the police barriers and burning cars. The hunters were closing in. He could see their yellow eyes glowing. He had to do something fast. A searchlight rushed across the parking lot to the dirt pile, but Gnat had already leaped from sight, scooting along with the bus down the abandoned street. A bullet whizzed by his head, puncturing the side of the bus. Gnat whirled around. The vampire hunters were standing around him in a half-circle.

"Gnat! Gnat!" a voice called out.

Gnat slowly reached down to his side. He knew better than to lunge quickly when vampire hunters had your scent. His hand clenched around his inferno gun.

"Gnat, hurry up. Lunch is ready."

"Just a sec." The blazing light of the enormous flat panel bathed him in a staccato barrage of images. It was too late. The vampire hunters pounced. "Demolished again," Gnat mumbled. He fell backward to the floor. His eyes were red.

Doug Corcoran's mother poked her head around the corner. "I mean it. Now," she ordered.

At first, Gnat remembered, Mrs. Corcoran had been extraordinarily sweet and patient with him. He was allowed to play all the games that he wanted for as long as he could stay awake. He never had to eat lettuce or drink white milk. She made Doug do all the chores and help him with his homework. All of that benevolence was on account of the tragic circumstances surrounding the disappearance of his father, then his aunt and uncle, their house, and finally his sister. The State Department for the Protection of Minors didn't even know what to do with him. They had asked him repeatedly whether he had been slapped or starved. When he said "negative," they had no recourse but to let him remain in Mrs. Corcoran's custody until suitable long-term arrangements could be made. Gnat didn't mind at all. He had full access to the sweetest gaming system he had ever seen or heard about.

Sure, Mrs. Corcoran's eyes grew sadder and wetter with every new chapter in the saga. He could tell that she felt responsible for protecting him from the tragedy of his life. At first, she wouldn't let either him or Doug outside without supervision for fear they would run away again. She brimmed with safety pins, washcloths, breath mints, and diluted bleach spray. Where these things came from was a mystery to Gnat because he never saw her carrying them, but in any pinch they would suddenly appear to solve any problem.

As the weeks wore on though, she became more and more bossy, sometimes even snapping at him. He heard her on the phone at night with her friends describing him as stubborn, odd, and precocious, that he was filled with wanton disregard for anything other than video games.

Odd is what really bothered him. She had said it like it wasn't just an opinion. On top of all that, she wouldn't keep him informed of Olivia's exploits. He knew everyone was looking for her and the bear. He even knew the national news had nightly stories. Mrs. Corcoran was bound and determined to keep all of it from him. She tried everything to divert his interest. Bribes. Yelling. Tears.

Gnat didn't care. Let her yell. Let her cry.

He dropped the game control on the floor and waddled to the kitchen. The thudding music of the video game continued to boom throughout the house.

"Go turn that off," she sighed. "Please, go turn that off."

Gnat sat down at the table and began to eat through a bowl of corn chips. He could hear her fumbling with the power switch and cramming the game console into the drawer.

"Hey, Gnat," Doug said, joining him at the table.

Gnat bounced a clear rubber ball on the floor. When it hit, a series of colored lights flashed inside. He held it up to his eye.

"Don't let Mom catch you throwing that at dinner."

"It's my disco pearl, not hers."

"Disco pearl? Isn't that a little bit too much like Olivia's pearl?"

Gnat didn't answer.

"I talked to her this morning," Doug whispered.

"Olivia?"

"Yeah. She's in Texas. She said 'hi.' "

Gnat shoved a handful of corn chips into his mouth. He chewed the chips with a frown on his face.

"She wanted to talk to you but she had to go. Something was happening."

Gnat grabbed another handful of chips and stared right at Doug. He was looking straight through him, ignoring his attempts to talk about Olivia.

"You know what? Fine. I've got things to do. I just thought you would like to know."

Doug went back to his room and slammed the door. He was getting sick and tired of walking around on eggshells. Gnat didn't even seem upset. He never cried. Yet Mom let him do anything he wanted.

If anyone was suffering since Olivia left, it was Doug. He had to share his room *and* his bathroom with a little pig. Gnat messed around with his research and moved books out of order. The Mutch twins had been crueler now that he didn't have Olivia to protect him. They made sure to sit next to him on the bus no matter what seat he picked. They loved emptying his bag and spreading his books and pencils all over the bus. Cuke threw his homework out the window one morning. The bus driver Mr. Ott didn't tell them to stop even if he sat in the front seat. Doug thought he saw him chuckle in the rearview mirror one afternoon. Thankfully, summer school was almost over and he would have a few weeks of peace before fall school started.

Doug looked out the window. The forest was returning to normal after the hurricane. Trees were sprouting new shrubby tops so it barely looked like a storm had passed at all. The same couldn't be said for the town of Lyonia. Huge piles of rubble lined the streets. Shattered glass littered the ground. Half of the school was roped off for repairs. People argued at the grocery store. People yelled at the gas station. He's just sick and tired of all of it.

He leaned over his desk and grabbed his pencil case. He had been trying to draw a giant tardigrade. The Bobwhite Witch had called them "Crogan horses." He wrote the name carefully at the top of the page. Underneath, he wrote *Echiniscus corcoranae*. On some he wrote, *Echiniscus douglas* or *Echiniscus douglasii*. He hadn't really decided what he wanted to name it. Corcoran's tardigrade or Douglas's tardigrade? There were hundreds of species of known tardigrades. He didn't even know if he had picked the right genus. Scientists would never accept "Crogan Horse" as a legitimate name. There was so much to figure out and it was all very complicated. He had to get it right because this was the chance he had been working so hard for.

Hundreds of failed sketches were piled all over his small desk. On one of the drawings, he got the foot right but the rest looked all out of proportion. He tried to simply draw the face, but he didn't know how to draw something that was supposed to be clear. He had even tried to cut out the pieces from several drawings that he got right and glue them all together. That one looked horrible, some kind of psycho tardigrade. Now, he could barely remember what the giant tardigrade really looked like because he had looked at so many books in the meantime.

Some days he gave up and tried to draw the cave urchins. He wasn't any good at those either. They looked like tennis balls. He had one hundred pages of tennis balls. He just wasn't any good at drawing. He couldn't even remember the Junonian words that he blurted out whenever things got rough. He had seen other discoveries in Junonia than the tardigrades and urchins; brief glimpses of grotesque cave animals down innumerable tunnels as he had ridden the tardigrade to the surface. He couldn't really picture those animals. He couldn't describe them. He just knew that he had seen them. They'd just been flashes of tubercled, goggle-eyed, slimy-skinned, multi-legged monsters. In short, he had nothing. If he was ever going to have a discovery named after him, he would need schematics and descriptions. He would need measurements and comparative analysis. He would have to write articles, maybe even a book. There would be a million questions from scientists all over the world. Skeptics and doubters. He would need proof.

He shoved his chair back. He went to his closet and pulled out a pair of old sneakers. He found a windbreaker with a hood. He put some blank papers in a clipboard. He grabbed his pencils. He knew enough to bring pencils because pens don't always work. He snuck into the hall and found a small digital camera and some batteries. He packed two flashlights. He found a tape measure.

Doug could hear Gnat playing video games in the other room again. He snuck down the hall and knelt down behind him.

"Gnat," he whispered.

No response.

"Gnat, I'm going back. In the morning, I'm going back. Don't tell."

No response.

"Mom is running errands all day and leaving us to take care of ourselves. I will be back by dinner."

Silently, Gnat stared at the TV screen. He set down his controller, turned off the switch, and put the game back in its cabinet. He walked down the hall to their shared bedroom and quietly began to pack.

5

Origami

It was a rare overcast morning. Doug could smell nauseating, tangy smoke in the air. Gnat trotted alongside him, wearing a snorkel and mask that were too big for his head. The mask was fogging and sweat dripped down his face. Doug didn't ask him why he was wearing it. After twenty minutes he heard something sniffing behind them. Doug whipped around expecting to see a bear.

"Cheeto! What are you doing here?"

"He wants to come with us," Gnat answered.

"He can't. He's too small. Go home!" Cheeto's fur raised on his back. He growled and showed his teeth.

"He is *not* too small."

"He won't be able get in. He will get hurt. Besides it is too far for a little dog to walk."

"How do you plan on getting him back to home base?" Gnat mumbled. By now, Cheeto was hiding close behind Gnat's legs.

"Why don't you take him back? You're both too little."

"I've already been down there twice, Sweetheart."

Doug laughed. "Well, that's true. But if Cheeto goes with us, he has to go all the way with us. We can't leave him out here in the scrub. There are coyotes, bobcats, and panthers. And who knows if the bears are still nice with Olivia gone."

"He doesn't fear panthers."

"That's the problem. Cheeto doesn't fear *anything.*"

"He can stay with me if he wants."

"All right, but if he gets hurt or tired, you will have to dump out your backpack and carry him."

"Come on, Cheeto. We are going to Jun . . . Junyano."

"Junonia. You can't even say it right."

"Jun . . yah . . nio."

"Ju . . NO . . nia. Forget it. Just try to keep up. We have to get home before dinner."

"We're going to be in big trouble if Mom catches us."

"She isn't your mom. She's my mom. You're just visiting," Doug snipped.

"Is there a fire? It stinks."

"Yeah, hopefully it's far away. It's from the drought."

"Well, we don't like it."

"We?"

"Me and Cheeto. Come on, boy."

"You don't have to smell it for long. There's the entrance." They entered the clearing in the woods. A slant of sunshine beamed through the smoke and illuminated the sand, making the tiny flecks of quartz sparkle. The ancient tortoise burrow sat in the middle of the clearing.

"Who first?" Gnat asked.

"I'll go." Doug adjusted his jeans.

"You take point."

"What does that mean?"

Gnat shrugged. "You take point."

Doug walked to the middle of the clearing and started stomping around the burrow. Nothing happened. "Maybe it's gone."

"You have to run." Gnat remembered what Olivia had instructed Hoolie to do last time. "You have to run, then jump without fear."

Doug looked at Gnat. "You've got to be kidding."

"Don't you remember?"

"It doesn't make sense. A hole is a hole. It doesn't change just because you run without fear, or if you stroll calmly, or if you do cartwheels."

"No cartwheels. Run, then jump," Gnat responded. "Without fear."

"And a hole certainly doesn't appear because you aren't afraid of it. How do you suppose the hole knows what you are feeling?"

Doug scuffed his feet and dug a trench around the burrow. He jumped up and down. He clawed handfuls of sand. He walked over to the edge of the clearing and found a long stick.

Gnat took off his snorkel mask, wiped his sweating face, and set the mask down in the sand. He picked up Cheeto. He was barely able to hang onto the struggling dog. "Stand back," he ordered.

"Just wait. I'll figure it out."

"Stand back."

"Hold on. I've almost got it."

"AAAAAAAAAAA YAHHHHHHHHHHHHHHH!" Gnat's voice echoed through the woods, much louder than necessary. In a half-run, half-waddle, he stomped past Doug and leapt into the air, landing right in the middle of the burrow. In a blink, Gnat and Cheeto sunk beneath the sand as if they had just jumped off a dock into a lake.

Doug lunged with his stick to the precise spot they disappeared. He scratched around. Nothing. That burrow looked the same as it did a few seconds ago, an old abandoned tortoise hole.

"All right." Doug walked several steps back. Halfheartedly he yelped, "Aaaaa yah." He loped forward and jumped into the burrow. Several seconds of tumbling and inhaling sand later, he dropped through the ceiling and came crashing down on the giant pile of white sand inside the aquifer.

Gnat had already shaken the sand off and climbed down to the cave floor. He clicked on his flashlight. The cave was much different from their first visit. Instead of water, an endless slab of black ice extended into the darkness. Beams of blue light fell like shimmering streamers, but they dulled and disappeared as soon as they hit the ice. Enormous, sharp icicles hung down from the ceiling. Some of the beams of light passed through the icicles, splitting into bursts of broken rainbows. But the most noticeable thing was the incredible quiet, a great and yawning stillness. The air was stale and suffocating.

"Let's go," Doug said.

"Helllllooooo," Gnat shouted. His voice tailed off, absorbed by the overbearing silence. "Helloooooo," he repeated. Cheeto rolled around on his back in the sand.

"Let's go get some pictures and get out of here," Doug started striding along the tombolo. "If you see any tardigrades or urchins, let me know."

"Heeeeeeeeeeeeeeeeeeeeeeelp!" Something dropped from the ceiling behind them and landed with a thud on the sand. Cheeto yelped and skirted behind Gnat. Doug and Gnat whipped around. Their flashlights swung all over the sand hill. They couldn't see who it was, but they heard a stifled whimper in the dark.

"Who . . . who's there?" Doug called out.

"Identify yourself," Gnat said.

The voice groaned louder.

Doug slowly walked around the hill of sand, probing the darkness with a flashlight until the light came to rest on a crumpled figure.

"Who's there?" Doug asked again. "Who are you?"

The figure slowly stood up.

"Oh no," Doug whispered. "Oh no, no, no. Larry."

Larry Mutch wiped the sand from his jeans and rotated his right shoulder as if to stretch a knot out of his muscle. Doug could hear bones cracking in his neck.

"I don't know what you are up to, Corcoran, but you are in huge trouble," Larry announced.

"Why did you . . . how did you find us? I can't believe you followed us here. This . . . this can't happen."

"I followed you and the midget. I knew you were up to no good. I knew it! Well, check it out," Larry said looking around. "This explains all of your secrets. What is this place?"

"None of your business," Doug's mind raced trying to think of a way to send Larry home. He knew there was no exit nearby.

"It's my business now, Corcoran." He poked Doug in the chest. "This is a cave. A crazy ice cave."

"Yeah, it's a cave."

"You are trespassing in *my* ice cave," Larry growled, stepping close. "It's mine now."

Doug gulped.

"Relax, Corcoran." Larry shoved him and laughed. "I'm not gonna take your secret hideout. I can't wait to show Richard though. We could have a mean game of Gomer-Hunt down here."

"You can't." Doug said. "I mean, you can't show anybody."

"How are you going to stop me, Prawn Bait?"

"You just can't. This isn't one of your jokes."

"Nobody tells me what to do. How do we get out of this place anyway?"

"We have to walk that way." Doug pointed down the tombolo. The cave was too dark and enormous to see the end.

Larry suddenly looked a little nervous. "Well, how far is it?"

"It takes awhile."

Cheeto snarled.

"Yuck. Keep the little rat away from me."

"He's not a rat," Gnat said.

"He looks like a rat. My uncle's pit bull is a real dog."

"If he's so tough, how come he isn't down here?" Gnat argued.

Larry paused. He didn't have an answer. "I haven't forgotten your hand in all of this Natty Nat. You better check yourself and mind your own."

"Let's go already or we won't get home by dinner," Doug interrupted.

"Let's go already or we won't get home by dinner," Larry mocked, giving Doug a shove. "You better get us home before that. I have practice this afternoon."

"No one asked you to come down here." Doug's voice trailed off as he realized how foolish it was to say that.

"You better check yourself too, Corcoran. Your girlfriend isn't here to protect you anymore. From now on, I'm in charge. You little cupcakes couldn't find your way outta here with a map and a bag of chips."

Doug and Gnat looked at each other. Gnat shrugged.

They walked quietly, looking around, straining their eyes into the darkness. The sand was hard beneath their feet so it was easy to walk fast. Every few minutes for amusement, Larry would kick Doug's ankle from behind, sending him tumbling to the ground.

Soon, they found the mammoth bones at the battle site. Larry swung a long bone like a baseball bat. He wrestled a sharp blade from one of the bones and wielded it like a ninja. He threw a knuckle bone across the ice. It clattered and slid out into the darkness. He seemed completely unimpressed with the scientific significance of the giant bones.

Doug slid out onto the ice and pointed his flashlight down. The Bobwhite Witch was frozen exactly the way they left her, mouth wide open and eyes rolled back. A patch of hair clamped with the magical red barrette lay lifeless on top. The tips of her spindle-like fingers stuck out of the ice.

Doug remembered those fingers running deep into his hair and latching on as she shoved him through the woods that night in the hurricane. He had felt helpless as the witch rushed him away from his house, through the stinging rain, branches snapping against his face, and down into Junonia. He'd been so weak and groggy, it was like watching some other boy kidnapped by a monster, like he fell asleep on the couch and woke up after midnight to some cheap horror movie. He had wanted to fight, but he couldn't lift his arms. His head lolled and drooped. She was so strong. Stronger even than his dad. At least what he remembered of his dad when they wrestled in the living room.

"Aw, man! I caught the Bobwhite Witch! I caught the Bobwhite Witch! I'm gonna be famous," Larry yelled out.

Doug pushed the flashlight closer to the witch's eyes. Her pupils quickly shrunk to a pin prick. Her fingers started clenching above the ice. Doug jumped back. "Look at that!"

Gnat rushed over. "She is undead."

Doug squirmed. "Don't get too close. She'll grab you and never let go."

Gnat studied the trapped fingers stretching like an insect caught in pine pitch. He reached into his pocket and pulled out a marker, sticking it into the clutch of her fingers. Her hand clamped.

"Yikes!" Larry jumped.

"Why'd you do that? Get away from her," Doug shouted.

Gnat tried to take the marker back. It wouldn't budge. He thought of Miss Rinkle and how nice she was to him, so he didn't try too hard.

"Oh man, you were so scared, Corcoran! I'll bet you peed your dress. That was classic," Larry said, slapping his thigh.

"You haven't seen anything yet," Doug responded.

"What's that supposed to mean?" Larry snapped. Doug and Gnat walked away. "Hey, I'm talking to you. What's that supposed to mean?" Larry gave up protesting and followed behind them.

Thirty minutes later, they reached the end of the tombolo.

"We aren't finding anything," Doug whined quietly to Gnat. "All of the echinoids must be frozen under the ice. And the tardigrades are hiding. Or dead." The only good news was at least Larry wouldn't find out about his discoveries. They walked across the ice to one of the cave walls. Doug shined a light up into a tunnel entrance.

"We can go to the city," Gnat suggested.

"Do you remember how to get out?"

"City? What city?" Larry asked.

"Yeah, at the top. Up the stairs," Gnat answered.

"All right. I didn't get to see it the last time. If I can't find a tardigrade, at least I will have pictures of the city."

They found the circular tunnel leading down to the city. Doug climbed in feet first and let go of the edge. The water in the tunnel was frozen, sending him down at an incredible speed. Faster and faster he sped. When he hit the bottom, he slid across the frozen pool and slammed into the city wall. Moments later, Gnat spun out of the tunnel clinging to Cheeto. In a flash, he crashed into Doug and sent them all tumbling to a stop.

"Was that fun?" Doug asked picking up all of his equipment. "I'm not sure. Was that fun?"

"That wasn't fun," Gnat answered. "That was depraved."

"Yeah. Depraved. Let's do it again."

Silently, Larry shot out of the tunnel and across the ice like a missile.

"Wasn't that depraved, Larry?" Doug asked.

"Duh, what?"

"Wasn't that awesome?" Doug said.

"Sky Wave at Water Planet is way better."

"Gnat and I are going again."

"Wait. Look at this." Gnat walked over to the aqueduct that ran down the city. A thin cylinder of ice ran through the twisting trough that used to flow with water. He held the flashlight against the ice. Nothing happened.

"Uh oh," Gnat said.

"What do you mean, 'uh oh?' "

"This lit up last time. The whole city lit up."

"Well, it's not now." Doug looked at him skeptically.

"It isn't working." They looked up. Gnat pushed his flashlight into the ice again. The city remained dark above them. Their flashlights scooted around, casting deep shadows that only seemed to increase the murkiness.

"These are stairs," Larry announced.

"Obviously," Gnat answered. "My sister and I discovered it."

"New rule," Larry announced loudly. "No one is allowed to mention your sister."

"You just did," Gnat said.

"Starting now."

"Hold on, I want to get pictures," Doug said, rummaging in his backpack. He pointed his camera up toward the city and took a picture. A feeble flash of light emitted from the camera. He looked at the screen. The flash only reached a small bit of architectural detail. The rest of the picture was black. Doug snapped several more pictures and grimaced at the results.

"This whole trip was a waste." Doug's heart sank. "First no animals. Now I can't even get a decent picture of the city."

"And this goon is here," Gnat said, pointing toward Larry.

"I'm here all right," Larry responded. "This place is great. I'm going to use it for paintball. No, wait! I'm going to sell tickets so my customers can play paintball. No wait, I'm going to do both. I'm gonna be rich."

"I'm hungry," Gnat said.

"I should be able to get some pictures farther up, when we are closer."

"Enough messin' around. Show me the way out," Larry ordered.

"Do you want some?" Gnat opened his backpack and pulled out some snacks.

"Maybe you two can hold the flashlights so the pictures come out."

Gnat plopped down on the stairs that used to descend down into the pool of water. Cheeto stared at him with dewy, unblinking eyes.

"Here you go, boy," Gnat said, throwing the dog a miniature donut, then popping one into his own mouth. Powdered sugar immediately covered half of his face. "Want one?" he asked holding two out to Doug and Larry in his grubby hands.

"Sure," Doug answered, still craning his neck upward.

"Give me that." Larry sneered, taking a donut.

Gnat opened a Coke and drank half the can in one gulp.

Doug ate some carrot sticks.

They heard a twinkling noise high above them on the city's rooftops.

"Poltergeist," Gnat said authoritatively, "class five."

"I don't know about that," Doug answered.

"Maybe you're right. Could be a class four."

"Who cares?" Larry said.

A loud, groaning rush fell behind them, shattering onto the icy cave floor.

Doug jumped back. "Icicles!" Another large icicle fell from the ceiling, tumbling and crashing down the city stairs and verandas until it smashed next to them. The ice rang like thunder as it cracked the darkness. Within seconds, the air was filled with sharp projectiles and gigantic chunks of ice. Doug looked up into the darkness, but couldn't see anything until the falling ice was almost upon him.

"Quick, in here!" Doug and Gnat ducked inside a circular alcove in the wall alongside the frozen pool. It only went back a few feet, so they barely had any cover. It sounded like the entire cave was falling around them. The alcove walls shook and rumbled. Larry somehow crammed in next to them, his knees up to his chin.

Icicles were dropping faster, tiny darts and enormous daggers the size of boulders.

"Cheeto? Where's Cheeto?" Gnat panicked.

"Cheeto!" Doug called out. "He's over there." He pointed to the other side of the pool. "Come on, boy!"

Cheeto took off running toward them. With surprising speed for a little dog, he leaped over a large icicle chunk. He slipped and spun away just as a long, thin icicle pierced the air in front of him. Struggling to gain a foothold, he ran though a rain of ice, finally sliding safely into Gnat's arms. Gnat could feel his tiny heart pounding. As scared as he was, Cheeto had enough energy to growl at Larry and Doug.

"That was wicked cool," Larry shouted.

"That was not cool. Cheeto was scared," Gnat scolded.

"What time is it?" Doug murmured. He answered his own question. "Eleven o'clock. The ceiling must be warming up from the midday sun."

Gnat reached out and snatched a thin icicle several feet long. Like all of the ice since the temperature change, it felt warm like plastic. He knocked it against a bigger chunk. It clanged musically. He hit a second one and it made a brighter note. Grabbing another icicle, he started banging them against every surface. Doug joined in, laughing. They tried to make a song but it only sounded like wind chimes crashing down the stairs. Larry rolled his eyes.

Gnat stuck the icicle in his mouth and pretended to smoke a cigarette.

"Hey, don't eat . . . what does it taste like?"

"Water," Gnat said snapping the icicle in half and handing it to Doug.

"I guess we won't die of thirst."

Larry tore the camera from Doug's hands and flung it across the ice, shattering it into a million pieces.

"Wh . . . Why did you do that?" Doug screamed.

"I don't need you and your cheese log friends stealing my paintball arena."

"That was my only camera."

"Aww, don't cry."

"My dad gave that to me."

"Whatever."

"No, Larry. No 'whatever' this time. I'm sick and tired of your stupid antisocial tendencies."

"All right, Corcoran, I've been trying to be patient with you and your fancy words. Keep pushing me and I will settle your account right now and find my own way out of here. I don't need either of you two fools"

"P . . . P . . . Pushing you? *I'm* pushing *you?*"

"Y . . . Y. . .Yes, you are." Larry imitated Doug's stutter and shoved his head. Doug's hand formed into a tight fist. This was the limit. He couldn't take it anymore.

"It's stopping," Gnat said, pointing up. Cheeto's growling increased at the rising tensions.

Doug jumped out of the alcove. When Larry stood up, Doug shoved him back into the wall. Larry swung his arm. Doug ducked and landed a punch on Larry's stomach. Larry stumbled backwards, coughing.

"That was a good punch, Corcoran," Larry smiled. He stepped closer. "Do you want to try it again?"

Doug wound up for a bigger swing, but before he could propel his fist, Larry gave him a huge shove. Doug slid on the ice and crashed his head on a big icicle. Groaning, he reached back to the knot on his head. His fingers stained with blood. Larry rummaged through Doug's bag and stole his flashlight.

"There's more of that coming your way, Corcoran," Larry warned. "I used to think you were all right, but enough is enough." He bounded up the stairs and disappeared in the darkness.

Doug stood up and walked over to his broken camera. He picked up the useless pieces and put them in his bag.

"Do you think you can fix it?" Gnat asked.

"I don't know. I'm not a mechanical engineer."

Doug and Gnat started quietly climbing stairs. It was tough walking because each stair was covered with a thin glaze of ice. The spiraling ramps and ladders were the hardest to climb, especially when they had to carry Cheeto.

"This trip isn't going the way I wanted," Doug said.

"What are you talking about?"

"First Larry. Then no tardigrades or urchins. Then . . . then Larry again."

"Since when did coming down here go easy?" Gnat answered.

It was true. It hadn't been easy either of the times they had been here before. Doug looked at Gnat and patted him on his back.

"I remember this," Gnat said, arriving at a landing. He pushed on a large operculum door. It swung open and they went inside. Hundreds of bottles lined the walls. "This is where the pink sparks escaped."

"Pink sparks? You never told me about that."

"I forgot. They flew away."

"What were they?"

"I dunno. They were alive."

"Like fireflies?" Doug shined Gnat's flashlight into each bottle: colored liquids, tiny shark teeth in oil, dried flower buds, gossamer fluff.

"Smaller. Brighter."

"These bottles look like chemicals. Maybe medicine. A few of them, well, who knows?" he said, looking into a bottle filled with hundreds of smooth, white pebbles.

"Hey, what's this?" Gnat pulled a cube the size of a grapefruit from behind the bottles. It was made entirely of a thin paperlike material, like tissue. It was very light, almost like it was filled with air. He turned it over and around in his hands. A tiny latch made of paper seemed to hold it all together.

"It looks like a Christmas present," Doug said, "but made of tissue."

"There are five of them back there." Gnat unhooked the latch. Immediately, the paper box started to unfold. It flipped and opened in great triangles and folded sheaves. It slapped against the shelves, knocking bottles over. A thin green oil spilled and turned to smoke as soon as it hit the air. The pebbles scattered. Over and over the paper loosened and flattened out onto the floor until only an enormous flat sheet remained.

"Wow, that was cool."

"Look, there's writing." They stepped onto the thin paper to get a better look. Small letters were delicately written in faint greenish-blue at the exact center of the sheet. Part hieroglyph, part script, it was a language neither of them could read.

"What does it say?"

"I don't know."

"You speak Ju . . . NO . . . nia," Gnat said. Cheeto squirmed in his arms.

"I speak it, I don't read it. I can't even speak it very well."

"Try."

"Chek . . . lin . . . moforsa," Doug mumbled. "I don't know. These aren't even letters. Checklin moforsa. What does that mean?"

"Aaaaaaaaah!" Larry flashed across the room and tackled Doug sending everyone tumbling. Cheeto clamped onto his pant leg. "How do I get out of here? How do I get out of here?" Larry screamed.

"Let go. Get off me!"

"Tell me or I will beat you senseless."

"I . . . I don't know! Only Gnat knows the way to the surface."

Suddenly, the thin paper folded over on itself, trapping them inside. Again and again, it folded, twisted, creased, and collapsed. It folded faster and faster. Doug screamed and tore at the paper, but it was too tough to rip. Larry pounded uselessly with his fists. Cheeto dug as hard as he could. They could barely breathe. Their flashlights grew dimmer as the layers piled up. The paper pressed in closer and heavier. Complicating then simplifying, it returned to its original cube shape, the size of a grapefruit. It sat in the middle of the room, rocking back and forth as the kids pounded their fists helplessly against the paper walls. Then, it turned inside out. With a faint pop, they disappeared altogether.

6

Grub

Olivia sprawled on Hoolie's back, exhausted and unable to move. Her shoulder was so painful that it sucked the energy from her. Time lost its demarcation. Hours smeared together. All she could remember was non-stop, endless running. The scraggled land brushed past. Great prairies with nothing, nothing but brown grasses as far as the eye could see. Rattling, blowing grasses. Rabbits and gophers scattering to their straw homes. Starlings flew in cloudy, swooping flocks. Purple lightning unzipped the sky and crashed with a force she could feel in her bones. But no rain. No rain. Just dry grass and impossibly dark nights, speckled with galaxies spinning. Thirsty insects rose on cellophane wings. Long highways with no signs and no lights.

On the wide horizon, drought fires glowed like the end of the world.

They ran over the charred earth, black trees crumbling, smoldering bodies. They ran through deserts of lime green glass that shone like goblin ice. They ran over dried earth sprouting with petrified dinosaur eggs that bloomed from the ground like gigantic mushrooms. One night, they made congress with other bears who ran alongside. Strange, cinnamon bears who regarded Hoolie with suspicion.

Days passed. They stopped only once to drink long, slow gulps from a warm, twisting river. Then Hoolie swam across and began to run again.

Always running. His muscles burned like a red engine. Hoolie ran like there was nothing else to life but running. In a groggy blur, Olivia hung on until she could no longer feel her fingers digging into his thick fur. Her shoulder felt like solid glass shards sending electricity down her arm with every stride that Hoolie took. She wobbled and almost fell. The pain was unbearable, but the thought of falling off was even more unbearable. Days passed, lost in time. She couldn't remember where she was, who she was. Memories mixed with dreams. In a blur, her father called *Butterfly, Butterfly* from somewhere distant, somewhere just out of sight. She would run to him and leap weightlessly and tell him about Florida. And her mother suddenly home from Iraq. They would all visit the prairie, including Gnat, flying kites high into the blue sky.

The land began to rise, unnoticeable at first, but soon undeniably. The land sloped upward. They passed small towns who painted their names with white rocks on the hillsides. Days passed. The brush thickened and rose into small trees. Small mountains rose and fell. Large mountains loomed on the horizon.

One day they ran among tall trees once again. Tall, safe trees. Lungs heaving, Hoolie found a small creek tumbling over a rocky ravine. He crashed to the ground, tossing Olivia into the leaves. Neither of them moved.

In time, Olivia awoke and forced herself to stand up. Every muscle in her body ached. Her left arm wouldn't move. Her shirt sleeve was stiff with dried blood. She felt around until her fingers disclosed where the metal had punctured her shoulder. A pinch of skin oozed thick liquids. It made her woozy. She dipped her hand into the flowing creek and drank. Something white jumped out from the stones at the bottom.

"Squeak!" Squirt had wiggled out of Olivia's backpack during the night and was eagerly feasting in the underwater dead leaves. He flushed pink when he saw Olivia.

"Hi, Squirt. I can't feed you. I'm out of food." Olivia's voice was weak and raspy. Squirt roiled beneath a small waterfall. He was used to the quiet, dark water of his home. The waterfall was like a rollercoaster for him.

Olivia opened her backpack and filled the thermos. The creek was only a trickle of how it once flowed before the drought. She poured water onto Hoolie's muzzle, wetting his nose and mouth. His tongue lapped out and he cracked open his eyes. She worked the mats out of his fur and checked his paws for spurs. His foot pads were rubbed raw and bleeding. His loyalty to her was so strong that he had been running in agony.

"Come on boy. We are safe here for now. You did good," she laid her head on his chest and they both fell into a deep sleep.

The sun blazed through the dry leaves high up in the trees. A cicada buzzed in the beaming light. Olivia had no idea how many days had passed while they slept.

"I am so hungry," Olivia moaned.

Hoolie rolled to one side, rocked back and forth, then thrust his body upward until he stood. He shook his body, sending dirt and leaves flying. He was hungry too. He saw a giant tree that had fallen years ago. He walked over, put both front paws on the log, and pushed with all his strength. The log snapped free and he rolled it over to Olivia. He sat down triumphantly.

"I'm not going to eat a log," Olivia laughed.

Hoolie pushed the log closer.

"I am not going to eat a log. You eat it."

His claws dug in and pulled the bark away from the wood. With a big heave, he tore the log into halves. Squirming in the mushy wood were hundreds of swollen, white grubs. Their juicy bodies bristled with tiny hairs and legs. Curved like the letter "C," they twisted in the sudden light.

"Oh, no way," Olivia turned away. Hoolie ploughed his head into the wood and gulped mouthfuls. He looked up and pushed some of the wood even closer to her.

"You can see their pincers," Olivia protested picking one up in her fingers. "Do you really think that I'm supposed to eat *this?* This is not human food, Hoolie. This, this is bear food, or bird food. This is nasty. You can see the guts through its skin. Is that poop down there at the end? And look at its gigantic eyes. How can you eat something that is watching you? No way. *No way.*"

Hoolie took another mouthful. The sight of him eating heartily made her even more hungry. Scrunching her face, she closed her eyes and popped the grub into her mouth. She quickly chewed twice. The juice of the grub made her gag. Its stiff hairs poked her gums. She swallowed.

"Blech." She ran to the creek and took a long drink. "That tasted like . . . like Crunchberries. That is disgusting . . . gross. I wish they didn't squirm." But it felt good to have something, *anything,* in her stomach. She grabbed another grub. Olivia loved Crunchberry cereal, but she sure wasn't going to admit it now.

"That is nasty," she said, examining the writhing creature closer, then tossing it into her mouth. Soon she was eating grubs one after another.

Hoolie grabbed a pine log in his mouth and pulled it closer. Inside were countless smaller, darker grubs. It was harder for Olivia to pick them out of the wood.

"Ugh, bitter and sandy," she complained. Still, she ate until she was full. She watched Hoolie carefully remove each grub from the log and place them on the back of his paw before gobbling them down.

"Why are you doing that?" Olivia scratched one of his ears. Suddenly angered, Hoolie lunged toward her, swiping with his giant paw. Realizing he lost his temper, he paused, then laid his head on her lap.

"I know you didn't mean it. Eat and drink as much as you can. I think we should get moving again tonight." She walked back to the creek and washed her face and hair. Her shoulder hurt. She pulled her shirt over to take a look. The dried blood stuck so she peeled it off slowly. Her heart sank. The wound looked horrible. Yellow and purple bloomed beneath her skin. Jagged lines of purple spread out from the wound. Dried, black blood flaked from her arm. In the center, a pouty hole opened like a bruised bull's-eye. It made her cry just seeing it. She knew she really needed a doctor, but she also knew that if she went to a doctor, it would all be over. Hoolie would be shot and killed just like his father. The Cult of Wardenclyffe would have the Pearl. The rain would never return. And she would never find Aunt and Uncle. More than ever, she knew she must keep going forward. She cleared her brain of all other things. *Just for now,* she told herself. Forget about air conditioning and soft beds. Forget about French fries and toasted cheese sandwiches cut into triangles and chicken tenders. Forget about television shows. Forget the pain. Olivia threw away the old bloodied shirt and winced herself into one of Chuck's new shirts.

Miles away, three remote-controlled black drones flew high over the landscape in formation. On the bottom of each drone, a 360-degree infrared camera scanned the landscape for the tell-tale heat signatures of a bear and little girl. Every time a red or white image appeared on camera, a drone would break formation and circle around the target until its identity was confirmed. Deer, farmers, hikers, gophers were all scanned, tracked, and identified without their ever knowing. The drones completed their search of the foothills and moved on to the mountains.

Olivia tried walking once the sun went down. She walked for over an hour. The pain in her shoulder flared with every step. Before long, she was riding Hoolie again. Mountains came and went. They ran up the switchbacks and down gullies and gorges. Stubby cactus grew fatter and taller. They followed the sandy dry river beds laid like veins in the desert. They snuck past ghost towns and a bright white church in the middle of nowhere. They ran through vast forests of cholla trees whose little bundles of itchy spines soon covered Hoolie's thick fur. He looked like a large running cactus.

Neither of them noticed the tiny glint of light following them high in the sky.

7

The Stabilimentum

Olivia stood with her back toward the edge of a cliff, watching a small battalion of helicopters and all-terrain vehicles converging toward her from the distant desert. A billowing cloud of dust blew upward into the sky behind them.

Olivia panicked. "They found us. We have to go. How did they find us?" She turned around and frantically searched for an escape route. There were no trees or bushes. There weren't even any large boulders or crevices to wedge into. The only trail was the one that they arrived on, and that led back toward the helicopters. She carefully leaned over the cliff. A thin trail dropped over the cliff's edge and dropped into the canyon. It was so steep Olivia got dizzy trying to follow it with her eyes. Her stomach turned sour. Far below, a silvery river curled around boulders. Several ravens circled in the hot air between her and the river.

"We have to get out of here," she yelled, looking one more time along the ridge for an escape route. "We have no choice. The only way out is down there." She wasn't sure if a bear could even climb down a tiny trail like that, much less a ten-year-old girl with an excruciating shoulder. Still, she scrambled over the edge and started shuffling down. She hugged the edge of the cliff. One thing is for sure; she knew enough not to look down. Just the thought of the height made her woozy. Above her, Hoolie

groaned. She looked up to see him lying on his belly with only his face hanging over the edge.

"Come on, Hoolie. You must. It will be all right. Just don't look down." Hoolie huffed loudly.

"Now! You must come with me," she commanded.

After a few more failed attempts, Hoolie finally managed to get all four of his paws onto the trail. He dug his claws into the rough dirt. Step by step, they descended the cliff. Halfway down, they heard a loud screech. Looking up, three helicopters roared over the canyon and disappeared over the other side.

"We lost them. We lost them. Awesome!" Olivia cheered. "We have to keep moving and get to the bottom." In places, the trail was so thin, she had to turn sideways. The canyon winds buffeted against her. Her head swirled whenever she thought of the nothingness that surrounded them. Only the vertical cliff wall and thin trail anchored her to the world. The raven swung by again, hanging in the wind just a few feet away.

"Hello, Crokley," she called out to him. She could barely turn her head to look at the raven for fear she would catch a glimpse of the river far below. Her voice was so small in the bigness of the wind and canyon. "Crokley, could you go up there and see if the helicopters are gone?"

The raven didn't move except for the ruffling of the wind over his back.

"Pleeeeeeeease," Olivia whined.

Crokley shifted the front of his wings, catching the wind, and soared wildly upward. "Always say 'please' to a raven," she announced to Hoolie. Crokley rose high above the ridge line and started slowly circling. With a loud squawk, he dropped like a stone. Three dark drones were crisscrossing the ridge and surrounding landscape, much closer to the surface than before. Crokley dove to get out of the way.

"What are those?" Olivia said as the drones overlapped the sky above her. A little red light blinked on one drone, and suddenly all three rose higher until they disappeared into the indigo sky.

Soon, the throb of helicopters could be heard in the distance once again.

"They are coming back. Hurry, Hoolie."

Finally they reached the bottom. The silver river wasn't silver at all. It was muddy like chocolate milk and thundering over large boulders. Helicopters echoed against the cliff walls behind them.

"This way." Olivia clambered up and over a large rock and started running upriver along a stony sandbar. Hoolie shook the water from his fur and slogged after her. The river's edge was cluttered with old tree trunks. It was slow going as they climbed the slippery trees and rocks. They waded through streams that joined the main river from side canyons. They pushed through a thick stand of tamarisk trees.

A siren blasted down the canyon from ahead.

"What . . . what's that?" Olivia screamed above the roaring water. It reminded her of the tornado sirens she would hear back in Wisconsin. The oncoming helicopters pushed closer. The noise was deafening: river, helicopters, and the loud siren.

Upriver, a gigantic dam blocked the entire canyon with its smooth concrete sides. Behind the thick walls, a vast reservoir of water filled the upper canyon. Hundreds of power lines strung from a large building next to the dam. Untold millions of gallons of water were held from rushing into the canyon. The air practically hummed with the power of the restrained water and the electrical generators. Because of Olivia's mistake with the Pearl, the water was freezing from below into a huge block of ice, creating extraordinary pressure on the dam walls. The Pima Power Authority was forced to regularly release huge amounts of water to avoid structural damage. A speaker that looked like a giant's trumpet on top of the main building blared the siren again. It echoed down the river. It was a danger warning for any foolish people who might be hiking in the canyon below.

The dam vents opened up. A violent wall of water gushed out and pummeled down the canyon. A huge groaning pressure blast preceded the wall. Nothing slowed the water down. Boulders rolled, tree trunks dislodged and tossed in the unstoppable flood like tiny canoes. On top of the dam, three men with ATVs scanned down the river with binoculars.

Two helicopters flew around the river bend. Hoolie stopped and turned to face them, his fur flying in the wind from their blades. Each helicopter had a shooter holding a giant gun watching them out the open side door.

"Hoolie, no! Keep running," Olivia screamed, "up there!" She pointed ahead to a small waterfall.

Hoolie turned just as a woman in the helicopter shot a net from the giant gun. The net snagged on a fallen tree, just missing him. The helicopters rose higher to get a better aim.

Olivia slipped on a rock. Her shoulder flared with painful fire. Her vision sparked blue and blurred with pain. Hoolie grabbed her by the back of her shirt and helped her up.

A net exploded overhead and settled like a sheet over them. A large boulder at the base of the waterfall kept the net from completely entangling them. Olivia found an edge and slid out from underneath. Carefully, she held the edge up so Hoolie could walk through without touching. The woman in the helicopter threw the net gun angrily into the back. She picked up a rifle. Olivia looked upriver. The blood drained from her face. Tears formed in her widened eyes. The wall of water turned the corner of the canyon and sped toward them, throwing rocks and logs ahead. The sheer cliff walls on either side were smooth and unclimbable. There was no escape. It was a simple choice now, die in the flood or let the Cult of Wardenclyffe capture them. Before she could raise her hands, the rushing water loomed over them like a terrible skyscraper, sending the helicopters out of reach. She grabbed Hoolie's neck. "I love you," she screamed. "I'm sorry."

Over his back, she saw a small crevice behind the waterfall. "Quick, in there!" She leaped ahead, sending both of them tumbling into the thin crack just as the surging water crashed over.

The noise of the water hit Olivia like a punch to the head. She looked back. The storming river made her weak in the knees. It was so close it felt like it would suck her in and pull her away. She threw up.

Outside, the helicopters flew away, announcing on the radio that the flood swept Olivia and the bear downstream. They would have to search on foot to find them once the waters receded. One man sitting next to the pilot turned off a video camera and lowered it from his shoulder. It would be twenty-four hours before they could get into the canyon.

Olivia struggled to her feet, wobbling. Hoolie seemed confused. Nothing in his bear-life prepared him for this. He had seen so many new things in his time with Olivia, but cliff walls, net guns, and flooding rivers were overwhelming.

"There is no sense going back toward the river," Olivia mused. "Let's see how far back this goes." She reached into her pocket and felt Squirt wiggling. "Good boy," she called to him.

Slowly their eyes adjusted to the dim light. With one hand on the side of the crevice, Olivia started walking away from the opening. Hoolie followed inches behind her, bumping into her every time she slowed down.

"Geez, are you scared or something?" Olivia whispered nervously.

The crevice grew darker until they couldn't see anything at all.

"Hey, I have an idea," she said, grabbing Squirt from her pocket. He was weak from the dry desert air, despite how careful Olivia had been giving him water at every available opportunity. "Come on, Squirty, I know you can do it. Light up. I remember you doing it before in Junonia."

Squirt spun a quick circle on Olivia's palm. She gave him a gentle kiss on his star. He settled into the middle of her palm and strained, pushing his cool blood to the surface. A faint glow rose from his white body until he looked like a burning coal.

"You sure get warm when you do that."

They continued inching along the crevice. The stone wall felt smooth as it curved and undulated under her hand. Like a wave, like water. They squeezed through twisting passages. From above, a faint light grew as they moved along. She could see a thin sliver of sky high above. Soon, they didn't need Squirt's light anymore.

"Why don't you ride for a while?" Olivia set him on her shoulder.

The sunlight shimmied down the soft, curving walls like silk curtains. The light coaxed subtle color from the stone, reds and oranges up near the top, royal blues and dark purples under her hand. Somewhere in between, emerald, turquoise, gold, and pink emerged from the wall as if they were souls of the stone. Each color seemed to flow around and over the smooth walls. It was like walking through a rainbow and a river at the same time. A thin trickle of sand streamed down from the ceiling. Olivia ran her hand through the sandy blur.

"A sand waterfall!" Olivia's voice chimed. "Isn't it beautiful, Hoolie?" She cupped her hand until the sand overflowed and trickled through her fingers. The colors on the wall whirled and spun.

Hoolie was unimpressed and simply wanted to find a way out.

With every turn in the canyon, a new spectacular display rose upward toward a thin shard of sky. There were larger sand waterfalls, some of them tumbling over smooth outcroppings of stone. Thin rays of sunlight pierced the air. Olivia couldn't imagine how high the walls were. There would be no way to climb out. The walls were too smooth.

The silent color washed over her. Her eyes dazzled. The walls seemed to move. Colors shifted, panes of glass rotating, overlapping. Left or right, up or down, backward or forward ceased to mean anything. The only landmark of direction was a particular splash of color and even that shifted as soon as her eyes locked onto it. Olivia walked, now putting the heel of one foot directly against the toes of her other foot to keep from losing her balance in the spin. The beauty was so overwhelming it frightened her. Faster, she stepped. One hand on the wall. One heel against her toes.

Finally, a light appeared in front of her. A normal, blotch of sunlight that didn't shift and spin.

"There," Olivia called out. Having a signpost, a beacon, made walking easier as they rushed forward. They stumbled out of the crevice and into the blaring sun. Her shocked eyes flushed white.

"I can't see." She rubbed her eyes. "Where are we?"

"Squeak!"

"Ugh, can you learn to talk for once?" She squinted, adjusting to the bright sun.

A bright and wide desert valley opened up in front of them. A sandy river bed filled with round stones meandered along the valley floor. All around grew cactus of the same kind Olivia had seen in countless cartoons. Thick, spiny columns divided into branches that looked more like the arms of bandits surrounded by cops, or like a faithful choir singing. Except these cactus were not only green; some were purple, pink, or gray. And they were taller than she imagined. Taller than any tree she had ever seen. Even taller than redwoods.

"Look at this desert, Hoolie. We could carve a door and live inside one of these cactuses. I say we live in a pink one."

Hoolie huffed and thumped the ground.

"Fine. Purple then."

Lemon and tangerine birds exploded out of a hole in one cactus, chattering at the wind then disappearing behind a stony ridge.

On both sides of the valley, mauve mountains rose up into the bright blue sky. One was so tall, she could see snow at the top. The hot valley sand wavered in a glossy mirage. The mountains appeared to be floating over the ground like ships moored in a calm harbor.

"There weren't any mountains a minute ago. Where are we?" Olivia was sure they hadn't seen any mountains before they climbed down the cliff, just miles and miles of flat desert.

"Squirt, be careful," she called out. He had already found a mud puddle in the river bed.

Her feet crunched as she walked. A blanket of broken crystals covered the ground. Facets and shards sparkled in the sun.

"Look, crystals!" Olivia scooped up every color she could find. Pink, purple, brown, blue. She held each up to the sun. Soon, her pockets were so full, she was forced to dump them all onto the ground. "I can't carry all of those. Let's find the perfect one. Look at them all, Hoolie!"

After a few minutes of stooping down for crystals, her shoulder started throbbing. The pain brought her back to the reality of her situation. They would have to find food soon. She and Hoolie both knelt down and drank from the puddle. The water tasted grimy, but it cleared the desert dust from her throat.

"Who are you? How did you get here?" a voice shouted behind her. Olivia and Hoolie both jumped, surprised that someone had snuck up behind them.

Olivia turned around. A girl about her age stared blankly at her. "I said, who are you?"

"Who are you?" Olivia shot back.

"I am Terrilyne Yazzi, and you don't belong here."

Olivia looked for any sign of friendliness or anger. She couldn't tell because the girl's expression was like a stone.

"Aren't you scared? I have a bear."

The girl stepped closer. "Not really, although he is a big bear. I've seen bigger." They sized each other up. Terrilyne's face never showed any emotion. "You have the eyes of a baby bear."

"E. . . . Excuse me?" Olivia said.

"The eyes of a baby bear. Lightish blue with a bit of pink around the edges. I've never seen anyone with eyes like that."

Olivia remembered her eyes when she had looked into Chuck's mirror back in Texas.

"Well, they weren't always this way."

"Well, they are now. I like them."

"Thank you," Olivia said.

"Whew! You smell something awful."

"Sorry."

"Just stay downwind if you don't mind."

"There isn't even a breeze."

"Then I'll just have to hold my nose. You still haven't told me who you are."

"Olivia. Olivia Brophie. This is Hoolie."

"How did you get here?"

"We walked."

Terrilyne looked at her skeptically. They stared at each other for a long time.

"No one has ever walked here before."

"Well, we walked. No one has probably ever walked as far as we have either. There was a desert, then a dam, then a cave."

"A dam? There aren't any dams around here."

"There *was* a dam."

Terrilyne stared. "What is wrong with that?" she pointed at Olivia's shoulder. A thick splotch of blood had soaked through her shirt.

"I dunno." She didn't want to tell this girl the truth.

"It looks bad. My dad's a doctor. He can look at it."

"I better not. We have to keep going."

"Where are you going?"

"I'm not sure. Hoolie knows though."

Terrilyne stared at her blankly. "You better come with me." She said it with such conviction that Olivia agreed. "Besides, it's getting late and it's almost dinnertime."

"Just make me one promise."

"It depends on the promise."

Olivia sighed. "Don't call the cops on me, or tell anyone I'm here. And your dad has to promise too."

"Why? Are you a criminal? What did you do?"

"I didn't do anything. I just can't let them catch me."

"All right."

"Do you swear?"

"Absolutely. We don't want any cops here either."

"Come on, Squirt!" Olivia called out.

"Who's that?"

"Squirt? He's a cave urchin."

Terrilyne watched Squirt crawl out of the creek and into Olivia's hand.

"Olivia, you sure are interesting."

"You are pretty interesting yourself. You live out here, huh? I don't see a town."

"Well, since you are here, I might as well tell you. I am a daughter of the Thirtieth Millennial. I am Hohokam. Our people have been living here for over thirty thousand years." She paused dramatically for effect.

Olivia wasn't impressed. "Don't you get bored living in the same place so long?"

Terrilyne looked irritated. "Thirty thousand years is a very long time.

I don't think you get it. We've been living here longer than people have lived in any city in the world. People from your world don't even know we exist. Your fancy American archaeologists don't have a clue. They only know the word Hohokam. They use it to describe other people, other traditions they don't understand. Ha!"

"So you're hiding?"

"I guess."

"Ho . . . hokam." Olivia repeated the name. "I don't get how no one knows you are here though. What about planes? What about spaceships?"

"Yes, well have you ever seen a spider web with a bright white zigzag through it?"

"I saw one of those in my aunt and uncle's garden in Florida."

"That zigzag is there to draw the attention of the spider's prey. Flies and moths mostly. Bugs," Terrilyne said, "are paying so much attention to the bright zigzag that they fly right into the spider's web."

They walked in silence for a while.

"Hohokam is just like that. Hidden in plain sight. Anyway, that is how my dad describes it. He says our zigzag shows people what they want to see instead of what is really there. This whole valley and the eastern mountains are ours. No one from the outside has ever been here. At least in my life. Well, until you."

"Whose mountains are those?" Olivia pointed to the west.

"Those are outside of our land."

"Is that snow up there?" Olivia squinted.

"My dad says no one can remember the snow staying up there this long into the year before."

Olivia felt guilty, knowing it was probably because of her messing up all of the water with the Pearl. "Where did all of these crystals come from?" she asked, kicking a small pile with her shoe.

"We made them."

"Seriously?"

"Who would joke about something like that? We made them. We've been making crystals for thirty thousand years. That's why there are so many. These are all the flawed ones. The practice ones. Trash, really."

"That answers what you do for fun out here in the middle of nowhere. I suppose you don't have any TVs either."

"Of course we have TVs. Who do you think we are?"

"My aunt and uncle didn't have a TV." Olivia suddenly missed them badly.

"What are they, hippies?"

"I suppose. Sort of," she said, not entirely sure what a hippie was. "Ouch!" A sudden sting penetrated the side of her neck. Instinctively, she reached back with her hand and punctured her finger on a bundle of spines caught in her skin. The wounds burned like acid.

"Look out!" Terrilyne pushed her backwards. "Watch where you are going."

On the ground in front of them, three more spine bundles were hopping high into the air like out-of-control super balls. Each time a bundle hit the hot sand, it let out a loud pop and jumped up in another direction.

"What in the world?" Olivia winced. She finally removed the spine bundle from her neck and threw it aside. The welt was burning hot.

"That's a jumping cholla," Terrilyne said, pointing to a tree completely covered with billions of spines. "If you get too close, those spines will leap out at you. And they hurt something awful."

"How close, exactly?" Olivia asked.

"Don't you know anything?" Terrilyne laughed. A huge, bright smile spread across her face. She slowly shuffled closer to the cholla. One of the spine bundles started wiggling free of the trunk, then leapt through the air as if shot from a rubber band. Terrilyne jumped backward just as the spines flew toward her. The spine bundle hit the ground and started popping every direction. Terrilyne giggled, dancing around to avoid getting hit.

"Look out! Don't let it get you!" She pushed Olivia to the side and ducked beneath the flying spines. After a minute, the spine bundle started weakening. It barely popped and only jumped a few feet in the air. Terrilyne found a large rock. With precision timing, she launched the rock high in the air so it landed square on the spines, smashing the threat into the ground.

"Now, imagine if there were hundreds of those jumping around. You would be covered in no time."

"I get it. I get it. Geez, that stings."

From that point on, Olivia made a wide circle around each jumping cholla tree. Sometimes there were so many that it was hard to find a way through without getting too close. But there was always a worn path through the crystals on the ground that wound its way through. She played it safe and stayed on the path.

"That reminds me, we have to get all of those out of Hoolie's fur too. They aren't the jumping kind though. It's because we ran through a forest of them."

"There are chollas that *don't* jump? Cool."

"Why don't you just cut all of the chollas down?"

"You don't think there is a reason why they are here to begin with? Why would we cut them down?" Terrilyne looked at her confused.

"So they don't jump on you. So you don't get spines hurting you all the time."

"Since when do you kill something just because it has spines." She wasn't asking a question.

Olivia didn't have an answer. They passed some other people that nodded at Terrilyne but simply gawked at her and Hoolie. "Why do you guys make so many crystals?"

"I will show you the tetracomb, if Dad will let us."

"The tetracomb? What's that?"

"I'll tell you later. There's our town." Terrilyne pointed up to a red cliff wall at the base of the eastern mountains. Hundreds of wooden ladders and scaffolds staggered thousands of feet up the cliff, leading to row upon row of homes carved deep into the stone. Olivia couldn't tell if they were caves or not, but the front of each home was walled up with large bricks.

Spiral designs decorated the base of the cliff. Handprints and sun symbols were delicately chipped into the stone. There were designs that looked more like technical diagrams. She saw a figure that reminded her of the Bobwhite Witch, part human, part bird. But the most remarkable thing, the thing that Olivia just couldn't figure out, was that the entire mountain floated above the ground. Ten feet. Maybe more. Certainly enough for her to walk under without stooping. In fact, she couldn't even jump up and touch the bottom if she wanted to. She looked into the empty space between the mountain and the ground. She couldn't see any supports holding it up. She couldn't see any chains holding it down.

"Um, Terrilyne?"

"Yeah?"

"The mountain is . . . the mountain is . . ."

"Is what? Spit it out."

"It's floating. Somehow. The mountain's floating."

"Big whup. You've never seen a mountain before?"

"I've seen plenty of mountains. I've even climbed my share lately. I've just never seen one floating. How is that even possible?"

"Geesh, you're funny. Come on, let's go home. I can't wait to show you to my parents."

High above the homes, Olivia could see a line of small satellite dishes sticking out from the rock.

"You live up there? That far up?"

"Of course."

"I don't think Hoolie can climb those ladders."

"I don't think he should try. He should stay down here."

"He won't leave my side. He's kind of attached."

"Ha! You don't have to worry. You're safe here. He isn't afraid of jaguars is he?"

"Jaguars? You mean like tigers?"

"Yeah, like tigers."

"I suppose he won't like them very much."

"He should stay close to the town then."

"I thought you said it was safe here?"

"They won't hurt anyone. They hunt higher up in the creek beds. But they might be walking around."

"Hoolie, stay here. I will be all right. I'll check on you later and we can get those spines out." Olivia grabbed his cheeks with both hands and kissed him on the nose.

Terrilyne stared at her. "You sure are interesting." With that, she started to climb. Olivia followed but the climbing was slow with only one good arm. The ladders were rickety and she thought they would crash down at any second. Terrilyne scrambled quickly and without fear.

"Here is my house. Come on!"

Olivia looked over her shoulder. The sun smeared on the horizon, burning red across the valley. She saw Hoolie curled up at the base of the cliff far below, already asleep.

8

The Crystal Farmers

Olivia wasn't sure what to expect when she entered the cliff house, probably a fire in the middle of the room and an old wooden bucket in the corner. She certainly planned on it being dirty and filled with desert sand. When she walked inside though, it looked like any house. The walls were painted cool green. There was a big kitchen. From the living room, several hallways led to the bedrooms. Lights seemed to emerge directly from the rock ceiling. Instead of a fireplace, a large TV hung on the wall in the corner.

"Look what I found!" Terrilyne yelled as she jumped inside. "Hello? Mom? Dad? Look what I found. I mean, look who I found! Helll-loooooo."

"What are you so excited about?" Her mom emerged from a back room. "Oh dear." She saw Olivia standing in the doorway, covered head to toe with dirt and dust. A large blood stain ran down her shirt. She was way too skinny.

"Her name is Olivia. I found her by the west branch. She has a bear that she kisses!"

"Where? Where did you come from? How did you? . . ." But Terrilyne's mom could barely get out her questions before she rushed over and gave Olivia the longest hug of her life. "Poor thing. Come in, let's get you cleaned up. Then you can join us for dinner and tell us your story." She hurried Olivia down the hallway and into the bathroom.

"There are towels under the sink. Yell if you need anything."

"Y . . . yes. Please, can I have a bowl? A big bowl?"

"Terrilyne! Bring Olivia that bowl on the counter, please."

Olivia took the bowl and closed the door. She could hear Terrilyne whispering excitedly with her mom out in the hallway. She filled the bowl with water and plopped Squirt in. Then she took a long, hot shower. Her wound looked worse than ever, even after she cleaned up. A fresh set of clothes including shoes were folded neatly inside the door. She dressed, picked up Squirt's bowl, and wandered back toward the front of the house.

"Oh, there you are!" Terrilyne bounded over. Several pots of food boiled on the stove, and the oven filled the room with a warm buttery smell. Terrilyne's mom and dad paused from their cooking.

"Good evening. I'm Dr Yazzi." Her dad strode across the room with his hand extended. Olivia shook his hand although it made her feel awkward, like it was inappropriate. She had never shaken an adult's hand before.

"I'm Olivia Brophie."

"Hmmm. Yes, so I understand. Is that the cave urchin?" he asked, peering into Squirt's bowl.

"His name is Squirt."

"Very interesting. I have never seen such a creature. Do you mind setting him down and letting me take a look at your shoulder?"

"I . . . I don't know."

"Olivia, I am a doctor. The way my wife and daughter describe it, you really need medical attention."

"I guess." Olivia stared at her feet. "Do you have a phone?"

"No, I'm sorry we don't have phones."

Disappointed, Olivia followed him toward the back of the house. Dr. Yazzi was short and stocky. A thick tuft of hair stood up from his head like a black fire. When they reached the end of the hallway, he opened a small, rounded door and ducked into a back alley carved entirely out of the solid stone.

"This is the way to my office," he said, hurrying down the alley. The dark passage soon opened up into a larger street lined by small store-fronts. Most of the stores were dark and uninhabited but some of them had colorful fruits and vegetables arranged neatly. One appeared to be selling uniforms that looked like space suits. Light shone from circular patches in the ceiling. Several people walked past staring at Olivia. One mother scooped her child behind her.

"Never mind them," Dr. Yazzi said. "No one here has ever met some-one from outside. Including myself. These stores are mostly empty, but once a long time ago, this street bustled with people. Much like New York must today. Here is my office."

Inside his small, clean office he examined her shoulder wound.

"I have many questions for you," he announced, "not the least of which is how you came to be injured." He pulled some gauze out of a drawer and soaked it in some liquid. It felt cold against her skin as he wiped it all around the wound.

Olivia didn't say a single word.

"You have a chrysina charm on your necklace. Where did you get that?" Dr. Yazzi pointed at the grass-green metal beetle she had found where her aunt and uncle's house had once stood. The charm was so intricately fashioned that a green light seemed to emanate from within.

"I've had it," Olivia mumbled.

"Those charms are very powerful in our history. You are lucky to have one."

Olivia didn't feel very lucky.

"And where did you get those beads?"

"Coral snakes gave them to me because I gave them some blueberries."

"Well that makes sense." Dr. Yazzi said that without even the slightest sarcasm. No one had ever believed Olivia about the coral snakes. Not even Doug or Uncle.

"The good news is I don't see any permanent damage. From the looks of it, you have had this for a while now. The infection is spreading. The bruise is yellowing and that is a good sign, even though it looks awful. It must be very stiff?"

"Yes sir." Olivia felt dizzy thinking about what he might do to her shoulder.

"Can you lift your arm up like this?" He held his arm straight out to the side.

Olivia slowly lifted her arm up. Pain shot down her side.

"I see. Well, your muscles are still intact. You might have some torn ligaments, but I won't know for sure until we contain the infection." He rummaged around in a cabinet and emerged with a syringe filled with clear liquid. "This is an antibiotic. I'm going to put this in your good shoulder so it isn't too painful."

Olivia grimaced but it didn't hurt at all.

"I'll bet your shoulder will feel a million times better in the morning. Come on, let's go get some dinner. I'm hungry."

This time, as they walked back home, the street didn't seem so big to Olivia. In fact, it seemed quite small and cramped. Like a cave.

"The stories tell of great heroes who wore the chrysina charm. Heroes that carved the canyons and forged the stars in the sky with pure silver. Heroes that defeated the stinking mud dragon and rode a thunder cloud over the sea. Only someone with an important purpose can find a chrysina charm."

"Is that all true?" Olivia asked.

Dr. Yazzi winked at her. "Some people believe that every human being has an important purpose, whether they have a charm or not."

When they made it back inside the house, a large dinner table had been set up. It was covered with food. A giant bowl filled with hundreds of small flowers sat in the middle. Every color Olivia could think of was represented in the bowl of flowers. A basket of warm fry bread steamed under a thick napkin. Countless plates of hot food filled the rest of the table. There were several new people standing around Squirt's bowl and discussing the strange creature.

"Olivia, I would like you to meet John Whistle, our . . . how would you understand? . . . our mayor. And this is Leonard and Lucy Ganado. Lucy is my sister and Terrilyne's aunt. Chubascos, here, is their son, their first son because Lucy is pregnant and I think she will have another boy."

"You have no idea either way," Lucy snipped with a smile.

With each introduction, Olivia shook their hand and muttered, "Hi." Everyone was nice, but they seemed a little nervous. They certainly chattered more amongst themselves then they did with her. John Whistle's graying hair flew around his head like he was sticking his head out a car window. Chubascos looked older than her. Probably twelve. He was taller than her too. His eyes were startling chocolate and bronze. She could tell that he was looking at her with those eyes whenever she was paying attention to something else.

"Enough staring. I'm sure Olivia is hungry," Terrilyne's mother announced. "Let's eat already." She beamed over the table in Olivia's direction. "Why don't you sit over here next to Terrilyne?"

Olivia's stomach growled as she sat down. "Oh, just a sec." She jumped up and tore a fry bread in half. She tossed a piece into Squirt's bowl. No one could see what was happening, but the bowl started rocking back and forth violently, sending water splashing upward. Chubascos could barely contain himself from running over there to look inside but he seemed compelled by politeness to stay seated.

As each bowl passed around the table, Terrilyne whispered to Olivia. "Try this. I love this."

To Olivia's surprise, even the bowl of flowers was passed around. Everyone filled their salad bowls with huge piles of the colorful blooms. "Here, try putting honey on your bread." Terrilyne drizzled honey across the table and onto Olivia's fry bread. "Whoops," she giggled. Her mom seemed annoyed but didn't say anything.

"So, Olivia, how did you come to find our land?" John Whistle casually asked.

Olivia stared at her plate, her mouth full of food.

"John, don't you dare!" Terrilyne's mom blurted out.

"Excuse me, Amythie, but it is a simple question." John seemed challenged by the assault.

"Let the poor girl eat. Look at her. She is a sack of bones."

"It isn't too much to ask. She shouldn't eat too fast or she'll get sick."

"She deserves a chance to get settled."

"A few quick responses from a stranger to our land is not an undue burden."

"She isn't a convict."

"Are you sure about that?"

The group at the table didn't seem worried about the conflict between Amythie Yazzi and John Whistle. Olivia stuffed a huge forkful of flowers into her mouth. They were pretty good. They practically melted in her mouth and disappeared with a slight wisp of fruity flavor. She never figured a person could eat flowers.

"I walked," Olivia said after swallowing.

"You *walked?* Really?" John mocked.

"Yes, I walked." Olivia looked him right in the eyes. She had stood toe to toe with the Bobwhite Witch; she wasn't about to be intimidated by some stupid mayor of this stupid place. Terrilyne stopped chewing and watched the standoff closely, a hunk of bread hanging out of her mouth.

"Well, there you go, Leonard. I told you there is more to the story. She insists that she walked!" John proclaimed with exaggerated glee.

The adults started talking quickly amongst themselves. The longer the conversation lasted, the louder it became. Although they were arguing about her, Olivia was much more concerned about putting as much food into her stomach in the shortest amount of time as possible. After a while, she leaned over to Terrilyne. "Can I save some for Hoolie?" she whispered.

Terrilyne slowly nodded, scanning the adults to see if anyone heard.

She whispered out of the corner of her mouth. "I can help you. We have lots of food, but they won't like us feeding an animal." Methodically, Terrilyne started grabbing fry breads and handing them under the table to Olivia when no one was looking. She slipped them into her backpack between her feet. She worried that the blue light of the Pearl would catch someone's eye, but it was soon covered in a pile of bread. Only Chubascos caught on that Terrilyne was up to something. His eyes squinted into mere slits as he watched.

"And what do you plan on doing with her bear?" John Whistle slammed his fists on the table and stormed out of the room.

The dinner table went silent.

"Terri is stealing bread," Chubascos announced, breaking the awkwardness.

"Am not."

"Are so."

"Am not. If I'm stealing food, where is it?" Terrilyne stood up and did a twirl with her hands above her head.

Chubascos seemed stumped. His eyes narrowed even more.

"Children, settle down," Lucy snapped.

"There is some confusion, Olivia," Dr Yazzi apologized, "because we did not believe that there was a way for any outsider to enter our land. Some among us believe that you are not so innocent to just wander here from a vast desert." He glanced toward the doorway that John Whistle had stormed through moments earlier.

"Well, it's true. I walked through the crack behind the waterfall, through the colors." Even Olivia thought *that* sounded like a lie.

Dr. Yazzi looked stunned. "Remarkable," he leaned closer to the other adults and they whispered some more together.

Chubascos put a lima bean in a spoon and launched it over Terrilyne's head. Terrilyne glared at him and mouthed something Olivia didn't quite catch.

"What kind of name is Olivia anyway?" Chubascos blurted out. No one paid him any attention.

"I'm going to go check on Hoolie." Olivia stood up and grabbed her backpack.

"Can I go too?" Terrilyne asked her mom as she jumped up from her chair with lightning speed.

"Of course. Just don't be too long."

The two girls rushed out the door and scrambled down the ladders to the sleeping bear. Hoolie's nose twitched and he woke up.

"This is fry bread, Hoolie." Olivia took out a stack of bread thicker than a dictionary and held it out for him. The bear grabbed the entire stack, set it down on the ground, and proceeded to swallow each piece, one at a time. As the last piece of bread came out of the bag, a bright blue light shone into the darkness.

"What's that?" Terrilyne asked.

"Nothing." Olivia zipped up the bag. "Do you want to help me get the cholla spines out of Hoolie?"

"Of course!" Terrilyne seemed thrilled with the idea of doing the mundane chore. "You said that these aren't jumping chollas right?"

Olivia nodded her head.

"Absolutely amazing."

They each grabbed a stick and started wedging the spiny bundles out of Hoolie's fur.

"I'm going to get more out than you," Terrilyne challenged.

"No way."

Soon, they had a big pile of spines. Hoolie was more than happy letting them pull the itchy spines out of his fur. He rolled over and groaned.

"Girls, come on home," Terrilyne's mom yelled from high above.

"Just a sec, Mom!" Terrilyne turned back to Hoolie's fur. "You know, you never told me where you were walking to."

Olivia thought quietly for a few minutes. "Sky Island." She finally let it out. "I'm looking for Sky Island."

Terrilyne looked scared. "Don't let anyone hear you say that," she scolded.

"Why? What's wrong? Do you know where it is?"

Terrilyne nodded her head. "That's Sky Island over there," she whispered, pointing to the tall western mountains. They were little more than a jagged shadow against the dark sky now. A chill went down Olivia's skin. "I'll tell you more about it tomorrow. Just promise not to tell anyone. I didn't call the cops on you so you have to promise."

"I promise," Olivia said even though the thought of waiting for an explanation drove her crazy

Back at the house, the kitchen was cleaned up and everyone was sitting around talking when they walked in.

"Come in, Olivia. There is a lot to talk about," Dr Yazzi began. "First of all, how are you feeling?"

"I'm a little tired."

Dr. Yazzi smiled and glanced at Amythie. She didn't protest but silently made it obvious that the questioning shouldn't go on too late into the night.

"It is only fair that you know about who we are first, since you're our guest." Everyone circled around her smiling. "We are the Hohokam people. We have lived here for . . ."

"Thirty thousand years," Olivia interrupted.

"Why yes, I can see Terrilyne has been talking. Many years ago, our land was much more expansive. But in recent centuries it has shrunk considerably in order to accommodate Americans. Our lifestyle is incompatible with the restrictions of your computer age. You see, Olivia, we are crystal farmers. A long time ago, our ancestors learned how to grow crystals from their basic ingredients: silicates, oxygen, water."

Olivia's eyes widened.

"Crystals are built by perfectly aligning the molecules in a rigid structure. It takes a lot of patience and precision in order to manufacture them. In nature, it would take thousands of years to create just one of those small crystals. We have learned how to speed up the process. All of those small ones you walked in on took up to one hundred years apiece."

Chubascos blurted out, "Tell her about the big ones!"

Dr. Yazzi laughed. "All of those small crystals are rejects. They were seeds in the manufacture of our larger crystals, six feet tall, to be precise. Our large crystals have to be perfect in every way. Perfectly clear with no striations. The faces have to be even and identical. There cannot be any impurities. Here. Here is a small one that started out perfectly until someone brought dust into the lab four thousand years ago." He held up a palm-sized crystal. It was so clear, it was almost invisible in his hand. The light seemed to magnify and grow through its sides. He handed it to Olivia.

"It's . . . it's like water." It felt cool in her hand.

"Oh it is much clearer than water," Dr. Yazzi bragged. "Even you Americans don't know how to make something so pure and perfect. Do you know what twinning is?"

"Twinning? Is that when you have two kids born together at the same time?"

Leonard and Lucy looked at each other. Everyone was very interested in Dr. Yazzi's story even though they must have known what he was talking about.

Dr. Yazzi considered what she said. "I suppose you can look at it that way. Imagine this one crystal only six feet tall." He took it back from Olivia and held it up in the air. "It takes five thousand years to grow a single six-foot crystal. That is seven hundred generations of Hohokam people. No one who is born today will live to see the completion of the crystals they started. Nor will their children or grandchildren. And so on."

Leonard held Chubascos around his shoulders.

"In that six-foot crystal, every silicon dioxide molecule is perfectly aligned and oriented. No two molecules in the crystal are closer or farther apart than they are to any other molecule. This is very difficult, particularly because oxygen atoms prefer to bond with just about anything other than a silicate." The entire room started laughing and nodding their heads.

"So true, so true." Lucy grinned.

"So true," Chubascos repeated.

"Twinning occurs," Dr. Yazzi continued, "when two crystals grow together." He held up a new one that looked like two crystals glued together. "These two crystals are called twins. Twinning is very common in geology, but it is never perfect. The difficulty of growing two perfect twins six feet tall is astronomical. Our twins must be perfectly aligned to each other, so a single twinning plane bisects them symmetrically. A twinning plane is the line where each crystal meets the other. Now, you remember what I told you about each molecule in each crystal being perfectly aligned?"

The room vigorously nodded their heads. Olivia stared, trying to keep up.

"If you were to grow two perfect crystals that were perfectly twinned, the single row of molecules in the twinning plane have to be aligned into two different directions. If you look at the crystal on the left," he said, covering up the other with his hand, "the twinning plane is perfectly aligned to the left. But if you look at the crystal on the right, the twinning plane is also perfectly aligned; this time to the right. So which one is it? Is the plane aligned to the left or to the right?" He poked at Chubascos' shoulder.

"Both, both!" everyone shouted.

"That is correct. The twinning plane is the only way a molecule can exist in two different places at the same time. Our ancestors discovered this secret and we have been making perfectly aligned and twinned crystals ever since. Only a tiny fraction of the crystals we start growing will actually grow perfectly to completion. That is why there are so many broken ones scattered throughout the valley. It takes a very controlled, clean environment to grow them. We do it deep in the mountain. Maybe tomorrow I can show you."

Olivia thought for a moment. "But why, why do you make them if you don't ever see them finished?"

The room went silent.

"We need them for the tetracomb."

Terrilyne nudged Olivia with her elbow.

"But that is a subject way too complex for tonight. I will give you a full tour tomorrow. Now that I told you our story, why don't you tell me how you came to find our valley?"

Olivia yawned. Terrilyne's mom shot a glance over to Dr. Yazzi. It was a warning to keep the conversation short. "Hoolie and I were hiking up a river. And Squirt too. He was in my pocket. We were hiking up the river and found a waterfall with a crack behind it. There was also a giant dam. We went into the crack and just kept walking. It was very beautiful and colorful in there. And quiet. There was a sand waterfall. I will never forget it. The colors were spinning and spinning, but we just kept walking. And here we are. Terrilyne scared us."

"Remarkable." Leonard sat back in his chair.

"I can hardly believe it," Lucy responded.

"She's lying," Chubascos said. Terrilyne kicked him in the shin.

"I am not," Olivia shot back.

"Not only that," Dr. Yazzi said, "but she has a chrysina charm and a bear."

"And the eyes of a baby bear," Terrilyne piped in.

"And a cave urchin." Lucy smiled.

"Yes, I suppose she does. Tell me, Olivia. It is our understanding that there are hundreds of miles of nothing outside of our land. How did you find the river in the first place?"

"Hoolie and I ran. Mostly, Hoolie ran and I rode him."

Dr. Yazzi grimaced.

"It took us a long time." Olivia looked down at her feet.

"And the dam. You say it was large?"

"We never really saw the whole thing. We just heard the siren and the water came down."

"The closest dam to our land is over one hundred miles away, to the best of our understanding, of course."

"And how did you get that shoulder wound?" He pointed at her shoulder.

"I slipped and hit it on a truck."

The answer didn't seem to satisfy, but it was plausible enough for the night.

Olivia faked another yawn.

"That's enough," Amythie jumped in. "It's time for bed. Come on, girls. Olivia, you can sleep in Terrilyne's room."

As they walked back toward the bedroom, Terrilyne whispered, "They are freaked out. There are old stories of a light door to the outside, but no one has ever believed it. You never told me you had a chrysina charm. Show me. I've never seen one."

"I'm sorry. Sure." She held the green beetle up in the light.

"Ha! Don't be sorry. Tomorrow, because you are here and my guest, Dad will show us the tetracomb!"

9

The Tetracomb

Olivia stood in the doorway of Terrilyne's cliff home. The sun was coming up over the mountain behind her and shining across the valley onto the western mountain. Sky Island. An entire mountain that no one outside this odd place knew existed. It was invisible to the outside. She knew her aunt and uncle were up there somewhere on those ragged peaks. If they were still alive anyway. Either way, she had to find out. She vowed to herself to hike over there today.

"How does your shoulder feel this morning?" Dr. Yazzi asked from behind.

"Pretty good, I guess." Olivia stretched her arm outward.

"That is excellent progress. Just what I hoped. We should give you another dose of antibiotic." He pulled back the sleeve of her shirt and injected again. "Terrilyne says that you want to see the tetracomb."

Olivia could see Terrilyne peeking around the corner down the hall.

"I suppose so," Olivia answered, but she really just wanted to leave.

"Yeeeeeeeeeeee YAH!" Terrilyne screamed and ran back to her room, crashing into the doorjamb and tumbling to the ground. Olivia could hear her moaning in pain.

Dr. Yazzi laughed. "Most Hohokam never see the tetracomb until their eighteenth birthday. Terrilyne doesn't want to wait eight more years. I guess she's pretty excited."

Olivia rolled her eyes and stirred Squirt's water until it spun in a whirlpool.

"It really is quite an honor. Everyone will be talking about it." The doctor paused, watching Olivia for any signs of interest before continuing. "Access is limited to a select few. Everyone contributes to the seed farm. Even the children. But as the crystals age, we must limit any risk, so appropriate certifications must be earned. We have twenty certs in all. Only someone at level twenty has access to the fifth millennium."

Olivia sighed.

"You and Terrilyne will have to adhere to the prescribed protocols of course."

Olivia stared at her feet.

"Well, for myself, I'm a level twenty. I can show you the certification exam for level twenty if you would like. It is quite descriptive and illuminating as to the rigors and discipline needed to achieve the honor."

Terrilyne sprinted out of her room wearing a ski mask. "I'm the tetracomb burglar!" she screeched. She had pulled her long dark hair through the mask's mouth-hole.

Olivia burst out laughing.

"Terri! Quit burglarizing and shape up. We can't take the tour with you acting like a Dark Eye."

Olivia's suddenly had interest. "Dark Eye?"

"I'm so sorry. I meant no harm from it, Olivia. Dark Eye is what we call outsiders. It's meant as an insult. Nothing personal to you, of course."

"I've been called that before. Where did you learn that name?"

"Dark Eyes have been part of Hohokam stories forever. No one made them up. They are part of our history."

Terrilyne skipped in a circle around the living room, reciting:

"Dark Eyes, Dark Eyes
Watch your back and say good-bye.
When you sleep they come alive
Dark Eyes, Dark Eyes."

"All right, let's calm down. Has everyone eaten breakfast?"

Both girls nodded. They had each wolfed down another big bowl of flowers. Olivia was still kind of hungry, but she didn't want to complain.

Terrilyne leaned over, cupped her hand over Olivia's ear and whispered, "There are crystals in your ear."

"What?"

"I said, there are crystals in your ear." Terrilyne paused for effect. "Everyone's got 'em."

"Really?"

"Yup. Why do you suppose it is?"

"I don't know." Olivia slipped her backpack over her shoulders.

"Oh, you don't need to bring that," Dr. Yazzi said, pulling at one of the straps.

"I want to bring it."

"Very well. Let's go, ladies." He proceeded to march out the front door and down the ladders. "I can show you the certification exams later today," he said hopefully as he climbed down. Terrilyne grew impatient with Olivia's slow progress down the ladders so she rushed across a platform and swung down another ladder in order to get ahead.

Once on the ground, Hoolie joined them and they walked along the cliff base to a large arched doorway. A stone stairway rose from the ground to the door.

"Dr. Yazzi?"

"Yes, Olivia."

"Why is the mountain, your mountain, floating in the air?"

"What do you expect a mountain to do? Now, come along. There is much to see."

"I told you," Terrilyne added.

Hoolie followed them up the stairs. Dr. Yazzi took out a large key and opened the door. A dark tunnel shot straight back into the mountain. "This walk will take a few minutes," he announced, "but your bear will have to stay here."

"His name is Hoolie."

"Of course. Pardon my insensitivity. Hoolie will have to wait here if you don't mind."

Terrilyne nervously sensed a potential impasse. "He will be all right, Olivia. He can have my sandwich." She pulled out a squashed sandwich from her pocket.

"Wait here for me," Olivia ordered and handed him the sandwich.

"Very well. Let's proceed. Perhaps I should explain a few things. Do you both know what neutrinos are?" Dr. Yazzi asked.

Olivia shook her head. Terrilyne shook her head too even though she had heard this story before.

"Neutrinos are rare cosmic particles that are expelled from super novae and imploding black holes in outer space. They are particularly rare but also exhibit very interesting behavior. Nothing can stop their progress. Not a giant slab of steel. Not even the entire planet Earth. Not even the Sun. There are neutrinos passing right through us right now as they fly through space." Dr. Yazzi took a long breath.

"Neutrinos also travel faster than the speed of light. In that way, they exist at every point along their path simultaneously. The precise moment they are created at the super nova, they are created at the end of their path and at every point in between. They are timeless."

"Ah, here we are. The sprouting room." Dr. Yazzi opened a side door. All three of them stepped into a small room and he closed the door. A huge fan blasted air from beneath their feet and at their sides. "This is to remove any loose foreign matter. Here, put these on." He handed a hairnet to each girl.

Terrilyne started giggling.

"Now, now. Calm down. In some ways, the sprouting is the longest part of the process. There is not much we can do other than provide the necessary environment for creating the molecular kernel."

Dr. Yazzi opened the second door and a rush of hot air greeted them. The large room was scorching hot. They walked briskly past rows and rows of stone troughs carved directly into the stone floor. Each trough was filled with clear water. Olivia could see thousands of tiny disks hung on strings, and thousands of those stings hung on racks. The racks of disks were submerged in the troughs of water. As far as her eyes could see, there were troughs and racks. Dozens of Hohokam of every age wandered through the pathways tending to the troughs; adjusting the temperature of the water or stringing new racks.

"After twenty years of bathing in these incubators, every sprout passes through a pure emerald laser to assess its quality. Any impurity, any speck of dust, or any irregularity of growth invalidates the sprout. Only one out of ten thousand is pure enough to pass to the next step. The rest are decomposed to unbounded molecules and sent through the process again."

"There are two other rooms just like this one in the mountain. We do this in case one room becomes contaminated. Every step of the process has this kind of redundancy."

They left the sprouting room and continued walking down the main tunnel. "The next room is where the twinning begins. Two pure sprouts are leveled and aligned, then fused onto a single disc. In each remaining room, we paint a layer of pure silicon dioxide onto the twinned sprout and incubate it in increasing concentrations of heated silicon dioxide solution. Eighteen steps and forty-five hundred years later, we have this." Dr Yazzi took out another key and opened the final door. "Level Twenty."

He made the girls put on metallic suits the color of gold and masks that covered their entire heads.

"It is much hotter in here than the other rooms. Without these suits, we wouldn't survive two minutes."

Terrilyne giggled again. The whole ordeal reminded Olivia of the tour her class took of the Sassy Swiss Chocolate Factory, but it definitely didn't smell as good.

Inside the finishing room, there were only thirty twinned crystals remaining. But what crystals! Six feet tall and clearer than glass. Tall clear tubes had been lowered around the crystals and filled with thick fluid. Olivia had to look very closely in order to even see them inside. A lattice of emerald lasers constantly scanned up and down each crystal, measuring and evaluating. Yellow and blue light split from the crystals and shot throughout the room, casting colorful dots on the walls and ceilings. Green light from the lasers collected in a thin vertical line at the exact middle between the two crystals.

"Notice how the emerald laser finds the twinning plane, like a moth to a candle, like water finds the lowest point." Dr. Yazzi beamed, pointing to the bright green intersection between the two crystals.

"Think of it girls. All of those generations. All of those years. These thirty crystals started in the sprouting room before the Egyptians built the pyramids. Terrilyne's grandfather and grandmother, their grandparents, their grandparents and on and on, all played their role tending to these very crystals. Hopefully, we pray, one of these will finish without any striations. This is the most sensitive, and least understood, of the steps. Eventually, every crystal in the tetracomb will need to be replaced and that is why we continue to grow them. It is the greatest honor for any generation to harvest a crystal for the tetracomb. And yet," he placed his gloved hand on the cylinder, "not a single one of us has actually touched one. We are forbidden to do so."

Dr. Yazzi paused, thinking to himself.

"Dad." Terrilyne waved her hands.

"Dad!" she yelled louder.

"Yes, well on toward the tetracomb." Instead of leaving by the door, they walked to the back of Level Twenty. On the back wall there was a huge door, twice as large as a garage door. Dr. Yazzi pulled on a thick rope and slowly opened the door. After they passed through a large airlock, he opened a second door to a balcony. A blast of sunlight overwhelmed their eyes and they all turned their heads to the side as if the light were painful. The desert sun felt cool after spending time in the scorching hot Level Twenty lab. The balcony overlooked a majestic horseshoe-shaped canyon. On three sides of the canyon, smooth reddish-pink stone soared high above the sandy ground. The fourth side of the canyon was open to the main valley. A breeze blew through Olivia's hair.

The canyon floor was cleared of all vegetation. In the very center, five of the large, twinned crystals stood in a circle, equally distant from each other. Sunlight shattered through the crystals, casting rainbows in every direction, splashing against the canyon walls. It was quiet. No birds. Nobody talking. A deep purplish haze filled the circle between the crystals. Every few seconds, Olivia could see a bright red streak spinning inside.

Terrilyne bounced up and down. "Look," she almost shouted, "the tetracomb!"

"Come girls," Dr. Yazzi whispered. He led them down a staircase cut directly through the stone. When they emerged on the canyon floor, Olivia felt electricity in the air.

"Do you remember what I told you about neutrinos? Nothing can stop a neutrino. Not planets. Not stars. Black holes and twinned space is the only thing in the universe that can alter their flow. The tetracomb doesn't stop neutrinos; it redirects them. It's a neutrino trap, calibrating and evening their flow. It's this flow that hides the entire valley from the outside. There is no way to enter or see inside a neutrino bubble. Even jets flying into it think they are flying straight, but are actually diverted circularly around. This is why we were all surprised at your arrival Olivia."

"That's not all, is it, Dad?" Terrilyne asked, her eyes shining in the light.

"No, indeed. Throughout our history, we have been building tetracombs in this very spot, but every millennium the crystals are shifted twelve degrees around the circle. After thirty thousand years, every space has been occupied by a crystal, increasing the power. Remember that neutrinos are timeless? The space inside the tetracomb is thusly hyperbolic.

It is the intersection of time and space. The river of neutrinos that flows through the tetracomb right this second has flowed through the tetracomb since the beginning and will flow until the tetracomb is destroyed. Inside, it is every time and no time. It is everyplace and no place."

Dr. Yazzi stepped into the spinning purplish haze. His body started to blur and blow away like snow off a rooftop or sand off a dune. In a second, he disappeared completely. The spinning red particles briefly increased and brightened. A few seconds later, he suddenly stepped out again, smiling and holding a handful of small yellow flowers. He split the bouquet between the two girls.

"I just traveled to a mountainside in the Italian Alps over six thousand years ago. We can control the twinning with these." He held out two smaller crystals. "One is for time, one is for coordinates. You must be very careful which two crystals you enter the tetracomb with. We have a library of these that I will show you later."

Olivia felt her hand tingling. She looked down to see the flowers blurring into dust, whispering away in the breeze and finally disappearing in a shower of green sparks. She looked over to see Terrilyne's flowers disappear too.

"My turn, my turn," Terrilyne squealed.

"All right, your turn. Ocean beach or Italian Alps? I only brought two."

"Beach!" Terrilyne snatched the two crystals from her father's hand.

"Don't forget, Terrilyne. Do not ever let go of those." He looked very serious.

Terrilyne turned to face the tetracomb. She took a long deep breath. Slowly, she stepped into the blur. Just like her father before her, she phased away in the neutrino wind. Moments later, she reappeared.

"Dammit!" she yelped.

"Terrilyne! That is enough," Dr. Yazzi scolded. "I don't ever want to hear that language again."

"I almost had a shell. A big one too." She stomped and threw a handful of sand onto the ground.

"Would you like to try?" Dr. Yazzi asked, turning to Olivia.

"I . . . I don't know."

"Come on. You can do it," Terrilyne said.

"Okay."

"Beach or mountain?"

"Mountain," she decided, as she had already seen the beach in Florida and should go somewhere with flowers. Dr. Yazzi handed her two crystals. One was smoky brown, the other had a pinkish tint.

"Promise me, Olivia, to not let go of these. Whatever happens on the other side, do not let go."

Olivia stood facing the tetracomb. Her legs felt very heavy. Maybe this wasn't such a sharp idea. Terrilyne started pushing her.

"Go ahead, it's easy," she encouraged.

Olivia took a cautious step forward.

"It doesn't hurt." Terrilyne gave another push.

She took a deep breath and stepped forward into the tetracomb. A quiet rush caught her like wind in a sail. "And don't eat anything," Dr. Yazzi called out to her.

She turned around to look back at him, but he was gone. Terrilyne was nowhere to be seen either. The wind rushed through her, pulling. There was no resisting it. She let the wind take her. Red sparks spiraled and left trails in her eyes. A knot of nausea settled in her stomach like a stone.

And then she stood in the middle of a grassy mountain meadow. Everywhere she turned, jagged peaks rose above her into the impossibly blue sky. They weren't just mountains. They were mountains the way she always imagined them. Feathery clouds climbed each snowy summit and rolled over the other side. The view went on forever. Some large boulders emerged from the meadow as if they had been placed there by a tasteful gardener. A stream gushed past her feet and plummeted over the cliffside on its way to a distant valley. She dipped her hand in. It was incredibly cold. Ice melt from higher altitudes. She realized how long it had been since she felt crisp, cold water. What a wonderful sensation on her parched skin! It ran through her body with a shiver. The entire meadow burst with flowers of every color and size. Tiny blue butterflies swarmed around her in complicated patterns as they explored all the different flavors of nectar.

Olivia's hand hurt from clenching the crystals. Dr. Yazzi's warning about letting go of the crystals was clear. She quickly switched them over to her other hand, hoping it didn't break the rule.

Behind her, a rumbling came across the meadow. In the distance, she could see a herd of horses running toward her. Tawny roans and spotted mustangs circled, investigating her as anyone would a strange creature. Their eyes looked right at her. Ponies bucked and cavorted as they ran. Satisfied that she was a friend, they ran up the hillside and around boulders. They ran for the pure joy of spring. Olivia could feel the ground shaking beneath her. Finally, they settled down to eat the fresh grass.

A sensation swept over her, like someone very large and powerful had grabbed the back of her shirt. She fought the feeling but there was nothing she could do. The mountainside swept away and in that instant, she was standing in front of Terrilyne and Dr. Yazzi again. A big smile was plastered on her face.

"What did you see? What did you see?" Terrilyne screamed with excitement.

"Flowers. And horses. And mountains everywhere."

"That smoky quartz crystal in your hand is finely tuned to that very meadow," Dr. Yazzi said. "It is one of the safest places someone can twin for the first time."

"And cold water. Lots of cold water. I didn't drink any though."

"That was smart of you," Dr. Yazzi said. "I'm glad you heard me before you twinned away."

"Did you bring back anything?" Terrilyne asked.

"Um . . . I forgot. There were so many ponies. I couldn't help watching them play."

"I want to see the ponies. Let me go!" Terrilyne yelled out.

"You were only gone for a few seconds. It felt like longer didn't it?" Dr. Yazzi ignored his daughter.

"It was a long time. Maybe an hour."

"I said I want to see the ponies."

"Time moves at a different rate when twinning. What seems like only seconds outside, is actually much longer in there." He nodded toward the tetracomb. "It is indeed unfortunate that we cannot control the duration of the visit. The laws of the universe seem to have an unmodifiable need to reunite disparate time elements. What triggers the settling is completely unknown to us. If you aren't in contact with your crystals when the settling occurs, your molecules will simply degrade and dissipate into nothingness. You will die just like that." He snapped his fingers. "Just like those yellow flowers I gave you earlier. The settling has caused many heartaches in our history. Of course, if you hang on to your crystals, you can return to your destination as many times as you'd like."

Olivia felt a little queasy.

"Olivia, I tell you this, showed you all of this, for a very important reason." Dr. Yazzi grabbed her shoulders and looked straight into her eyes. "I tell you this because you have come to us. You are an angel and you are one of us now. I'm sorry, but you can never leave."

"We're going to be sisters!" Terrilyne squealed as she twirled in a splotch of rainbows.

10

Sisters and Monsters

"You can't keep me here. That's kidnapping," Olivia announced at the dinner table.

John Whistle glared at her across the table and pointed his fork at her. "We can't let you leave. It's too dangerous. You should make the best of it and be happy that's all we're doing to you."

Amythie jumped in. "That isn't it at all, Olivia. We love you and want you to be happy. Terrilyne told us that you don't have a family. You can live with us. Hoolie can even stay in the valley."

Olivia kept her big trap shut. She never really told any of them about Gnat. How could she expect them to understand what has been happening to her since leaving Wisconsin? She could tell that everyone in the room really believed that this was the right thing to do. There would be no convincing them tonight. She stared at her bowl of flowers. She pretended that John Whistle wasn't creeping her out. She even ignored Chubascos who was busy making ridiculous faces at her.

"She knows too much," Leonard added.

"We need her to show us the light door so we can make sure no one else gets in. Can you imagine?" Lucy said.

"She won't show us, I suppose," John snipped. "How can we be sure she won't escape?"

"She is an innocent child," Dr. Yazzi said. "I've spent enough time with Olivia. I can say with complete authority that she entered our land accidentally."

"It isn't a matter of accidents or a matter of innocence. It's a matter of thirty thousand years of history. It's a question of what she represents." John was turning red in the face again. "If we let this slide, we could lose everything. We could lose everything for the entire history of the Hohokam. Are you prepared to risk our ancestors *and* our children?"

"We all know our history, John," Lucy rolled her eyes.

"If we do not act with compassion, if we do not act on trust, then we would be the ones putting everything at risk," Dr. Yazzi argued. "What is the point of our people if we choose to act like Dark Eyes?"

John slammed his fists onto the table. "Now I'm a Dark Eye because I want to protect my family? *Our* families? I, for one, will be watching her very closely."

Amythie placed her hand on Olivia's cheek and smiled. "The adults will clean up after dinner. There is a clear sky and a big moon this evening. Why don't you kids go watch the Gila monster wake up?"

Terrilyne pushed her chair back from the table so hard she skidded halfway across the room. "Come on, Olivia. Let's leave mean old John Whistle to clean up after us."

"Terrilyne!" her mom called out to her, a slight smile on her face. The front door slammed and the three kids were gone.

Instead of climbing down the ladders to the ground, Terrilyne and Chubascos climbed their way upward. The higher they went, the older the wooden ladders seemed to get. Up past the satellite dishes. Up over the curving cliff wall. The heights and shabbiness of the ladders were bothering Olivia less and less the longer she lived there. As long as she didn't look down, she could almost keep up with Terrilyne. The sun was quickly setting behind them.

As they climbed, Terrilyne yelled out to the sky, "We are the Hoonaw Kookam, the Bear Sisters. And the whole world is ours!" She swung one leg over the side of the ladder and waved her arm over the valley below. The ladder tilted and creaked.

"Hoonaw Kookam. I like that," Olivia laughed.

"Well I don't like it," Chubascos said.

"That's because you're a smelly sowi," Terrilyne shot back.

Chubascos mumbled something under his breath and kept climbing. Terrilyne slid down the ladder like a firefighter until she was next to Olivia.

"It means he's a smelly jackrabbit," she whispered. "Don't you think?"

Olivia blushed. "I dunno."

"Of course he is," Terrilyne said. "Of *course* he is," she yelled loud enough for him to hear.

Finally, they stood on top. The stone summit was smooth. Ghostly figures were drawn into the stone beneath their feet. Figures with long fingers. Clawed and wretched. Faces with no eyes. All mouth. Bodies twisted and stretched. Haunted nightmares. Olivia took care not to step on any of them. Far below, the houses were finishing up dinner. She could see a few lights shining out onto the desert. The moon rose, washing the entire valley in pale light. As she walked, the painted figures seemed to turn and follow behind her, arms reaching, mouths yawning. She could feel them watching her like a breath on her neck. As soon as she spun around to look, the figures froze. She could never catch them moving, but she was sure of it.

"They are following us," Olivia said.

"Who?"

"The . . . the paintings. On the rock."

Terrilyne giggled.

"Over here," Chubascos announced, rushing across the summit.

"Don't worry about them," Terrilyne told Olivia. "They are just scared of you."

"Scared?"

"They are scared that more people will come here, the same way you did."

"Oh, you mean Mr. Whistle and the others. I doubt that."

"John Whistle wants to kill you," Terrilyne said as if she were just commenting on the weather. "He thinks you are up to something."

"Well, he wouldn't be the first."

"Don't worry. The people won't let him do it."

"I'm not afraid of John Whistle. He can say whatever he wants."

"Here. This is where we wait," Chubascos said, sitting down in a spot with a wide view of the several smaller, rounded hills. "That is his house." He pointed down at a large circular cave on the other side of a canyon. Several minutes passed. Moths of various colors and sizes started landing on Olivia. The ghostly rock figures closed in around them.

"It won't be long now," Terrilyne said. "He should be waking up."

"I can't stay, Terri. I like you and all. I like your family. But I have my own family. I just don't know where they are right now. I also have . . . other things." Olivia swiped at a yellow moth that landed on her forehead.

"Like Sky Island?"

"Yes, like Sky Island. I have to go there. Things are very complicated."

"You can't go there. You just can't. It's forbidden. Besides, we have a truce with them."

"With who?"

"The people living up there. They are very bad people and they have missiles that they will shoot at us if we ever cross the boundary."

"They are Dark Eyes," Chubascos said.

"I thought you guys said I was the first Dark Eye to ever come here?" They both fell silent.

"I thought you guys said no one could enter this valley from the outside."

"They have been here for two hundred years," Terrilyne mumbled. "They arrived in the middle of the night and there was nothing we could do. They wanted the tetracomb but they didn't know how to work it. They don't know about twinning. They only know it protects this whole area from the outside. So we made a truce. They get the western island. We get the eastern island and the valley. No one goes over there."

"Who are they? What are they doing?"

"They have no name. We call them Dark Eyes."

"I know who they are," Olivia answered angrily. "They are the Cult of Wardenclyffe. They have my aunt and uncle. I'm sure of it."

"You can't go over there. The faino peplas will catch you before you even get close."

"The who?"

"Faino peplas are small black birds that sit all the time on top of every bush near the boundary. There are thousands of them. Half machine and half bird. Their eyes notice every movement. Any sign of you and they will hunt you down."

"The faino peplas don't scare me," Chubascos said. "I saw them once over the river wash."

"You're a liar," Terrilyne accused.

"There has to be a way to get past them," Olivia interrupted.

"Why do you call them the Cult of Wardenclyffe?"

"I don't know. My uncle can tell you all about it when I find him."

"Why don't you just ask them?"

"Listen. Those people are very bad," Olivia answered.

"I know that."

"Yeah, we know that," Chubascos repeated.

"Maybe, but they want to control everything. Not just your valley. They want to control the whole world. The whole universe even."

"Pffftt. No one can do that."

"Yes, they can. You know the drought. You know why it doesn't rain anymore?"

"What about it?"

"Well, not everything is as simple as you think," Olivia caught herself.

"Look! There he comes!" Chubascos screamed.

Slowly, a very large, squarish head appeared in the cave far below. Even from this far away, Olivia could see the creature's black, shining eyes set behind a gigantic mouth. A body emerged on stubby legs. It was an enormous lizard.

"That thing is bigger than an elephant," Olivia said.

"Of course. The Gila monster is bigger than a whale," Chubascos countered.

"He has lived there longer than the Hohokam," Terrilyne whispered.

"If you get too close and inhale his breath, you will turn into a raging maniac and run off into the desert to die a thirsty, shriveling death."

The lizard turned and started slowly climbing the cliff above its cave. The stars and moon gleamed off its polished scales.

"What does he eat?"

"Mustangs."

"Lots of 'em."

"Horses? He eats horses?" The thought of it made Olivia's skin chill. She thought of that speckled pony she saw playing on the alp. How shy and sweet it was.

"Yeah, and peccaries. He hunts them farther down in the box canyon over there."

"Probably not a good place to go play with your bear," Chubascos whispered with sinister glee.

"He couldn't catch us. We're too fast."

"You don't think desert mustangs are fast?"

"I don't know. I've never seen one."

"Well, they are plenty fast and the Gila monster does just fine. I've even seen him do it. He swings that giant head across the ground and scoops up everything."

"Well, he doesn't look very dangerous," Olivia said.

"He has claws the size of couches and with one bite he could crush a truck. What more do you want?"

After the long climb, the Gila monster reached the rounded top of the cliff. With a sigh, he settled down to bask in the moonlight. His long body curved against the stone. He let out a wide yawn.

"And he loves to nap in the moonlight," Chubascos added.

"Okay. Okay, he's pretty cool I guess."

"You guess? You guess?" Terrilyne joked.

"He's way more awesome than anything you've ever seen," Chubascos replied.

"Have you ever heard of a place called Junonia?" Olivia wanted them to know something that was truly amazing.

"Junonia? Of course."

"We know lots of stories from Junonia," Chubascos agreed. "Big whup."

"The Junonians were friends with the Hohokam before they were destroyed in a war."

"Really? How could they be friends from so far away?" Olivia was stunned.

"I guess we just twinned there. They were a peaceful people but they didn't have twinning like us. They were very smart though. Eventually, their enemies found where they lived and then that was that. They had amazing powers that are lost forever."

"Well, I've been there. I've been to Junonia."

Terrilyne's and Chubascos' eyes widened.

"Seriously?"

"Yes. It's where Squirt lives. Also, the Crogan Horses and the floating bridge."

"The Anaspidean? You saw an Anaspidean? You have to tell us everything."

Olivia told them the entire story. The Bobwhite Witch. The secret entrance to Junonia. The mammoth bones. The aqueducts that light up when the giant lens is lowered. The horn that calls the Anaspidean. When she was done, she opened her backpack and took out the Pearl. Its swirling blue light splashed across the rock they were sitting on and into the darkness. The blue light sent the ghost images in the rock scattering back to their shadows. The musical chimes inside the Pearl hummed in her hands.

"This is all that is left of Junonia. This is the Pearl of Tagelus, and the Cult of Wardenclyffe will do anything to get it. They will start wars and betray their own families. I was running from their helicopters when I found your valley."

"Whoa," Chubascos said. touching the Pearl's smooth surface.

"It's so beautiful." Terrilyne was in awe.

"You have to help me. I need to save my aunt and uncle. I need to start the rain again. I need to find my mom and dad."

The three of them sat quietly for a long time. Blue light from the Pearl shone off the Gila monster's scales across the canyon like a million glass beads. A cool breeze quietly blew across the vast desert.

"I will help you escape," Terrilyne finally said.

"Me too," Chubascos said.

"Can we still be sisters?" Terrilyne asked, laying her head on Olivia's shoulder.

"Of course. I would like that," she answered. Olivia couldn't see the tears running down Terrilyne's cheek.

11

The Enfoldment Box

"The middle one is not Walleri. He is not Dark Eye. The armor is unique. The animal is too small. The small child is a Dark Eye. The tall one is a partially developed Dark Eye."

"They rode an enfoldment box to get here. How did they get one of those? None of them are missing."

"Look, the middle one wakes."

Doug rubbed his head and sat up. Circled around him were fifteen small people wearing bright red clothing. They were very pale, a paler pale than anyone he had ever seen. Thin hair wisped on their heads like yesterday's mist. None of them were wearing shoes. "Who are . . . Where am I?" Doug asked. His voice boomed in the room. All of the strange people stepped back.

"Whoa. Aliens," Gnat blurted out, suddenly awake. Cheeto stretched and stood up. The fur on his back bristled. Larry jumped to his feet.

"We will not hurt you. Or your animal. Are you here to kill us?" the pale people asked.

"Uh . . . no. I mean, we aren't going to hurt anyone," Doug answered. He noticed that the pale people were all talking in unison. He couldn't figure out how they all knew what to say at the exact same time. "Where are we?"

"You are in Junonia. You arrived by enfoldment box," they all said at once.

"Junonia?" Doug looked around. "What do you mean? Is this some kind of joke?" He stood up. Even though he was only ten years old, he was already several inches taller than the pale people.

"You arrived by enfoldment box, but you are not from Junonia. Who are you?"

"I . . . I am Doug Corcoran. This is Gnat and Cheeto. Um . . . and Larry." Doug held his hand out to shake their hands. The entire group of people took another step back, looking fearfully at his sudden gesture. Doug noticed how incredibly thin their arms and legs were. They stood high on the toes of their tiny feet.

"You guys are *all* wearing red?" Larry laughed uneasily. "Not cool."

"And you will not hurt us?" the group spoke simultaneously.

"No. Of course not. How could we possibly hurt you?" Doug answered.

"Your animal might hurt us."

"Cheeto? He won't do anything if you don't attack us."

"Well I'm gonna to hurt you if you don't show me how to get home," Larry threatened. "I'm gonna hurt you all the way to Sunday."

"This Dark Eye will hurt us." The Junonians looked nervously at each other.

"No! No one is going to hurt anyone. Larry, tell them that you won't hurt them."

"Mind your own business. I *am* going to hurt them if they keep us here. This is kidnapping."

"He isn't going to hurt you. I promise," Doug interrupted.

"You may have weapons. Do you have weapons?"

Doug laughed nervously. "Mom won't even let me have a BB gun."

"Ha!" Larry laughed.

"BB gun?" the Junonians asked.

"I have my disco pearl," Gnat said as he threw the rubber ball to the ground and held the flashing lights out in his hand. The Junonians jumped.

"That's not a weapon. We do not have any weapons. We won't hurt you. That's *not* a weapon," Doug argued.

"Hhhmph," Larry said. "We'll see."

"Then it is agreed. You may stay."

"We don't really want to stay," Doug said, walking toward the operculum. "Gnat, Cheeto, let's go home. We're probably in trouble as it is." The pale people split apart as they walked forward.

"You are welcome here. You may stay," they repeated.

Doug pushed open the operculum. He couldn't believe his eyes. The city was alive. Junonia was alive. The aqueducts sparkled and shone, lighting the entire city. He looked down. The pool that was frozen only moments before was lit like a spring on a summer day. Everywhere more pale people were walking and going about their day. He looked up. The city was so high he could barely see the ceiling. White birds the size of hummingbirds flew across the chasm, from veranda to balcony, circling around in the empty space. Doug thought he could see small silver chains hanging from their feet. Tiny bells hung at the end of each chain. The faint twinkling echoed throughout the city.

Doug stumbled back into the room. "Where . . . where are we?"

"You are in Junonia, as we said," they answered.

"What time is it?"

"Time?"

"What is your time continuum?" Gnat interjected.

"That doesn't even mean anything, Gnat. This isn't a video game," Doug snapped. "What is the time? Is it still morning?"

"We do not understand what you are asking. You are in Junonia."

"Just tell us the time already. I have to get to practice," Larry said with more than a hint of frustration.

"Time? It is thirty-fourth marking in the sixth dune."

Doug ran his hand through his hair. "That doesn't make any sense. What are you talking about?" He looked at his watch. It said noon.

"This is ridiculous. Get out of my way." Larry pushed though the crowd and out the operculum. Within seconds he was stumbling back into the room. He looked pale. Without a word, he sat down against the wall.

"You should beware of this Dark Eye child." The pale people pointed at Gnat. "The parents will be searching for it."

"My father is lost," Gnat replied, irritated. "My mother is on a mission."

"Then you are an orphan."

"Olivia will find us."

"Olivia. What is Olivia?"

"She is my big sister. She has been here before and will find us. She will bring bears too."

The people looked nervously at each other. "You will not let Olivia hurt us?"

Gnat looked at them suspiciously. "She doesn't listen to me."

"All right, no one is hurting anyone," Doug shouted. "We aren't hurting you. You aren't hurting us. Can you just take us to the surface? We *have* to go home."

Something was up. Something bad. Doug had a sneaking suspicion that things were way more complicated than he initially thought. They were on another planet. Or lost in time. His head swirled with the possibilities. He had read countless stories that started this way and none of them ended well. Slowly, he came to the realization that he should just ignore his suspicions. They were just stupid stories anyway. People don't just wake up on another planet. It was best to just go along with it for now. Scientific inquiry would resolve this once he learned more. Facts not fear. He was sure that he would find out soon enough what was happening.

"It is time for harvest. You may go with us." All but one Junonian left the room. The single Junonian continued. "We harvest on the surface."

"My name is Doug. This is Gnat and Cheeto. And Larry over there in the corner. What is your name?" Doug repeated their names, this time without sticking his hand out.

"Name? We do not understand."

"What do people call you?"

"We are Junonians."

"You told me *that* already. I mean *you* specifically. What do your friends call *you?*"

"We are all Junonians."

"So you don't have a name of your own?" Doug thought for a second.

"I say his name is Anachis," Gnat said.

"What kind of name is Anachis?" Doug whispered to Gnat.

"Ana . . . kis," the Junonian said.

"See? He likes it." Gnat grinned.

"Anachis." Doug rolled his eyes, pointing at the Junonian. "Doug." He pointed at himself. "Gnat, Cheeto, Larry." It reminded him of some Tarzan cartoon.

"Come," Anachis said. "We leave for the surface."

Doug noticed that Anachis's skin was thicker than human skin, giving his flesh a blobby look even though he was very skinny. It looked like some kind of thin jelly covered his entire body. His skin was partially clear on its edges. His fingertips were almost completely transparent; the tiny bones showed inside. His ears were smaller than Doug's, something he thought he would never see.

Doug walked over and started pulling on Larry's arm to help him up. Larry whipped his arm away and slowly stood up on his own. They walked back out into the city.

"Awesooooome," Gnat called out, holding Cheeto in his arms and looking at the busy city.

"This is not awesome," Larry finally said. "This is weird. Don't either of you nerds think this is weird?"

Gnat shrugged.

"I just want to go home now. This is weird."

"We are going home now, Larry. We'll just follow these guys to the surface," Doug said, rolling his eyes.

Instead of walking upward toward the surface though, they were led back down the stairs and ramps toward the pool. As they walked, other Junonians joined them from side streets and other apartments. He counted thirty-five Junonians in the group now. They walked very closely together, too close for comfort. Yet they never stumbled. Their legs seemed to work like a single creature. Doug could feel one right behind him.

"Anachis, I thought the way to the surface is up. Where are you taking us?"

The entire group responded in unison. "Anachis is leaving for the harvest. You will follow us and return to your home." Doug suspected that they all thought their name was Anachis now.

Soon, he saw why they were descending. Lined up in the pool at the bottom of the city there were five tardigrades. Their giant clear bodies took on the color of the water. One snapped angrily at the tardigrade in front of him. Each of them had a reddish saddle bag draped across its back.

"Crogan horses," Doug said excitedly.

"Yes, they will not hurt you," the Junonians assured him.

"I know. I've ridden one before." Doug folded his arms with satisfaction.

"Then we were right that you are not a Dark Eye." They nodded to each other. "They will not hurt the child or the little animal either."

"What about me? What about me?" Larry asked.

The Junonians looked nervously at each other.

"What? What is it?" Larry asked again.

A tardigrade lunged its head toward him, extending its neck like rubber to an incredible length and snapping its jaws. The growling scream that came out of its toothless mouth was deafening. Larry slammed backwards into the banister and tumbled to the ground.

"Whoa. What is that thing?" Larry yelled. "Make it stop!"

"Actually, it's a tardigrade, which is incredible considering how small they typically are. Tardigrades are usually microscopic. These people call them Crogan Horses," Doug said authoritatively.

"I have no idea what is coming out of your pie hole. You sure seem to know a lot about this place. This is one of your tricks, isn't it?"

"No one is trying to trick you, Larry."

"I know you know more than you are telling me, Corcoran. If I find out that you are holding out on me, I'm going to make your life miserable."

"Well, there is one more thing," Doug answered, hiding a small smile from Larry's view. "Tardigrades are fearsome predators. Top of the food chain at their scale. I'm really glad they like us."

The tardigrade swung its head around again and snapped at Larry.

"They like you," Larry yelled. "They like *you.*"

Doug looked up. More tiny white birds swirled in the air, swooping through the archways and columns. Junonia was beautiful. The most beautiful city he had ever seen. It was no longer the moldy relic they had explored earlier with Olivia. It was alive with music and light. The walls and architecture swirled and sparkled with white and pink enamel. He wished he still had his camera.

A large trumpet-shaped bowl was passed around to the entire group. Each Junonian reached in and grabbed a handful of blue powder. One by one, they threw the powder onto a Crogan horse. The blue color stained and ran down the sides of the giant, clear beasts. Anachis held the bowl for the boys. Gnat reached in with both hands, waddled over to the edge, and hurled the bright blue powder through the air. Half of it landed on the horse, half of it blew back and settled on the Junonians who laughed appreciatively. Larry took a pinch and threw it, simultaneously cowering for the next attack. Doug grabbed a small handful of powder and examined it closely, trying to determine what it was. The color was unlike anything he'd ever seen. It didn't smell. It felt like baby powder with a bit of sand. He didn't dare taste it. Grimacing with his inability to identify it, he tossed it far from the tardigrade's head so it didn't get in its eye.

"Why are we doing this Anachis?" he whispered.

All of the Junonians within earshot answered, "We thank the generosity of Crogan. We thank the wisdom of Tagelus."

"Tagelus!" Doug yelped. "He is here?"

"Tagelus is here. Tagelus is all around us."

"Can we meet him? Where is he?"

"We do not understand. Tagelus is all around us. Tagelus is here."

"He is a ghost," Gnat explained.

"They must not understand," Doug added. "Tagelus lived so long ago."

"Where's all the ice?" Gnat asked.

"I don't know. I don't know," Doug whispered. He had been thinking about the enfoldment box. He had been wondering how everything could have changed so quickly. The knot in his chest grew heavier.

"We leave. Mount the horses," the Junonians called out. High above them, a horn sounded throughout the cavern, sending birds twinkling into the air.

Doug easily climbed on top of the tardigrade that he had thrown blue powder on. He reached down and helped Gnat up behind him. Gnat clung tightly to a squirming Cheeto. "Don't let go," Doug warned. The tardigrade's cold, firm body felt familiar under him. "I told you I rode one last time, didn't I?"

"Yeah, yeah," Gnat conceded. "A million times."

It took ten Junonians to convince a tardigrade to allow Larry onto its back. Its giant clear body writhed wherever Larry touched it, as if the mere contact was torturous.

One by one, the tardigrades crossed the pool, each with multiple Junonians riding. Doug could hear them coaxing and talking to them.

"Good boy, come on." He offered up the only thing he could think of and patted its thick neck.

"Giddyap!" Gnat called out, just as their tardigrade squished down like a water balloon and entered a tunnel. A single, glowing antler grew out of its head and lit the way forward. Water rushed and sloshed down the tunnel, completely soaking everyone within seconds. Doug gasped for air. Cheeto buried his head in Gnat's chest. After a few minutes, they emerged back up in the main cave and onto the tombolo.

The cave seemed a lot smaller than what Doug remembered. It was narrow enough to see the cave walls on both sides. Countless cave urchins covered the walls and ploughed through the sand. Flashes of color spread through them like waves.

"Squirt!" Gnat yelled, echoing. "All Squirts! Giddyap!"

"Look at how many there are now. Where did they all come from?" Doug asked.

The urchins dropped from the cave walls into the water as soon as they saw the tardigrades approaching, causing a great splashing in every direction. They ejected so much pink ink that the water changed color. Amphibious creatures slithered away from the stain into the depths of the lake.

Doug saw groups of Junonians digging sand from under the water, sifting through the grains with shallow pans, and collecting bits of something into pouches. The remaining sand was dumped on the end of the tombolo, allowing them to work farther and farther into the lake.

Like a train, the line of tardigrades crossed the water and entered another side tunnel. They spiraled upward, passing through smaller caverns. Streams cascaded down smooth rock into quiet blue pools. They entered one tunnel where the rushing water was so deep only their heads remained above water. Gnat held Cheeto over his head. Larry's tardigrade writhed and fought. Several times, it rotated Larry completely under water, trying to dislodge him from its back. Clear mosses hung down from the ceiling. Small canary snails crawled everywhere, eating the moss and algae.

They arrived at a subsurface landing and the horses came to a halt. Through a thick curtain of moss and vegetation, they could see sunlight breaking through the leaves. A small spring emerged onto the surface and trickled away out of sight.

"This was way easier than crawling up the tortoise hole," Doug said, swatting at a mosquito that was looping around his head. "I wonder where we are. I've been to every spring around here and I don't recognize this."

"Giddyap. Let's go, ride 'em," Gnat called out.

"I don't think we can. The tardigrades need to stay in the tunnels. The sun will probably kill them."

Larry fell off into a heap on the ground.

The Junonians dismounted the horses and started handing out sacks.

"You can help us harvest?' the Junonians asked.

"Maybe a little bit." Doug was curious. "But we have to get home. What are we harvesting?"

"We pick the jumjams, only the white jumjams."

"Well, okay. We'll just follow you. What exactly is a jumjam?"

"It's candy," Gnat suggested.

"It isn't candy. Nobody harvests candy."

"I'm hungry."

"Me too. Let's follow them until I can figure out where we are. We're already going to get in trouble for leaving the house. Mom is going to know because we're all dirty and wet."

"I'm not picking nuthin'. I'm going home," Larry said, hopping to his feet.

"I wouldn't do that. Do you know where we are?" Doug asked.

"I know where I'm not," Larry said. "I'm not at home and I'm not staying with you losers." Larry plunged through the opening and disappeared from sight.

One by one, the Junonians pushed through the curtain of vegetation. Doug and Gnat joined the line.

"Stay with us. Stay close," Anachis urged.

The bright sun blasted them as they emerged. Doug's heart sank when his eyes focused. The entire world was white sand. He whipped around. As far as he could see there were dunes. Patches of yellowing grass were scattered here and there. Occasionally a stand of stunted trees rose up in the valleys between the dune tops. A hot wind blew grains of sand like smoke along the ground. A flock of tiny white birds flew out of a nearby crevice and looped into the sky. The twinkling bells faded into the wind.

"Oh no," Doug whispered loudly.

"What? Where are we?" Gnat asked.

"I think we're back in time. That paper box, that enfoldment box must have taken us back in time. I thought about it when we woke up, but now I'm almost sure. Just look at the landscape. Almost no trees. No topsoil as far as you can see. We should be seeing the radio tower or hearing traffic from the highway. There aren't even any jet trails in the air. This isn't good. This really isn't good."

"Awesome. Back in time."

"Gnat, this is serious. We're back in Junonia. My mom doesn't know where we are. Heck, technically my mom isn't even born yet. I mean, have you ever heard of anyone who went back in time? Time travel breaks the laws of physics. It isn't even possible for anything larger than a quark. Have you considered how in the world we're supposed to get home?"

"We can use the paper box."

"I dunno. That thing isn't a bus. We can't control it. We could end up with dinosaurs. Or dead."

"Stay with us," the Junonians warned. They moved quickly over the sand, clustered together in a group. Gnat and Doug had a hard time keeping up. Cheeto scrambled behind them, carefully sniffing the ground.

Over the next few dunes the sandy land opened up into a larger grassland. A small forest grew toward the north. Sandy ridges rose and fell endlessly toward the west. Doug and Gnat stood on the last dune gawking at the sight. A giant tortoise the size of a wheelbarrow slowly ate grass in front of them.

"Look at the size of that one," Gnat called out. "I'll bet you really want to put a flag on its hole."

"That is no gopher tortoise," Doug said. "That's a giant tortoise, like the ones in Galapagos. I can't believe we are this close." The tortoise raised its head with a mouthful of grass and calmly munched. It looked like a very old but gentle man as it looked at Gnat. Doug slowly raised his arm toward the tortoise's head. His hand was shaking.

"You're scared," Gnat whispered.

"No. No, I'm not. It's just . . . amazing." Doug's hand rested against the tortoise's cheek. The giant animal didn't stop chewing. "Dr Smeerczak will never believe this. Never."

"Who in the world is Dr. Smeerczak?"

"Look out there." Doug pointed across the grass. Far in the distance, a small forest grew out of the sand; it was scrub, just like their Florida scrub. A thin fog hung over the treetops. Large birds swung their heavy wings as they flew off to some far-off destination. A herd of elephants walked slowly toward the scrub. Their trunks swayed back and forth with every step. Dust billowed behind them. A baby jogged alongside, his ears flopping wildly in the air. He held his mother's tail in his tiny trunk.

"Elephants!" Gnat yelled.

"Those aren't elephants. Those are woolly mammoths. Like the skeletons we found in the cave."

"So woolly." Gnat looked more excited than scared.

"We really *are* back and time. *Way* back in time. I don't know how far back. Thousands of years at least." Doug pushed his hand through his short hair. Woolly mammoths, giant tortoises, Junonia. It was overwhelming.

In the grassland, the Junonians found a patch of jumjams and started picking.

"These are just gopher apples," Doug said aloud, tossing one of the white fruits into his bag. He couldn't stop staring at the mammoths. "It doesn't make any sense. It isn't even scientifically possible. But here we are. Thousands of years in the past."

Gnat ignored him.

"We have to get that enfoldment box. There must be a way to reverse it, " Doug said.

"That was my idea," Gnat said as he took a small bite out of a jumjam and scrunched his face. "You stole my idea."

"How could we reverse it though?"

"All you have to do is reverse the ions."

"You are just saying stuff that you don't even understand." Doug's voice was getting higher and higher.

"You can do it, fella. You are smarter than anybody," Gnat said to Doug as he handed the rest of his jumjam to Cheeto, who turned up his nose.

Doug pressed his lips together. Part of him wanted to cry. If he was their only chance they were in big trouble because he had no idea what to do or how to even begin figuring out what to do.

After an hour of picking on their hands and knees, most of the Junonians' sacks were full. Doug's and Gnat's were almost completely empty. They were too busy watching giant tortoises and mammoths. All of the Junonians suddenly leaped to their feet.

"What? What is it?"

"Be quiet. Stay with us," they whispered.

"What is going on?"

"It will hurt you."

A chill ran down Doug's neck. He looked around. Slowly creeping toward them in the grass, a car-sized cat took a cautious step. Its bright yellow eyes glowed. Two thick ivory spikes hung down from its mouth.

"Scimitar!" the Junonians screamed. In a flash, the entire group started running back across the grass, leaving Doug, Gnat, and Cheeto standing with their empty sacks. The scimitar cat leaped from its hiding spot and lunged toward them.

"Get down," Doug shouted to Gnat as he grabbed Cheeto. "Don't move." He pushed Gnat's head into the dirt and covered Cheeto under his arm so he wouldn't bark. Cheeto squirmed with all of his strength trying to break free. Doug clenched his jaws shut.

With a thunderous crash, the hungry cat passed within a few yards, focused on the escaping prey. It moved beautifully with long leaps, smoothly gaining ground. Its lungs heaved urgently. The Junonians rushed across the landscape like a herd of animals, clustered together, swerving and turning as a group. Once they reached the sand dunes, they had the upper hand. The cat slowed down in the shifting sand, eventually giving up as the Junonians disappeared over the next dune.

Slowly, Doug raised his head.

"Is it gone?" Gnat whispered.

"Shhhhh. Quiet." Doug was barely whispering. He watched the frustrated cat look back over the grasslands. He could almost see the disappointment on its face. The cat sat down and began to chew its hind foot.

"Ugh."

"What?"

"It's right there. We can't get up or it will see us." Doug rubbed Cheeto's ear as much to comfort himself as the dog. "There is no way we can run that fast. We have to stay here until it goes away. Whatever you do, just stay down."

Hours passed and the sun started dropping toward the horizon. Doug knew night would be even more dangerous. They wouldn't be able

to see where the cat was in the dark. He dug his fingers into the sand. He couldn't shake the picture of the cat leaping forward on its huge paws. Its body had rippled with solid muscle as it changed directions effortlessly. He smiled to himself as he realized that Olivia would probably think of a name and walk right up to it. Every once in a while, Doug stuck his head above the grass to look around. Far from looking relaxed, the scimitar cat appeared to be nervous as it scanned the surrounding landscape for anything to eat. Gnat and Cheeto took a nap.

Just before the sun went down, Doug saw three Junonians slowly making their way across the sand toward the cat. They looked so puny next to the predator. It would probably eat all three of them in one meal. Doug wanted to jump up and warn them to run away. They probably couldn't see it hidden in the grass. But he didn't. He was too scared.

Suddenly, the Junonians started waving their hands and screaming. The cat leaped to its feet and took off chasing them toward the forest. They disappeared into the trees.

"Get up, Gnat. We have to go." As he stood up, he realized that the rest of the Junonians were circled around them.

"You stay with us." They were smiling. "You stay with Anachis."

Gnat jumped up and gave the closest Junonian a hug.

"We can't run as fast as you," Doug explained. Inside, he suddenly felt a warm sense of compassion for these strange people. They risked their lives to come back for two kids and a small dog lost in time.

"Stay with us now. Soon the Walleri will wake and they will hurt us."

Doug hated to think about what a Walleri was. If the Junonians didn't mind taunting a scimitar cat but the Walleri scared them, it must be something awful.

12

The Music of the Tardigrades

"The enfoldment box only works one way. It returns anyone to the place the box was folded, to where it was made," Anachis explained. He was alone with Doug and Gnat in his apartment. A creamy light glowed from the curving walls. The ceiling spiraled upward into a pinkish point. It was like sitting inside a conch shell.

"Do you understand? We are from the future. We don't belong here," Doug said, hyperventilating.

"That has never happened before. We use them to bring large harvests home from far away or if we are lost. They are very dangerous."

"How are we supposed to get home?"

"We do not know. There is no way to reverse it." Anachis set a plate of fruit in front of them. Doug recognized the white jumjams but there were other fruits that he had never seen before: spiky red cranberry-sized fruit, a pile of clear mosses, thin spindle-shaped green berries, an oblong fuchsia lump that looked like it would glow in the dark. "You may stay here or you can live with the Dark Eyes on the surface."

"We'll stay here." Doug didn't like the idea of going to the surface again. Gnat sat in a ball on the floor and stared at his feet. Slowly, his hand reached out again and again to the fruit plate, but he didn't say anything. He also didn't try the clear moss.

"Your Dark Eye is young." Anachis pointed to Gnat. "Are you sure its parents will not come to get it?"

"His parents aren't even born yet."

"We are sorry. You are right. He is harmless until he grows. We have a hard time accepting that you are from another time. These are things that we are not familiar with, enfolding from the future."

"Yeah, me too." Doug paused. "Why don't you call me a Dark Eye?"

"You are not a Dark Eye."

"What . . . what am I?" Doug wasn't sure he wanted to hear the answer.

"We do not know. You look like a Dark Eye, but you don't feel like one. We don't know what you are." Anachis considered the issue. "It remains to be seen."

Doug sat quietly for a few minutes while Anachis watched him, studying. He could feel his own hands shaking. He thought about the enfoldment box. It must have been built back when Junonia was populated, but the bottles that were knocked off the shelves did something to allow it to travel back in time. He tried to remember which specific bottles crashed to the floor. He hadn't paid much attention because they were so surprised at the unfolding box. White pebbles certainly, because he remembered kicking them as he walked to the middle of the paper. A smoke filled the air too, but where did that come from? Even if he could recreate the same conditions, there was no reason to believe the box would return them home. The box did exactly what it was designed to do, return its contents to the place it was made in the first place. There really was no way to get home. He looked over at Gnat out of the corner of his eye. He was nibbling on a star-shaped lavender berry. He looked at Anachis, who stared without blinking back. Doug had the sneaking suspicion that Anachis didn't even have eyelids.

"How do you make an enfoldment box?"

"It is quite simple really," Anachis answered. "A paper is made from palmetto threads, very thin pine pulp, and powdered quartz sand. As the pulp dries, it imprints on the gravitational signature of wherever it was made. The palmetto threads are incorporated into the paper at a very high tension. Then the paper is folded into a box. The ink is made from horseshoe crab blood that has been slowly anodized. The words themselves are meaningless. They could be anything. The ink is really just a switch to refold. Sensitive to vibrations, it triggers the threads to return to their original shape. Once triggered, the momentum of the refolding box pushes it beyond that original shape and into itself. At the moment it inverses and ceases to exist in our space, it emerges in the location of its gravitational signature." Anachis rattled off the directions like he had it memorized.

"Can we trick it? Can we make it think somewhere else is its home?"

"Well, no. The powdered quartz has to align to the specific gravitational field of a location."

"Like a fingerprint," Doug suggested.

"What's a fingerprint?"

"You know, everyone has their own fingerprint?"

Anachis shook his head.

Doug held up his fingers. "These lines and circles here, see?" Anachis leaned closer and grabbed Doug's hand. His clear skin felt cold. Anachis held up his own clear fingers and slowly pressed his hand against Doug's. The reason for his confusion was apparent. He didn't have fingerprints.

"We have tried unsuccessfully to create an enfoldment box that goes somewhere else. It is impossible to get the . . . fingerprint correct. The paper must be fabricated at the location you want it to return to."

Doug's heart sank. Gnat was counting on him and he couldn't understand half of what Anachis said. How in the world was he going to reverse it?

"There must be a way. We have to try or we will die here."

"Yes, you will die here."

Doug felt tears welling up in his eyes. He tried to hold them back. He told himself that it wouldn't do any good. But one tear escaped, rolled down his cheek, and sat on the edge of his jaw. He didn't want Anachis to see so he pretended it wasn't there. It felt heavy, like a bumble bee glued to his skin, stinging and burning. He shrugged his shoulder up to his jaw, finally wiping it away.

"What is this material on your feet?" Anachis pointed to the bottom of Doug's shoes.

"That's rubber," Doug answered.

"Rubber. How do you make it?"

"I . . . I don't know. From a rubber tree."

"We would like you to make rubber for us."

"I can't. I mean, I don't know how. A factory made it."

Anachis considered this. "Here, we all know how to make everything. It is unfortunate that you do not know how to make rubber. We would very much like to make some of our own. Perhaps you can show us the rubber tree?"

"They don't grow in Florida."

"Florida?"

"Here. They don't grow here." Doug flung his hands every which way. He was so far back in time that Florida wasn't a state yet. Ponce de Leon hadn't even been here. And yet, here were a whole people. Kind, wonderful, beautiful people living their whole lives. Clear-fingered jelly people who all look and talk the same, but beautiful people nonetheless. "Rubber trees grow in other countries. Along the equator I think."

"Your people are traders then? That is good. We trade very little. Most nations want to hurt us so we do not trade with them."

"Why do they want to hurt you?"

"Most nations want to hurt everything. We cannot fight very well. We are small and frail as you can see."

Doug thought about the mammoth skeletons with the war armor. "How do you know they won't just come to Junonia and hurt you?"

"We said we cannot fight. We did not say we were helpless. We have some defenses. But we are very vulnerable outside of Junonia. When we leave, we stay out of the way and don't take much from the land."

Suddenly it clicked in Doug's head. The Pearl! The Pearl of Tagelus. Olivia said it changes the laws of the universe. That was their ticket home. All he had to do is find it and alter time. Doug chuckled to himself. Three months ago if someone had said something about time travel and a device from an ancient, secret city, he would have called them irresponsible and strident. That is what scientists said about such things. Irresponsible and strident.

A horn echoed throughout Junonia. Its deep mellow note filled every corner of the city.

"What's that?"

"The lights are going to go out. It's time to sleep."

"Good. I'm tired. Where's the bed?"

Anachis set the bowl of fruit on a shelf. He picked up a small bottle of milky liquid and released a single drop onto the floor.

"Hey!" Gnat woke from his thoughts. "The floor is sinking."

"It's not sinking. It's softening. This," Anachis shook the bottle, "is concentrated mucoloid."

Doug stared speechless.

"It temporarily nourishes the calcium carbonate and nacre matrix that make our buildings. The floor turns into our bed."

By now, they had sunk softly into the floor that felt like a giant marshmallow. The lights quickly lost power and dimmed. For some reason, both Doug and Gnat felt more comfortable closer to the walls. Cheeto curled into a ball against Gnat's stomach. Anachis settled into the center of the room, sinking out of sight. Doug tried to stay awake. He had to make plans. He had to find the Pearl and figure out how it worked. He was pretty sure the Junonians wouldn't like him taking it. They would probably kick him and Gnat out onto the surface if he got caught. It wasn't going to be easy. He was the tallest and biggest person in the entire city since Larry had run away on the surface. For the first time in his life, he was the strongest. Only now, being the biggest might be a disadvantage. It would make it harder to sneak around. He stuck out here like a sore thumb.

The lights of Junonia dimmed to a faint yellow before disappearing altogether. The darkness was complete. Doug couldn't even see his own nose. A faint yowling floated through the city.

"Crogan horses," Anachis whispered into the darkness. "They sing every night in their congregations."

Doug listened to the strange music of the tardigrades as they howled from their wet caves. Their countless voices merged, rising and falling in haunting waves. Deep growling notes and high trilling flutterings. Like distant wolves, song birds, and whales all vibrating from a single voice. Only more beastly.

No matter how hard he tried to stay up and listen, his eyelids dropped. He dreamed of a fierce scimitar cat flying across the plains, its claws digging into the wind. He dreamed of deep, flowing water rushing him along in darkness beneath the landscape of Florida, the current too strong for him to swim against. Swallowed by the cold, black water, he could breathe. Somehow, he could breathe under water. It was a fantastic moment. The best kind of dream.

The sonorous horn echoed once again in the darkness, waking him with its gentle nudge. *Now what?* he thought.

"Come." Anachis grabbed Doug's elbow and helped him toward the operculum door. They stepped outside onto the balcony. Even in the complete darkness, Doug could feel the yawning cavern opening up below.

"What is going on? Where are we going? I was sleeping so well."

"We wanted you to see sunrise."

"Sunrise? We just went to bed." Doug was suddenly afraid that the Junonians didn't believe in the greatness of sleep. What kind of sick place didn't like to sleep?

"No. We slept all night. It's sunrise. Look up."

In the dark Doug couldn't really tell which way was up, but he tilted his head back. Far above them, a spark appeared like a spinning star. The star grew brighter, spilling over the edge of the blackness. Molten glass.

The star caught fire, rushing along the aqueducts and troughs of the city, pouring down in waterfalls, splashing into terraced pools, sending bright rain falling downward. The light flushed along the thin aqueduct that was built into the railing Doug leaned on. He dipped his finger into the water. Cool and wet. Light lingered on his finger and dripped down his arm as he raised it to get a better look. Finally, the raging light crashed into the pool far below. The city shone as bright as ever. Up and down the city, hundreds of Junonians stood on their balconies and patios watching the new day arrive.

"Sunrise," Anachis said, smiling.

"You have *got* to show me how you do that." Doug thought about winning next year's state science showdown. This would be way cooler than the giant model of an anthill he did last year.

Gnat yawned and stretched his arms up. "What's for breakfast?" Cheeto walked off looking for a patch of grass that didn't exist.

All of the Junonians started walking toward the middle of the city. Climbing stairs, they formed into slowly accumulating groups. "Come," Anachis said as a group of others neared.

"Where are we going?" Gnat asked as they fell into line with the others.

"The Hall of Nations," Anachis and the Junonians around them responded.

"Why do you guys all talk at the same time?"

"It is important to be as one," they answered.

The Junonians converged on a walkway that turned off the main stairs, cutting horizontally through a side alley. Cheeto wove in and out between everyone's feet, growling under his breath at everyone he didn't know, which was pretty much everybody.

Curving around the last of the buildings, they crossed a small bridge over a waterfall. Doug looked down. The waterfall fell into darkness far below, a white curtain of rushing water disappeared from sight. Thin alabaster struts crossed over the chasm between buildings. On every spare inch of the struts sat the tiny white birds Doug saw yesterday. Some of them nuzzled their shoulders into their neighbors trying to negotiate just a little more space. The little bells hung below their feet on delicate silver chains.

"What are they doing?" Gnat whispered.

"Shhhhhh," Doug hushed, not really sure why everyone was being so quiet.

The entire group passed under a large archway. Bright pink conch pearls decorated the edges of the archway. Small figures were carved into the stone on both sides of the door. Each figure was unique. Doug recognized one of them as Junonian, but most of them were strange. One figure had a beaming sun where its head should be. One had the fin of a killer whale jutting out the top. One looked like it was half-bird, half-man. At the very top sat a keystone in the shape of sea urchin. "The Hall of Nations," the Junonians around them announced.

Inside, the Hall of Nations resembled a gigantic banquet hall. Long tables stretched from front to back in four rows. The ceiling was covered with millions of thin, circular, translucent shells hanging down on invisible threads, gently swinging in the drafts. Each one seemed to hold its own small flame, giving the room a shimmering light. The smell of cooking food filled the air.

"Breakfast." Gnat nodded appreciatively.

It was only after everyone took a seat that Doug saw a raised platform at the front of the hall. A single long table stretched across the stage. From off to the side, a line of Junonians filed out. Each of them wore an orange smock instead of the typical red the rest of the Junonians wore. They were also much taller and thinner than the others.

"Who are they?" Doug whispered.

"They are the Diadora," Anachis and a few others answered simultaneously.

"What are they, your leaders?"

"The Diadora foretell."

Before Doug could ask further questions, a low hum started across the crowd. Louder and louder the hum grew until it filled the entire room. Every Junonian joined in, eyes closed in pure joy. Over the humming, the Diadora chanted, "We thank the generosity of Crogan. We thank the wisdom of Tagelus."

Everyone responded, "We thank the generosity of Crogan. We thank the wisdom of Tagelus."

The humming stopped and hundreds of platters stacked high with pancakes were distributed to every table. Shallow bowls filled with syrups and mashed berries were placed between every diner.

"We don't get our own plates?" Gnat moaned.

A basket was handed along. Everyone took a utensil that looked like a wide, long popsicle stick. Using the stick, the Junonians expertly served themselves pancakes.

"We don't get a fork?" Gnat added.

"You don't have to eat," Doug said. He was so hungry, he would have eaten from the floor. He reached over and knifed through the stack. He dunked his pancake piece into the berry mash. The popsicle stick wasn't very easy to use. It was a balancing act. Half of the pieces he picked up tumbled to the table or floor where Cheeto snatched them up. The pancakes weren't particularly good either. They were dry and grainy. But the syrup and berry mash helped compensate. A lot.

He looked over. All of the Junonians were watching him and Gnat wolfing down their food. They glanced nervously at each other. They had finished eating long ago. Apparently Junonian appetites didn't compare to that of two human children. Another stack of pancakes arrived, just for the kids. Cheeto yelped, staring with glossy eyes. Gnat threw three pancakes to the hungry dog, who gobbled them down in seconds.

Finally, Doug and Gnat sat back and held their stomachs.

"Ugh."

"You didn't enjoy?" asked Anachis.

"It was great," Doug answered definitively.

A cheer let out across the room. Only the Diadora sat quietly, whispering among themselves.

"Do you have any chocolate milk?" Gnat asked. Doug smacked him on the shoulder. "Fine. Do you have any orange juice?" The Junonians stood up and simultaneously started filing out of the room.

"Where's Cheeto?" Gnat bent to look under the table.

"Cheeto, come here, boy." Doug started looking under some of the other tables.

The Diadora stood up and quickly snuck out a very tall, thin door at the side of the stage. Suddenly, the front door slammed shut. Doug whipped around. All of the Junonians were gone. Cheeto was gone. He and Gnat were alone in the Hall of Nations. The tables and floor were a mess of crumbs and spills. A series of loud clicks echoed through the room. Tiny operculum doors, only a few inches tall each, opened along the floorboards and the crown molding along the ceiling. Canary snails quickly slid into the room and down the walls. By the thousands they covered the chairs and tables. Each yellow snail shell was delicately inscribed with tiny words. Their tiny eyes were distinctly white with blue pupils. Faintly, Doug and Gnat could hear them warbling with happiness as they ate the sweet crumbs.

"They are cleaning!" Gnat yelled. "Look at that, they are cleaning!"

The leftover pancakes were swarmed with bright yellow snails. Before long, all that remained was a seething mound of warbling snails on top of a spotless platter.

Doug picked a snail up by the shell. The mollusk writhed violently and let out a piercing screech, almost higher than the human ear can discern. The high-pitch siren bore into their skulls so sharply that Doug immediately returned the snail to the table.

"Interesting defense mechanism," Doug said.

"Ultrasonic," Gnat confirmed.

"Ouch!" Doug slapped his ankle, smashing a snail in his hand. "It bit me." He shook the dead snail off his hand, sending it flying onto the floor. The surrounding snails quickly slid over to consume the remains. "Ouch!" He slapped another one away. "We have to get out of here before they eat us." Doug thought for a second. "This way," he jumped onto the stage, pulling Gnat, who couldn't quite get his balance. Their feet smashed snails with every step, leaving a gooey mess for the others to clean up. The startled and dying snails let out the high-pitched screams, filling the banquet hall with an unbearable noise that pushed Doug and Gnat faster toward escape.

"Through here." Doug opened the Diadora's thin door and slipped inside, slamming it shut behind them.

"What about Cheeto?" Gnat whispered.

"He must have left with Anachis," Doug answered. "He'll be all right. The Junonians are probably scared to death of him. Come on and be quiet." The dark hallway was so thin that Doug found it easier to walk sideways. Gnat had no problem walking straight forward. There was nothing beautiful about the passageway like the rest of the city. Doug could see the Diadora's lamp ahead, worming its way through the maze of hallways. Only occasionally would a dim reddish light cast just enough glow from the walls so that they could see where they were going.

Doug had a clever idea. He figured the Diadora knew where the Pearl was kept. If he could follow them to it, he would save a lot of sneaking around. Gnat stumbled along behind him, huffing and puffing. Carefully Doug peeked around every corner before pursuing. He kept hearing Anachis in his head: *Yes, you will die here. Yes, you will die here.* There were so many things he didn't understand. Time travel for one. But he knew, somehow between the enfoldment boxes and the Pearl, it was indeed possible.

They passed through a large spherical chamber. A narrow walkway cut through the chamber, halfway between the floor and the ceiling. Every surface of the wet walls, ceiling, and floor was covered with thousands of thin, spatulate flaps that fanned up and down. Crisply red, each flap folded innumerably upon itself like papery accordions. Moisture bubbled and foamed, brewing a froth that clung to the flaps and dripped to the ground. A humid breeze blew urgently through the chamber.

"Gills," Doug whispered.

"What?" Gnat asked.

"Gills. The walls are breathing. But for what?"

"Fish, of course."

"We aren't standing inside a fish," Doug argued.

They walked endlessly down another maze of tunnels. Always, just at the edge of sight, the faint light of the Diadora rushed ahead of them. Finally they came to a large vertical shaft. It was so wide that they couldn't see to the other side. Doug shuffled to the edge and looked down into the darkness. He looked up. Far above he saw the faint glow of the Diadora's light. He looked around to find out how they had walked so far up into the shaft. Suddenly, they heard a faint whistle and a wind blew through their hair. A large object swung past the opening so quickly that Doug fell backwards.

"What was that?" Gnat asked.

"I'm not sure." Doug snuck close to the edge again. He peered carefully into the dark. "Stairs," he whispered. "A spiral staircase is spinning turning around the edge. We have to jump on."

The staircase rotated counterclockwise around the circumference of the cylindrical shaft. Doug watched the stair speeding along the curve. It moved fast. It would be tricky to jump out into the darkness and actually land on a stair. There were no railings. He looked down again. Nothing. Nothing but an endlessly rotating stairway.

"Come closer, Gnat. We can do this."

"No. I'm not jumping out there."

"We have to. It is the only way home."

"Who builds a stair that moves?"

"I don't know. But that's what it is."

Gnat sniffed. He peered over the edge. The whistle blew his hair. The stairway rushed by and he stumbled back.

"All right. Let's get on the next one. We'll go together. We have to jump just before it gets to us or we will miss it." Doug pulled on Gnat's arm. Gnat dug his heels into the ground but Doug was too strong. Doug watched along the left wall of the shaft. Out of the darkness, a shadow rushed toward them.

"Almost . . . almost . . ." They heard the faint whistle. "Now!"

Doug jumped out into the dark pit. Gnat barely moved his feet but Doug's momentum pulled him along. Just as they started to fall into the darkness, the stairway rotated under their feet. Gnat tumbled too far and fell off the edge. He swung out over the empty shaft, his weight pulling Doug down to his knees. Doug gripped his hand so hard it hurt.

"Gnat! Hang on!" Doug grimaced with all of his strength. He couldn't get Gnat to budge. The darkness yawned below. If he let go, Gnat would certainly die. Gnat started to cry and kick his legs. "Don't kick, Gnat. I can't hold on."

Doug grabbed with his other arm. He could feel Gnat's weight slowly pulling him toward the edge. Gnat's huge eyes looked up at him. He didn't have a look of fear really, more of a questioning expression as if he didn't understand what was happening. Doug slipped closer.

"No," Doug said. "NO!" He shifted his feet right to the edge, then squatted down, falling onto his back. Gnat launched into the air and landed smack on top of him.

"We're okay. We're okay."

Tears streamed down Gnat's face.

"We did it. Come on. Let's go fast." They started running up the stairs. It was a weird feeling climbing up stairs that were moving. Doug felt a little dizzy. He pulled Gnat behind him and he bumped along like heavy luggage.

"Let's go, Gnat. We can freak out later." Doug realized he sounded like his dad. He always liked how Dad said "we" instead of "you" when referring to some emotional reaction. They jogged up the stairs. Doug couldn't see the light from the Diadora anymore. Before long, they came to the last stair.

"That's it. There aren't any more steps." They both stood on the last stair, riding as it rotated around the shaft.

"There it is," Gnat said.

"What? I didn't see anything."

"A hole. I saw a hole."

"I didn't see it. Where?"

"There." Gnat pointed. A small tunnel flashed by.

"That must be where they went. It is too small for both of us at the same time."

"Don't leave me," Gnat whimpered.

"It will be fine. You go first." Doug slowly pushed him toward the outside. As the tunnel neared, he gave Gnat a hard shove. Gnat tumbled into the door with a woof.

Doug rode the stair around the shaft one more time before tumbling into the tunnel himself. Gnat launched his entire body at him, swinging his arms wildly.

"No, no, no, no, no. I hate you. I hate you." He pummeled his fists into Doug's stomach.

Doug could feel the anger welling up inside him. He shoved Gnat backwards. "Stop hitting me. Stop it!" Gnat launched at him again. He dug his tiny finger nails into his arm.

"I hate you. It's all your fault."

"My fault? My fault? I didn't ask for this. I didn't ask for you to come along. I didn't ask for you to live in my house." Doug's face was red.

Gnat fell down crying. Doug kicked the wall. After a few minutes, Gnat stood up and started walking down the tunnel.

"Gnat. Gnat, come on. Wait up." He could hear Gnat sniffing. "I didn't mean it." But Gnat wouldn't respond. He strode along the tunnels without any hesitation.

Eventually, they came to the end of the last tunnel and they crawled up a tortoise burrow to the surface. Doug carefully stuck his head out. The opening was in a grove of small oak trees. No one was around, but he saw footprints in the sand. He reached down to help Gnat out. Gnat slapped his hand away and climbed out by himself. Pushing the branches away, they saw the fifteen Diadora in the clearing. Doug had a hard time seeing through the glare of the sun.

A person stood in front of them talking and gesturing wildly with one hand and holding a spear with a long, curved blade with the other hand. The strange person was much taller than the Junonians and wore elaborate metal armor made from millions of tiny pieces. The flensing spear's blade shone brightly in the sun. It was so thin that it shivered slightly in the breeze. But what flensing spears lost in rigidity, they made up for in razor-sharpness. With a single flip of the wrist, the flensing blade could whip through the air faster than the eye could follow. Everyone appeared to be uneasy with the conversation, shifting from leg to leg. The tall person filled Doug with dread.

Gnat snapped a twig under his foot. They both froze as the entire group in the clearing turned toward the noise. Their eyes seemed to bore through the leaves, searching for the source of the broken twig. Doug could see the tall person was a woman. She had a thick red band of paint across her eyes. Her nose and mouth merged into a sharp point.

"A beak," Doug whispered. "She has a beak. Like the sculpture." A chill flashed across his scalp: like the Bobwhite Witch. He looked carefully at the bird-woman. She was very muscular. Her long thick toes constantly clutched at the sand. After a minute, the Diadora and woman continued their conversation.

"Did they see us? Do you think they saw us?" Doug whispered.

"Negative," Gnat whispered.

"You have to be more careful."

"Shut up."

One of the Diadora bowed toward the bird-woman and handed her a small bag. She snatched the bag, inspected the contents, then ran off over the dune. The Diadora looked at each other for a moment, then started walking back toward the burrow.

"Quick, over here." Doug pulled Gnat behind a palmetto. Gnat shoved away from him. One by one, the Diadora climbed down into the burrow and disappeared. He heard them talking to each other. All he understood was the word, *walleri.* The last Diadora stared directly at the palmetto as he walked by.

"Do you think he saw us?" he whispered to Gnat, who didn't answer. "They said 'walleri.' That tall person was a Walleri. I'm sure of it." After a few minutes, Doug put his feet in the hole and started sliding down. He hit something solid. He worked his feet around in every direction. Everything was solid. He kicked as hard as he could. It didn't budge. He kicked again and again. Panicking, he slid down headfirst and started feeling around with his hands. "There has to be . . . a door knob or something." But there was nothing. They were locked out.

13

A Trap

Doug and Gnat waited by the door all afternoon. The roaring sun bore down on the sand. With so little vegetation, nothing stopped the landscape from turning into an angry oven. Soaked through with sweat, they sat in their little island of oak trees scanning the landscape for scimitar cats.

"We can't stay here forever," Gnat whined.

"Shhhhhh."

"There is nothing out here. We've been sitting here for hours."

"I said, shhhhhh!"

"I want to go. I'm cooked."

Doug stood to his feet and decided to try to open the door in the burrow again. He dug his fingers through the sand looking for an edge.

"It's no use. We are going to have to find another way back."

"Let's go then."

"Just wait just a sec." Doug grabbed a stick and drew a small circle in the sand. "This is the tortoise burrow. Try to remember the tunnel to the stairway. We have to work backwards, so the opposite of the way we actually walked. I know we took a right just before the burrow, so that turn was a left." Doug lined up facing the burrow so his line stayed in the same direction.

"It was a right," Gnat held up his right hand.

"No, it was a left. I'm sure of it."

"You are incorrect."

"Gnat, I watched you."

Gnat closed his eyes. His hand twitched like it was working a game joystick. "Right. Straight for 20 steps. Sharp right. Left." He stole a glance at the picture Doug was drawing. "Keep going left . . . more. Straight. There. That was the staircase."

Doug wiped the sweat from his eyes then drew a large circle for the staircase. "I hope you are right."

"I'm right," Gnat snapped.

"All right. All right. All we have to do is walk that direction." He pointed toward the largest circle. It doesn't guarantee anything, but at least it is a start. I don't remember the tunnels from the Hall of Nations to the stairway. Do you?"

Gnat shook his head.

"We have to try and stay over the general area of Junonia. If we get too far off, we will never find our way back. Keep your eyes open for that little spring we came out from last time."

"Let's go already, Professor."

They cautiously stepped out from the cover of the oak trees and started climbing through the low grass and cactus that grew on the sandy dune. Doug expected to be attacked by a scimitar at any moment. When they reached the top of the dune, he found a tree in the distance that they could walk toward. He had learned that trick from walking in the scrub at home. Finding something to walk toward was the only way to keep from going in circles.

The sky above them swirled with vultures. They could hear large animals bellowing in the distance. Mammoths maybe. Doug wished he had his sunglasses because the glare blasting off the white sand was overwhelming.

"It can't be too far," Doug said. "If we walk more than an hour, we should turn around and follow our tracks back here."

"Blah blah blah," Gnat mocked.

The wind picked up. Dark clouds were growing in the western sky. The vultures plummeted, pushed out of the way by something invisible. An enormous clear ball the size of a hot air balloon rode the wind, dropping toward the ground between gusts.

"Check it out." Doug pointed. The balloon soared just over their heads. It had a slight greenish tint as it spun in the sky. They watched the sun pass through its thin, clear walls as it flew off toward the east. Its walls were a little loose, as if it were not completely filled with air. "What in the world?" Another balloon tumbled across the landscape, bouncing with long looping arcs. More balloons rode the surge of wind ahead of the storm.

"Look out!" a balloon dropped from the clouds landing directly on them. It settled lightly like a parachute before floating back up in a swirl. Gnat rolled to the ground giggling.

"Here comes another. What are they?" Doug screamed.

Gnat lunged at the balloon as Doug ducked. He grabbed two fistfuls of the thin-skinned ball in his arms. For a second, it looked like he trapped it. Then the wind caught hold and lifted him into the air. A few feet off the ground, Gnat let go and dropped to the sand again. His hands were covered with a sticky green film.

"Haw yawww!" Gnat yelled. "Try it. Try it." He chugged off to grab another gigantic balloon. Doug ran to catch up. A particularly large one landed nearby. Gnat grabbed hold. Doug dug his fingers onto the thin wall, pinching it into a fold so that he could hang on next to Gnat.

"It is ours now," Gnat called out.

"Geez, this thing stinks. What is it made of?"

"It stenches awful."

A blast of wind crashed though, catching the ball like a sail and launching it upward.

"Hang on. We're too far up." They clenched the balloon with all of their strength as it spun wildly. Their added weight caused it to veer and jolt. For a few seconds, they hung from the bottom before a gust swung them to the top. Their weight caused them to sink down, stabilizing the spin of the balloon.

"Wooo hooo! Look at that," Doug yelled.

"We are flying. We are flying!" Gnat yelled back. Once Doug felt more comfortable, he stuck his head up over the edge of the ball. He could see the entire landscape from the clouds. A large herd of mammoths marched in the distance. There were other animals too. Gigantic, hairy animals pulled small trees to the ground. Doug tried to think of their names. He had seen their bones in a museum once.

"Giant sloth!" Doug announced into the wind.

Gnat looked at him with a combination of fear and confusion. He was hanging on too tightly to respond.

"Giant sloth. Over there." Doug tried to point by jutting his chin toward the towering beast. He didn't dare let go with one of his hands.

Gnat shook his head.

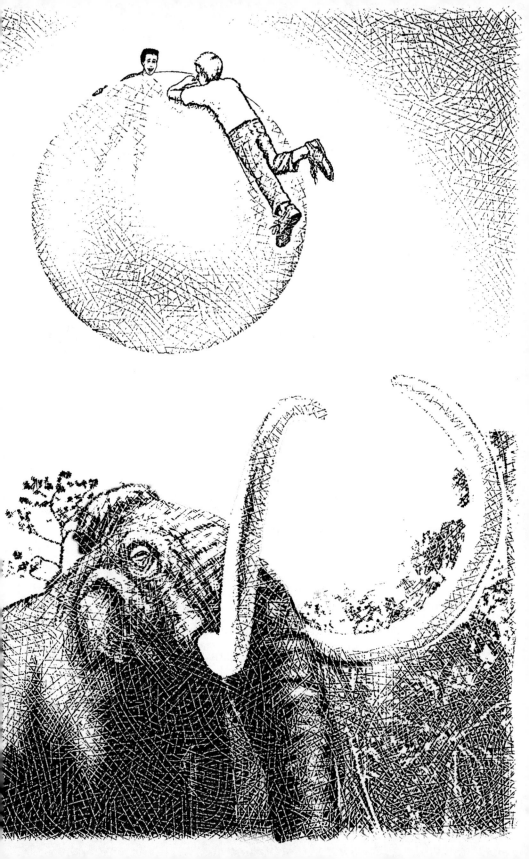

"Giant sloth," Doug said one more time.

Thunder rocked the sky. Beneath the storm clouds in the west, Doug could see the ocean. The ocean! So close. It took his mother almost two hours to drive to the Gulf from his house. Here, it looked like it would take ten minutes.

"This is where Lyonia is in our time," he yelled. "Can you believe it?" Vultures swerved by their heads. "I wonder where our school will be." Nothing looked familiar enough to tell.

The giant clear balloons blew onshore from the sea. There were piles of them riding in clusters on the waves, collecting in the bays all up and down the coast. Occasionally a stiff wind would catch a balloon and launch it into the air. As far as they could see, clear balloons tumbled across the land.

Finally, the balloon they were riding started dropping. Doug looked all around.

Gnat tumbled off the balloon and slammed into the ground. Doug let go and fell beside him. A thin layer of slime covered his entire body. He tried to wipe it off on his shorts, but it was too sticky.

Doug sniffed his hand and touched his tongue to a finger.

"Gruesome," Gnat said. The fear that gripped him so tightly only moments before seemed to be completely washed away.

"I think it's some kind of algae. It tastes like pond water."

"I've never tasted a pond." Gnat stuck his entire thumb in his mouth. "Blech. Salty."

"You stink like a pond too." Doug jumped to his feet and started scurrying up a large dune. At the top he yelled back to Gnat. "There they are! The Junonians are picking gopher apples again."

"I'm coming." Gnat huffed up the hill behind him.

"We found it. We found it!"

"You owe me."

"What do you mean? I'm the one who found it."

"Only cuz I pointed you in the right direction. You were lost."

"I was not. I was analyzing the situation and making an educated hypothesis."

"You were lost," Gnat said.

From the top of the dune, they could see the spring cave where it emerged from under ground. It was the secret entrance to Junonia where they had dismounted the tardigrades yesterday before heading out to harvest jumjams. About twenty Junonians were on their knees picking fruit about a quarter mile from the entrance. They were too far away to hear. Doug and Gnat watched them for a while. Suddenly, the Junonians startled and dropped their bags. They stood up in alarm. After a brief moment of doubt, they started running.

"Something is chasing them again. That scimitar, I'll bet," Doug whispered to Gnat. "Stay down. I can't see what it is." He squinted in the sun. Several shadows rushed incredibly fast across the sand toward the Junonians. A chill rushed down Doug's arms. He couldn't see whatever predators were making the shadows, but the way they ran was recognizable. "Those are dogs. Giant dogs."

"Wolves," Gnat suggested.

"Yeah. Wolves. White dire wolves." They watched the dire wolves herding the Junonians, surrounding them from different directions. Their white fur blended into the white sand so perfectly that most of the time Doug could only see their shadows. "Those are bigger than normal wolves," Doug whispered to Gnat. "Much bigger."

The Junonians clumped together, swerving and cutting simultaneously like a single organism. The dire wolves kept pace patiently, hanging behind, probing the edges, content to wait until a slower Junonian dropped from the pack or stumbled. The entire group ran closer and closer to the safety of the spring cave entrance to Junonia.

"Come on. Come on." Doug clenched his teeth "You can make it." He looked over to the spring cave. Something flashed and caught his eye. Something familiar. A flensing spear shimmered in the sun from behind the bushes.

"No!" He jumped up and waved his arms. "No! Go back! Go the other way!" he screamed as loudly as he could. But the Junonians were just too far away to hear. Doug ran and stumbled down the dune toward them screaming, "Go back! They are waiting for you. Go back!"

Three Walleri leaped from their hiding places just as the Junonians neared the cave. The Junonians skidded to a stop and were instantly encircled. They gave up and huddled together. The dire wolves paced back and forth around them, snapping their jaws in nervous hunger. One of the Walleri warriors put his hand on a wolf's head. The wolf jerked his head around. Dodging the bite, the Walleri smacked him on the snout.

One of the Junonians took the disruption as an opportunity to escape. He lunged away from the wolves and toward the cave opening. A Walleri swung his flensing spear. The blade lashed through the air like a lightning-quick wave, knocking the Junonian to the ground. Two dire wolves pounced and tore into the body. It was so far away it looked unreal. But Doug knew it was very real and horrible. He turned his head away. Gnat scrambled down the dune to join him.

"What's happening?"

"It's the Walleri. They have the Junonians trapped." He didn't mention the one who was just eaten.

"Is Anachis down there?" Gnat squinted his eyes trying to see the activity.

"I . . . I don't know."

The storm opened up with a violent crack of lightning. Thick sheets of rain pounded into the sand. Within seconds, Gnat and Doug were soaked. Their view of the scene blurred.

The Walleri quickly tied the arms of all twenty Junonians and marched them away toward the coast.

"We have to go warn the others."

"I miss Olivia," Gnat cried.

Doug wanted to agree. It would be nice to have a bunch of bears and their bear queen there. He would feel a lot safer. She would probably say something smirky to make them laugh.

Then there was the problem of Larry. Even if he was still alive, how could they possibly find him? They couldn't just leave him here, could they? Doug wished he could ask his dad. Dad always knew what to do when things were tough. He used to tell Doug that he needed to shape up and get his head out of the clouds. He had to learn more common sense instead of reading so many books about things that weren't useful. Dad always had a brilliant plan for everything. Everything except cancer. Doug could feel his muscles tense. He took a deep breath. *Keep it together.* They were trapped outside of their time, in a world filled with dire wolves, giant scimitar cats, and Walleri warriors. For the first time ever, someone was depending on him for his life, even if he was an annoying little brat. He can't keep expecting a little kid to get through this. He was going to have to figure out how to get both of them home on his own.

"We are going to see Olivia soon. We are going to get back to our time and she will come back with your aunt and uncle, I promise." Doug was trying hard to believe his own words. "Once we find the Pearl, we will go back and we will have the greatest story ever. Hey, we can even go back in time for dinner."

"We can go back to before Olivia and I even came to Florida and never even lost our dad and mom."

"No. No. If we go back that far, there will be two of us. Besides, you would go back without Olivia. It wouldn't make any sense." Of course, Doug didn't have a clue on what made sense when it came to time travel.

Gnat considered this while the rain washed down his face. "I wish we could go home," he mumbled and grabbed Doug's hand as they walked down the dune to Junonia.

14

Never-ending Pancakes

Junonians carrying platters of pancakes filed into the Hall of Nations like a parade, followed quickly by others bringing bowls of syrup and mashed berries.

"We are having pancakes for dinner too?" Gnat asked. Cheeto jumped up and started clawing at his leg.

"You should eat and keep your strength. . . ." But Gnat already had a mouthful before Doug could finish his sentence. Doug turned back to the Junonians sitting next to him. "I'm telling you, the Walleri were at the entrance. They were waiting for the dire wolves to bring them right into their trap. They killed someone right in front of us and kidnapped the others. And now Anachis is missing. I'm sure he was one of them."

"There are many ways to be hurt," the Junonians within earshot responded. For the first time, Doug noticed that the farther away the Junonians were from the conversation, the quieter they talked. Those farthest away were simply mouthing the words.

"I thought you said the Walleri didn't know where Junonia is."

"They do not know our entrance."

"Then how do you explain the missing Junonians?"

"It is true that the harvesters have not returned yet. But Walleri and dire wolves are enemies and they do not know our entrance."

"Well, they sure looked like friends. They took all of the Junonians away. I don't know where, and I don't know what they are going to do with them."

"The Walleri eat Junonians."

"What!?"

"The Walleri eat Junonians."

"We can't just let them get eaten. We have to go save them." Doug felt sick to his stomach.

"No. We will all get hurt."

"You came back for Gnat and me when the scimitar had us cornered. You saved *us*."

"Scimitar is a dumb cat. Walleri will kill us. There are too many. It is better this way."

Doug sighed. "I'm not saying it is safe. I don't understand why you don't care."

"You think we don't care?"

"We can't just let them get eaten. There has to be a way. I'm going back out there and save them. Anachis needs me."

The Junonians looked nervously at each other. Everyone ate pancakes in silence except for Cheeto, who growled as he ate.

"The Diadora would like to speak with you," the Junonians said as they stood up from the table and left. "We will wait on the bridge."

Doug's mind raced as he and Gnat shuffled forward toward the stage. Did the Diadora see them hiding behind the palmetto on the surface? The light shimmered on the walls and floor. They stood in front of the stage as fifteen Diadora stared down at them. They were intimidating up close even though they were extremely frail and thin. They had much clearer skin than the regular Junonians. Their long-fingered hands were completely transparent.

"What do you want, Aliens?" Gnat quipped.

"Gnat!" Doug responded.

"They aren't saying anything."

The Diadora finally spoke all at the same time. "Yes, you are indeed a young Dark Eye. You may leave. Take your little animal with you."

Doug and Gnat turned to leave.

"Not you. Only the Dark Eye."

Doug stopped and turned around. "It's all right, Gnat. I'll be out in minute."

Gnat eyed Doug, then the Diadora. He turned and plodded away.

The Diadora watched him, then turned to Doug. "We find you interesting. You arrived by enfoldment box. You are not a Dark Eye. You are not Walleri. And you are not Junonian. Yet Tagelus sings in you."

"I don't understand. Tagelus is here? Can I speak to him?" "Tagelus sings, but it is for us to listen. It is the river that flows from the stone. Tagelus is the clear water inside."

Doug's mind spun. Tagelus wasn't a person. Olivia had it wrong. The Bobwhite Witch had it wrong. Tagelus sounded more like a ghost or a church than a person.

"Tagelus gives us strength and direction in its flow. You as well. Tagelus collects in you more than anyone we have ever seen." The Diadora climbed down from the stage and surrounded Doug. Up close, their faces were very grim and severe. Their eyes conveyed no emotion. One reached over and placed his clear hand on Doug's face. "You are Diadora. We want you to stay and teach us."

CHRISTOPHER TOZIER

"T . . . teach you? What can I teach *you?*" He wanted to ask them about the Pearl, but he knew it wasn't the right time. He also couldn't forget about them talking secretly with the Walleri on the surface.

"You can teach us the ways of Tagelus."

"I am not Diadora. I don't even belong here. I don't know anything about Tagelus. I need to go home."

"Yes, we understand you arrived from the future in the enfoldment box. There is no return. We believe that you have been told that already."

"Anachis told me." Doug looked at his feet. "He said I would die here. And now he is going to die."

"Then you already understand."

"I understand, but that isn't the point." Doug stared deeply into their unblinking eyes trying to see if there was any clue that they knew he saw them with the Walleri. Their eyes were beautiful. Midnight and inky. Large, deeply indigo. Like galaxies. Like glowing fish of the deep sea. Their eyes drew him in. Calling to him. He tried to look away, but wanted to see. He *had* to see deeper. A wave of fear rushed over his body. He couldn't look away, he couldn't turn to leave. He was locked in and it felt like they were inside his head. There was no escape.

"You are Diadora," they said.

"I am Diadora," Doug repeated. "I am Diadora."

15

Hovenweep

A gigantic bonfire blasted from the largest pile of logs Olivia had ever seen. Sparks billowed into the sky, mixing into the stars until she couldn't tell which was which. Olivia dumped an armful of logs into a pile away from the fire. She was wearing some of Terrilyne's spare clothes. Her shirt was woven with bright ribbons and very soft yarn. She double-checked that two crystals were still safe in her pocket. The bonfire lit up the entire canyon so brightly that the purplish light of the tetracomb was barely visible. Globes of party lights lined the canyon walls. Clusters of very long balloons snaked on the breeze. There were five different bands and one gigantic stereo playing music. The mix of rhythms and singing fought the roar of the fire. The enclosed canyon seemed to amplify every tiny sound. People were dancing everywhere. Some were slow dancing as couples in the flickering shadows. Some colorful dancers were spinning faster and faster around the fire. Every few seconds, groups of people appeared out of the tetracomb carrying more wood, food, and various other packages. Hundreds of Hohokam people were packed into the canyon and it felt like half of them were staring at her.

"Hovenweep! I can't believe it. I can't believe it. I can't believe it." Terrilyne rushed up to her out of breath. "Can you believe it?"

"It's great."

"It's great? It's *great?* We are probably the only kids ever to go to Hovenweep. Hoonaw Kookam at Hovenweep! It only happens every five years and only a few from each generation are allowed." Terrilyne executed a perfect cartwheel and landed with a spin.

"Are there people here from thirty thousand years ago?"

"This *is* thirty thousand years ago, sillyhead. And there are people from the future here too."

Olivia looked around. "Really? Where?"

"AAAAAaaaaaaaaaa! I can hardly stand it!" Terrilyne screamed at the top of her lungs and started dancing.

Olivia laughed. "Come on, I'm hungry." She started pushing her way through the crowd.

"Just remember, we can only eat the food from our time. Dad said you wouldn't want to know what happens if you eat food from any other time."

"I want to know."

"Are you sure?"

"I'm positive. Tell me."

Terrilyne giggled. "You puke through time."

"Gross."

A woman in front of Olivia dissolved and blew away in the neutrino wind. A few seconds later, she reappeared from the tetracomb carrying a drum.

"Check it out." Terrilyne stood facing the fire. The heat blasted into them relentlessly. "Check it out. Just watch."

"What? It's a fire. Big deal." Olivia felt like her eyebrows were frying off. A large burning log started to dissolve. With a fizzing pop, it disappeared in a cloud of green sparks that rushed toward the sky.

"The settling. Nothing can stay outside its time," said Dr. Yazzi, who walked up behind them smiling, "even logs. Don't lose your crystals or that will happen to you."

A man threw a new log onto the blaze.

"Come on, kids. Have a popsicle from our table and watch the festivities."

"Prickly pear? That is all there is? We *always* have prickly pear."

"I think it's pretty good." Olivia licked one. "I heard the people from the future have rocket pops though."

Terrilyne scrunched her face. "Just once in my life, I want a rocket pop."

"I'll grab some elderberry and paloverde treats on my next twinning. Now hurry. You girls don't want to miss this."

They wove through the crowd toward the canyon opening.

"If one of us twins out of here, we have to promise to meet at our food table," Terrilyne said.

"OK."

"Promise?"

"I promise." Some of the people they pushed through actually looked like they were thirty thousand years old. Some of them wore clothes like the Native Americans Olivia had seen in picture books. Some of them wore fancy clothes that she had never seen anyone wear. But everyone seemed to be getting along and laughing like old friends. They all spoke a language that sounded odd but vaguely familiar, familiar enough for her to understand.

Finally, they found some space away from others where they could see. "Look up. Any second now," Dr. Yazzi said.

A purple firework exploded above them. Over the canyon wall, a large dragon-shaped kite flew out over the crowd. It was so big it filled the sky. One by one, orange fireworks lit on the kite, spinning and shooting bright fire.

"It's the Gila!" Terrilyne screamed, bouncing up and down uncontrollably. "It's the Gila!"

The kite swerved and veered in the air like a writhing creature. In a burst of light, the kite disappeared into smoke. Suddenly, ten people appeared out of nothing, floating in midair where the kite used to be. Red smoke poured out behind them as they parachuted to the ground. The crowd went nuts, screaming their approval.

"That's the forty-one hundred and ninety-fifth generation. They always like to make a grand entrance," Dr. Yazzi explained. One of the billowing parachutes settled on the bonfire. For a brief second, it looked like the fire would be extinguished before it burst through, evaporating the fabric.

The tetracomb sputtered. Six men marched out arm in arm. Each of them wore a different hat, but they all looked similar. The crowd started laughing. All six men were the same man of different ages. The youngest was in his twenties, the oldest in his sixties.

"Have you seen yourself yet?" Dr. Yazzi leaned into Olivia.

"Why? Do I have dirt on my face?"

"No." Dr. Yazzi laughed. "I mean, have you seen yourself from the future yet? There is no telling, you might be here. Some people are here ten times over."

Olivia spun wildly around. "Oh good. I can ask myself some important questions I have."

Dr. Yazzi laughed. "Time doesn't work the way they show it in movies. Information from the future won't do you much good. There are too many variables that will change. Even events in the past are subject to change. Chances are, anything you hear will be wrong."

"Oh."

"It's best just to enjoy it if you find yourself."

A group emerged from the tetracomb throwing snowballs at people.

"Over here!" Terrilyne jumped up and down. "Over here!" Someone launched a snowball high into the air. Olivia and Terrilyne both jumped up to grab it, causing the ball to explode in their hands.

"All right, girls. You have fun. John Whistle and Sally Ray are both here if you need something and you can't find me. I have some business to discuss."

"Ewwww. John Whistle is gonna get ya," Terrilyne said and pinched Olivia in the ribs once her dad was out of earshot.

"Quit it." Olivia looked around nervously. "He isn't trying to kill *you*." She turned around. There he was, in a small group of people. He looked over and winked at her.

"I see him." Terrilyne pointed the other direction.

"There's another one, over by the bonfire," Olivia said. "How many John Whistles are there?"

"They're all watching you too."

"We'll have to split up. It's time."

Terrilyne suddenly looked serious. "We have to hurry. We're gonna twin soon, I bet."

"All right. See you in a few minutes."

Olivia took off toward the staircase that led to Level Twenty of the crystal lab. She quickly wove through groups of people. Three John Whistles followed her. "Olivia!" they called, but she ignored them. Fireworks blasted overhead. Olivia ducked beneath a food table.

"Olivia, it's John. Didn't you hear me calling you?"

"Why are you hiding?" John Whistle number two asked. "Come out and talk to us."

A loud explosion echoed in the canyon. A pile of fireworks caught on fire. Rockets blasted in every direction. Spinners shot out knocking people to the ground.

"Everybody down!" someone shouted.

Olivia overturned the table and sprinted up the staircase.

"Hey! Get back here!"

"I knew it. I knew she was up to something." The John Whistles raced after her. Up on the terrace overlooking the canyon, she tried to open the door to the crystal lab. It was locked. She was cornered. The three John Whistles bounded up the last steps and circled around her.

"What are you up to, Dark Eye?" one said as he walked slowly toward her.

Olivia stepped over toward the edge. "Stay back."

"I'm not going to hurt you. I just want to know what you are really doing here on our land. Tell me the truth," the second John Whistle said.

Olivia stared him right in the eye. Slowly she pulled the two crystals out of her pocket. She looked down at them shining in her hand. She turned back at John and clenched her jaw.

"I'm never telling you anything." With one quick movement, she threw her crystals over the cliff. They landed in the bonfire with a thud.

"What are you doing? Why?"

"I'm not going to get caught," Olivia cried. "I can't do this anymore." She screamed out over the canyon, "Hoonaw kookam!" and crumpled to the ground. Her hand started to blur. A cool wind caught her hair. Blowing. Blowing her soul into dust and green sparks until there was nothing left. She was gone.

A small smile passed over the Johns' lips and they turned around to go tell Dr. Yazzi the news.

Back in the present day, Chubascos ran along a desert trail. He was very late. Clutched in his left hand, an extraordinarily large rattlesnake scowled at his captor. Like a jackrabbit he leaped over a barrel cactus. If you walked through the crystal lab it wasn't particularly far from the houses to the tetracomb. However, if you didn't go through the lab, you had to take the cliff-base trail all the way past the old observatory ruins and around the southern edge of the eastern mountain. It was at least an hour's walk. Chubascos had ten minutes to get there. Precision was critical. Tiny lizards zipped under his feet. He didn't bother going around the jumping cholla. By the time the spiny bundles jumped out, he was long gone. Chubascos loved to run. He was faster than all of the older teens. He looked at his watch and sped up. The rattlesnake swung in his grip like a rubber hose.

Finally he came to the tetracomb canyon. He peeked around the corner. Lucy Ganado was sitting on a stool in front of a long table. During Hovenweep, a librarian had to wait by the tetracomb to trade out timing crystals so attendees could return to the gathering relatively close to the time they twinned out. It was supposed to be a great honor, but it felt like a ripoff to Lucy. It was easy, boring work. All she had to do was simply help confetti-covered partygoers as they twinned back, talking loudly about meeting the ancestors. She would hand them a new timing crystal and a bundle of firewood or more food.

"Mommy!" She heard a scream. "Mommy!"

"Chubby? Is that you?" Lucy jumped to her feet and scurried toward the crying voice. She turned the corner and saw Chubascos pinned up against the rock wall. A large rattlesnake coiled at his feet.

"Oh, it's just a rattler, Chubby. Are you bitten?"

Chubascos shook his head. Tears streamed down his face.

"You are a little old to be crying." Lucy sauntered over to the snake. Her hand snatched out, grabbing it behind the head. She walked over to a sage bush and dropped the hissing reptile.

"There. No more snake. What are you doing out here? Why the big baby act?"

"I wanted to see you. I'm bored."

"All right, you can sit with me for a while. We should be getting some twinners soon." She put her arm around his shoulders and they turned to walk back to the tetracomb. "I've never heard you cry because of a snake before. You used to carry them around like babies." She couldn't see the sly smile on Chubascos' face.

Olivia was standing at the tetracomb waiting for them.

"Olivia, I see you've twinned back." Lucy looked at her watch. "Here, let me find your new timing crystal."

"Hovenweep is fantastic. So many people singing and dancing." Olivia smiled.

"I'm glad you liked it, dear," Lucy was more than a little jealous of the newcomer being allowed to attend.

"Do you mind if I have a new position crystal too? I left Terrilyne by the houses."

"What were you girls doing way by the houses so far away from the party?"

"She was showing me how they used to look. The paintings were much more colorful."

"Is that right, dear?" Lucy handed her two new crystals.

"Oh, and Terrilyne says to bring paloverde treats."

"Did she now?" Lucy grouched, rummaging around in a cooler. "Here, only a few left."

"Thank you, Miss Ganado." Olivia grabbed the package and rushed back to the tetracomb.

Terrilyne's plan was working perfectly. It was called doubling. It took a little bit of scheming, but Terri had found the right crystals from the future and brought them into the past for her to use. First, Olivia had twinned back about a half-hour. This created two Olivias in the present. The twinned Olivia went to Hovenweep originally and threw her crystals into the fire. The original Olivia hid near the tetracomb in the present and waited for her chance to pretend that she had twinned back. It was all quite confusing. To make it happen, all she needed was a distraction. Chubascos and the rattler fit the bill perfectly.

Olivia tried not to think about her twin dying in the neutrino wind. It must have been horrible. All she had to do the next time that Terrilyne came to her with the stolen crystals was to reject them and go about her business. Doubling was an old Hohokam trick. It was so old that no one even bothered trying it anymore. Besides, it was dangerous. If you made the mistake of starting the process a second time, you would die for real. It's very easy to make that mistake. They were counting on John Whistle not expecting a Dark Eye to know how to double.

Olivia walked into the tetracomb. "Goodbye, Miss Lucy. Goodbye, Chubby," Olivia stuck out her tongue at him and laughed. Within seconds, she was standing next to Terrilyne back at Hovenweep.

"Come on," Terrilyne urged. "We have to hurry. It won't be long before they figure out you doubled."

"You should have seen Chubascos. He was perfect. Crying like a little baby."

"Ha! I would like to have a video of that." They rushed along the lab tunnel. "They didn't lock any of the doors until a thousand years ago. I mean, a thousand years ago from our time. We are sure going to be in big trouble when John Whistle finds out you tricked him."

"You let me handle him," Olivia growled.

"I saw the whole thing. He was right there when you threw the crystals. He didn't even try to stop you."

"What if he goes back in time to try and stop the whole thing?"

"He might if he thinks you actually did something wrong. You have to make it look like you were just getting him back and playing a joke."

"He wouldn't like us running around in here. That's for sure."

"It's a good thing that everyone is at Hovenweep. There. There is the library." Terrilyne opened the door. Inside were countless shelves reaching up to the high ceiling. Row upon row of stone boxes were cataloged and organized for retrieval in tiny drawers on each shelf.

"There must be millions. How are we going to find the ones we need?"

"They are organized by location coordinates on this end of the library. Hohokam land is stored closest to us. The farther away you want to twin, the farther down the aisle you have to go." They walked partway down the aisle.

"Western Island. Western Island! Here they are."

"Just grab a bunch. Keep them in their boxes though. We will have to figure out coordinates when we get back."

"All right." Olivia loaded up her bag. Each of the stone boxes was etched with words and numbers she didn't understand. Soon the bag was almost too heavy to carry.

"Now we need timers." Terrilyne rushed to the other end of the library. Olivia noticed how beautiful the room was. Even though it was nighttime, a warm sunshine glowed in the ceiling. A tall crystal stood in the center of the library lobby, absorbing the glowing light and scattering it across the shelving. Along the walls, large six-foot twinned crystals stood in alcoves, reminding Olivia of how statues of famous authors sit in book libraries.

"What are these? Tetracomb rejects?" Olivia asked.

"Come over. Closer. And look up toward the light."

"There is something inside. A wisp."

"They are the phantoms."

"Ghosts? They are ghosts?"

"No, goofus. Phantoms. It is said that a phantom lives with every generation. Some say it hovers over our heads. Some say it lives within us. The phantom is tied by invisible thread to each of that generation, absorbing the spirit of its hosts. Upon the death of the last member of that generation, the phantom enters the stone that represents the legacy of its generation. If they lived a greedy and superficial life, the phantom will enter a dark and tortured rock, like a volcanic basalt or gneiss." Olivia nodded like she had a clue what kind of rocks Terrilyne was talking about. "If they lived a noble and pure life, the phantom will enter a crystal. Only the finest of generations will enter a twentieth-level twinned crystal."

Olivia stared up into a phantom. The white wisp had a form that seemed to come and go from existence. Sometimes, she swore she saw a face looking back at her. Sometimes, she had trouble seeing anything at all.

"If we are back in time with the first generation, why are there any phantoms?"

"Each of these alcoves is a mini-tetracomb. They are timeless."

"So they just sit there, forever into the past and into the future?"

"I . . . I guess."

"Creepy."

"It isn't so creepy. It's an honor."

"I feel sorry for them, stuck in there."

"Living outside of time is supposed to be the most beautiful thing in the universe. We can't even understand it. Besides, they want to be there. They are the ones that chose it remember?"

"I guess," Olivia answered as she squinted, pressing her nose against the clear crystal.

"Here are the timer crystals. Down here." Terrilyne rushed down the aisle, pulling Olivia along. "I might twin soon. We have to hurry." she scooped more boxes into the bag.

"Oh, don't forget the crystals we need so I can double to begin with," Olivia reminded her. She felt the phantoms staring at her. She wondered if they had ears and could hear what they were plotting.

"Should be right here too." Terrilyne ran her finger along the boxes. "Here. Let's go."

They scrambled out of the library and down the mountain's tunnel.

From weeks of running, Olivia was much faster than Terrilyne.

"Oh no."

"What?" Olivia turned around.

"I'm twinning." Terrilyne started to fade. "If they catch you, they will kill you for trespassing. They aren't very nice about things like that in the first generation."

"What? You didn't tell me that part."

"I'll twin back in a minute." Terrilyne blew to dust and disappeared.

Olivia waited in a shadow against the wall. "Come on, Terri," she whispered. Little sounds echoed from the tunnel. Minutes came and went. It was taking too long. It felt like an eternity. Voices seemed to reach out from the darkness. If she didn't bury the crystals before she twinned to the present, they would be destroyed in the settling and everything they did would be wasted. Then Olivia realized a terrible thing. They hadn't picked a place to bury the crystals. Terrilyne probably had a place in mind, maybe somewhere in the tunnel. It would have to be nearby. Somewhere that no one snooped around. Somewhere that no one would dig for thirty thousand years.

She couldn't wait for Terrilyne any longer. Olivia started running toward the tunnel entrance. She broke out into the cool desert air. Fireworks blasted in the sky over Hovenweep. The crowd cheered in the distance. Olivia ran off into the night like a fleeting shadow.

16

Baby Teeth

"John Whistle is awfully mad. I can't say that I blame him. What you girls did was very dangerous. One little mistake with those timing crystals and you would be dead Olivia," Amythie Yazzi scolded, trying to hide the smile that felt like it was going to explode out of her face. "And the ancestors are not very happy that the first time children are allowed at Hovenweep they pull a stunt like this."

"He deserved it. He hates Olivia," Terrilyne yelled, tears streaming down her face.

"That's enough. I'm counting on you to take care of Olivia. She doesn't know our ways and doesn't know how dangerous twinning can be. It is very disorienting to double. More than one Hohokam has sent the wrong twin into a doubling joke and both ended up settling. And you know it is against the law to go back to save someone. Now go feed Hoolie and then clean up the kitchen."

"Sorry ma'am." Olivia grabbed a stack of old fry bread and walked outside with Terrilyne. She couldn't help feeling bad. It made her feel guilty to have Terrilyne's mother yelling at them like that, even if she would do it all over again if she had the chance.

"Sorry, Terri, it is my fault you are in trouble," she said, climbing down the ladders.

"It's all right, sis. I've been in worse." She wiped her nose with her arm.

The sun was coming up over the eastern mountains. It was a beautiful morning.

"Hi, Baby." Olivia leaped down the final rungs of the ladder and tumbled into Hoolie's side. The bear rolled over onto his back. Olivia buried her face into his furry chest. "I brought you an extra big stack this morning," she announced. "I snuck some honey on the ones in the middle," she whispered.

"You sure are friends with that bear," Terrilyne said.

"He saved my life more than once."

"You never say much about how you got here. How you walked here."

"We saw a lot of things. I will tell you the whole story when this is all over."

"You're going to leave when we save your aunt and uncle, aren't you?"

"I don't know what's going to happen. I have a little brother. His name is Gnat. And I have to find my mother and father." Olivia was very sad. The Yazzis had accepted her as their daughter so easily. Terrilyne was the best friend she had ever had. More than a best friend. She couldn't imagine what it would be like to go back to Florida and not see her anymore. "Maybe you can come with me."

"You mean, leave Hohokam?"

"Sure, why not? Just for a while. Like a big slumber party. You can see the rest of America."

Terrilyne shuddered at the thought. "That is forbidden. I would like to see the ocean though."

"I just saw the ocean for the first time a few months ago." Olivia laughed. She remembered it wasn't so long ago that she didn't know very much about the world outside of Sun Prairie either.

"I could learn how to swim. Do you know how to swim?"

"Of course."

"And ski down a mountain."

"I've never skied."

"We could do it together then. And fly in an airplane."

"And go skydiving."

"And eat a bowl of cereal. I've never eaten cereal."

"You are going to love my aunt and uncle. They have every kind of cereal known to man."

"Oooo! And rocket pops!"

"Lots and lots of rocket pops."

"It will never be allowed. No Hohokam has ever left the valley."

Olivia looked over at the western mountains. Today was the day she would sneak into Wardenclyffe and find her aunt and uncle. A flood of memories rushed through her. Anger welled up in her throat. The Cult was dangerous and cruel. It would take everything she had just to find and get inside their hideout. She might not survive. It would be easier to just live here in Hohokam.

"Let's clean the kitchen and get going," Olivia said, standing up. "We have a lot to do."

An hour later, Terrilyne, Chubascos, and Olivia walked carefully through the jumping chollas. Hoolie took the long way around.

"It's just ahead," Chubascos announced. "Around that large boulder."

"Do you think the crystals are still there?" Terrilyne asked.

"They have to be. They have to be."

As they cleared the boulder, a large rounded cave opened halfway up the cliff. Chubascos stopped.

"I'm not going up there."

"Fine, you can stay here with Hoolie."

Chubascos stared at Hoolie's long claws. "Fine by me," he said proudly. "I'm not scared."

"All right, wait here." Olivia and Terrilyne started scrambling up the hillside. The crumbling rock and sand cascaded down with every step. Before long, they stood in front of the dark cave opening.

"Hello!" Olivia yelled.

"Shhhhh. What are you doing? I thought we were sneaking in."

"Hello, Moki. It's me, Olivia. I told you I would return."

Something large stirred deep in the cave. Hundreds of hummingbirds blasted from the cave into the bright sun. Every imaginable color shone from their feathers. Lavender. Emerald. Orange and crimson. Sky blue. Large iridescent gorgets. Forked tails. Thin, curving bills for sipping rare cactus blooms. They scolded the intruders before zipping off to find some nectar-filled flowers. Chubascos watched from the desert floor, shocked at what he was seeing.

"Moki. Moki. Moki. Don't worry," Olivia cooed as she entered the cave. The chrysina charm around her neck glowed a soft green.

Terrilyne hesitated. "Are you sure this is such a good idea?"

"It's okay. Stay with me." The charm provided just enough light to see a few steps.

Terrilyne entered the cave behind her. A wind blew through their hair.

"It stinks."

"Breathe through your mouth," Olivia warned. The cave smelled like sour apples and dust.

A few more steps and the source of the wind came into view. Two enormous nostrils opened and closed rhythmically high above their heads. The Gila monster's eye caught the light. Olivia could see her reflection in the black shine.

"Moki, it's me, Olivia. Do you remember?"

A deep moan emerged from inside the animal. The vibration knocked dust from the ceiling.

"Um . . . Olivia?"

"It's all right. We have an agreement. Don't we, Moki?"

Each of his giant rounded scales felt like smooth glass stones under Olivia's hand. With her other hand, she pulled the resistant Terrilyne along behind her. Slowly, they passed between his body and the wall of the cave. His foot looked like a baby's foot—plump, short toes—even though the foot was the size of a rhino.

"Just up here," Olivia said.

"Why'd you have to go so far back?"

"I had to be sure."

They came to a small side tunnel beyond Moki's front leg. His belly rose and fell like a bellows. The girls felt puny next to his body. If he shifted or rolled, they would be crushed.

"Here." Olivia dropped to her knees and started to dig furiously. Sand blew out under the blur of her hands. Terrilyne pulled the sand back into mounds. Deeper and deeper they dug.

"How far down did you bury it?"

"It has to be here." They dug deeper and wider. Finally, they hit something hard.

"There it is. It's still here!" Olivia grabbed the bag and shook the sand off.

"Let's get out of here. I can't breathe." Terrilyne held her nose.

"We have to fix Moki's cave." Olivia started pushing the sand back into the hole.

"How did you figure that the Gila monster's name was Moki?"

"I dunno. It just seemed right. And he likes it. I'm good at naming things."

"Do you even know what 'moki' means?" They stomped on the loose sand to pack it and Terrilyne took off for the fresh air.

"Hold on, one more thing." Olivia scrounged in her pockets and walked toward Moki's head. It loomed over her like a cargo van. "You kept your promise." She scratched his gigantic chin. Moki let out a rumbling groan. His large black eyes caught the green light from her chrysina charm.

"Here is my end of the bargain." Olivia held out a black, wrinkled object. Moki's mouth slowly opened. Strings of thick, rancid saliva hung like bungee cords between his top and bottom jaws. Thousands of tiny teeth lined his enormous mouth that looked more like a garage door than a lizard's mouth. Terrilyne wilted at the sight of Olivia standing in front of the yawning maw. Olivia gently placed the wrinkled object on Moki's tongue and rubbed his chin one more time. Slowly, his mouth closed. A noise similar to a squeaking whale echoed in the cave.

"Wha . . . what was that?" Terrilyne asked as they walked back out into the burning sunlight.

"That was an aji el diablo, hottest pepper in the world."

"I won't even ask." Terrilyne shook her head and laughed. "In two days, we have been to Hovenweep and inside the Gila's cave. No one has ever dared go anywhere near him, and you were inside his cave, petting and feeding him hot peppers."

"If you put it that way, it makes a good story," Olivia said.

"They will tell stories in the future about Hoonaw Kookam," Terrilyne answered, grabbing Olivia's hand. "You never answered if you knew what 'moki' means."

"No. It's just the name that made sense for him."

"It means 'death.' "

Olivia shrugged. "That doesn't make sense. He seems to be living forever." She dumped the bag of library crystals onto the ground.

Chubascos was in shock. "What was in there? Did you see the Gila? Did you see those hummingbirds? Were you scared? Were there bones in there? Did you find all the baby teeth that hummingbirds steal?"

"He was in there all right," Terrilyne snapped. "I touched him."

"Whoa."

"Olivia named him Moki."

"Death? You named him *Death?*"

"She fed him too. They had some kind of secret pact."

Olivia was organizing the boxes on the ground with the strange letters up. Hoolie sniffed her hair.

Chubascos grabbed Terrilyne's shirt and shook her. "Did . . . you . . . find . . . the . . . baby . . . teeth?" he shouted.

"No. We didn't see any baby teeth."

"I knew it." He looked disappointed. "I knew it."

"But we didn't look around a whole lot. We just walked in and dug."

"So they might still be in there."

"And besides that, I'm not a raging maniac after breathing his stinkiness."

"Guys," Olivia interrupted.

"You don't know how long it takes to go bananas."

"Guys!"

"What?" Terrilyne and Chubascos answered together.

"I need your help with these. I can't read the words."

"This is the ancient language that they used during the prayers and speeches at Hovenweep."

Olivia remembered twinning back to Hovenweep after the library heist and standing with the crowd as representatives from each generation gave invocations and recommendations on changes to Hohokam law. The speeches droned on for what seemed like an eternity. Voting followed. Amendment recommendations were debated. Voting followed again. For a party that started out with skydiving and disappearing fires it really was anticlimactic. She was still used to linear time and it was driving her bonkers that so many days passed with speeches, but only a few seconds passed in the present. She was crawling out of her skin to get back to planning her attack on Wardenclyffe. To make things worse, she couldn't understand a word of it. Besides, one of the John Whistles stared at her angrily the entire time once it became clear that she faked her own death. The whole experience was nerve-wracking.

"Well, can you read it?"

"Of course we can read it."

"So, let's pick out all of the timing crystals for today."

Terrilyne set aside twelve timing crystals.

"And get rid of any for a time that has already passed."

Five crystals were returned to the pile.

"There is one every hour for the next seven hours." Terrilyne put them in order.

"OK. So position crystals. What do we have?"

Terrilyne read carefully. "This is weird."

"What?"

"These are all for the western island, but most are duplicates. We only have two positions."

"They are all for the other side of the mountain though." Chubascos jumped in.

"No, they aren't. They are for the eastern side of the western island."

"No." Terrilyne ran her finger along each letter. "It says, 'Sunset— Western Island' on each of them."

"Yes, sunset is on the western side," Chubascos argued.

"No, it means when you face the mountain, you see the sunset. That would be on the eastern side of the mountain. On the western side, you would only see the sun*rise* and the mountain at the same time."

"I dunno."

"What do these other letters mean?" Olivia offered.

"Those are numbers. Exact coordinates."

"Those don't help unless you have the coordinate map," Chubascos added.

"And we don't have one of those, do we?"

"Nope."

"They measure all worldly coordinates as lines emerging from the navel," Terrilyne said as if reciting from a textbook.

"From whose navel?"

"Not a person's navel, sillyhead. The navel of Hohokam, the tafoni. The exact center of the universe."

"Where is that?"

"On the western island somewhere. No one alive has ever seen it. That's why the coordinates don't do us any good since Wardenclyffe took over."

They walked in silence some more. Hoolie could sense Olivia's nervousness. He stayed within one step of her the entire time, even pushing Chubascos off the trail a couple of times.

"If this doesn't work, the faino peplas will warn Wardenclyffe," Olivia said.

"This will work," Terrilyne encouraged. "I know it will work."

"I hope so. How long does it take to walk to the border?"

"Two hours."

"Hoolie can get me there in a half hour."

"Can you use the Pearl?"

"I can make a bubble if I need to. And green lightning. And I can make bugs do things. Oh, and I can stop gravity. But I can't figure out how to do anything with time."

"Or make it rain." Terrilyne punched Chubascos for saying it.

"We have to get going. It's almost afternoon already."

They walked in silence along the cliff base. An increasing sense of dread filled Terrilyne's heart the longer they walked. It was finally happening. Either Olivia would fail and be killed on the western island, or she would succeed and leave Hohokam forever.

"Terri," Olivia finally broke the silence, "I have to tell you something. Your mom and dad are going to be very sad when they find out that I stole crystals. And I'm sorry."

"It's all right."

"Everyone has been so great to me. Every other town I have been to, they tried to arrest me. But you all accepted me and Hoolie even though I wasn't supposed to be here."

"It's all right."

"No one called the cops. Your dad fixed my shoulder. Even the original generations were singing with me at Hovenweep."

"Yeah, they don't like John Whistle either," Terrilyne said. She grabbed Olivia's hand as they walked.

"If I don't come back, please tell them, please tell them . . ."

"Olivia, it's all right. You are one of us now. No one thinks you are a Dark Eye anymore."

"And if I don't come back, take care of Squirt. He likes to eat. Hoolie will leave on his own."

"I have to tell you something too."

"What?" Olivia sniffed tears back.

"I saw you at Hovenweep. I mean, I saw you from the future. You were old like my mom. And you were beautiful."

Olivia's mind swirled. "That doesn't mean anything. Your dad said you can't pay any attention to the past or the future."

"Nothing is for sure, but it means *something*."

"Did you talk to me?"

"No. I like my Olivia better."

The trail curved around a rock promontory. The tetracomb came into view. It hummed with energy.

"Why aren't there any guards? I thought only Level Twenty people could be here."

"That's the law. No one will break it so there's no need for guards."

"Except us."

Terrilyne turned pale. "Except us."

"I'm not scared," Chubascos said.

"Don't forget, first you need to double back to Hovenweep so we can fool John Whistle and sneak into the library."

Olivia reached out and took the crystals from Terrilyne. She stood in front of the tetracomb. Something wasn't right. How could they have the crystals if they hadn't already gone back and stolen them? But how could they go back and steal them without having the twinning crystals to begin with? Her head spun.

"No." Olivia remembered Amythie Yazzi's warning on doubling. "No, I've already done that." She put the twinning crystals in her backpack and set it against a large boulder. "I'll be right back," she said and disappeared into the tetracomb. A few seconds later, she returned. She tossed a gun onto the sand.

"Is that a gun?" Chubascos stepped closer.

"I suppose so."

"I've never touched a gun before."

"Me neither."

"How did you . . . where did it? . . . "

Before he could complete his question the gun dissolved into dust.

"So far so good." Olivia looked at her watch. "You guys need to twin there at two o'clock."

"No problem," Terrilyne said.

"I'm not afraid," Chubascos proclaimed too loudly.

"Oh, that's right. You've never twinned," Olivia said, patting him on the shoulder. "Don't let go of your crystals. If Wardenclyffe catches you, just pretend you're lost."

Terrilyne attached herself to Olivia. "Be careful. Be careful. Be careful."

"I will see you soon. Take care of Squirt."

"I love you."

"I love you too," Olivia peeled Terrilyne's arms from around her. "I have to go."

"Hoonaw kookam."

"Hoonaw kookam."

"Goodbye."

Terrilyne watched Olivia leap onto Hoolie's back and disappear into the mesquite brush. An overwhelming feeling of dread washed through her. This no longer felt like a game.

17

Tafoni of Sonora

Olivia jumped into a dry river bed that served as the border between Hohokam and Wardenclyffe land. The mountain loomed over her, its peaks far more jagged and sinister than they looked from far away. The entire mountain floated ten feet over the surface of the ground, just like the Hohokam town. She looked in the empty gap beneath the mountain. In the far distance, she could see the thin sliver of sunlight where the mountain ended on the other side. The gap was too high for Olivia to reach and climb up. Chubascos had come by earlier and hidden a ladder. She leaned it against the mountain and scrambled up. The dust and rock on the edge crumbled and fell to the ground below. She expected the mountain to tip slightly when she stood upright at its edge, almost like stepping into a canoe. Instead, the ground was as firm as ever.

Above her, a black pointy-headed bird sat on top of a tall mesquite, tilted its head, and watched her scramble along the rocks. Olivia could see its red mechanical eyes focusing and zooming as she walked. Just like that, she had been spotted. So much for a sneak attack. The bird let out a rasping chirp and flew to a closer branch. Up ahead, another faino pepla tilted its head and caught Olivia's movement. Another rasping chirp as it moved closer.

"Go away, leave me alone." She swatted her hands in their direction.

The two birds focused their mechanical eyes. Olivia jumped behind a gigantic purple cactus. She held her breath. After a few seconds, one of the faino peplas flitted around the cactus to a nearby bush and chirped.

"Leave me alone!" Olivia started running up the mountain. Almost every bush and tree had a faino pepla sitting on the top branch. Soon, hundreds of faino peplas followed her like a living thunder cloud. Every bird within sight tracked her progress across the desert, chirping the same rasping note. The noise was deafening.

Terrilyne had told her that the faino peplas only patrol the border of Wardenclyffe territory. If she can run a mile or so, the elevation is too high for them. Olivia jogged along a ridge that sloped upward into a rocky mesa. Faino peplas swarmed everywhere. She looked back down the valley. In the distance, she could see another cloud of birds shifting across the land. They were tracking another person.

"Run, Terri," she huffed between loud breaths. She strained to see Terrilyne and Chubascos, but they were just too far away. The air was so dry and hot she had to take a break. She put her hands on her knees. Every little branch around her had a faino pepla sitting on it. A thin cloud of dust streaked down the mountainside headed straight for her. She could hear the faint sound of dirt bikes. Her heart started pounding in her chest.

At least they didn't just shoot missiles, Olivia thought as she gritted her teeth. She stood back up and ran as hard as she could away from Terrilyne and Chubascos.

The rasping chirps and hundreds of mechanical, unblinking eyes relentlessly chased her. There was nowhere to hide. Seconds later, three dirt bikes jumped over a small ravine and circled wildly around her. The dust that kicked up from their tires choked in her throat. Small rocks kicked up by their tires shot through the air. Closer and closer they circled until she cowered near the ground. One of the drivers shoved her down into the dirt and pushed his hand on her head so she couldn't move. Once he had control of her, he stood her up and lifted his visor. A few long curls of greasy hair dropped out.

"Little Thing," he said, pinching her chin. "Do you remember me? I remember you!" He seemed genuinely excited. His smile made her sick.

"No. I don't have clue who you are."

"I can see you remember me, Little Thing. I can tell. I'm so glad you're here. I thought you died in the river. We searched for days."

"Get your hands off me," Olivia screeched. She writhed and twisted. For a second, she escaped but barely made two steps before she was face down in the dirt again.

"Aw, come on, Little Thing," he spit. "We're going to have some fun. I almost lost my job because of you. Wow." He kicked the dirt. "I can't believe you're really here!"

One of the other bikers yelled over the rumble of the engine, "Hurry up, Flinch. Quit screwing around."

Flinch grabbed Olivia's hair and pulled her toward the other man. It hurt so bad that tears came to her eyes. "You best check yourself, Carl," Flinch shouted and jammed a finger into his shoulder. "If you have something to say, just say it."

Carl revved his engine and stared straight ahead.

"I didn't think so."

Flinch slung Olivia on the back of his bike and headed back up the mountain. She considered jumping off the bike and running but they were going too fast and there were rocks and cactus all around.

"This has been a long time coming," Flinch yelled over his shoulder. "Just think, I had my hands on you in that tacky roadside store. Remember that? You didn't have the mark of the Guardian, so we let you go." He swerved, narrowly missing a rocky ditch.

"And the hurricane, do you remember that? We thought your uncle had the sphere and all along it was you." Olivia pushed her hands against his back trying to get some space.

"All this time, it was you. When we stop, you can tell me how you escaped the flood in the canyon. You really are amazing, Little One."

She could see him smiling through the opening in his helmet. She hoped they would hurry and get to the compound as soon as possible. She wanted to see if they had Aunt and Uncle. But halfway there, she felt a cool wind blow. The twinning had begun. As she felt the last of her presence blurring away, she reached over and grabbed Flinch's gun from his holster. And then she disappeared.

Olivia poked her head around a cluster of large boulders. Everything was silent. She scanned the tops of the bushes and trees. Not a single faino pepla could be seen. She felt a wet bear nose nuzzle into her hand.

"Come on, Hoolie. Let's go." She jumped on top of his back. "We have to get a mile up the mountain before they come back." Hoolie bounded up the dry river bed and blasted through the thorny bushes toward Sky Island. Carefully, Hoolie climbed the ladder. It strained and creaked, but it held. Chubascos had promised that it would hold.

Olivia looked along the ridge as Hoolie stormed up the slope. On the horizon, she could see the cloud of faino peplas that must be chasing her double. In the other direction, she couldn't see the cloud that chased

Terrilyne and Chubascos, but she knew they had led thousands of the annoying birds in the other direction.

All Hoolie had to do was run a mile before the faino peplas returned to their lookout posts. Hoolie could run a mile in no time. The plan was working.

She had no idea how far she and Hoolie had gone or how much longer until they ran a mile. Ten minutes passed. Fifteen. The land sloped upward. Hoolie could sense that other bears lived here. Their secret highways were clearly marked. Several rude raccoon-sized animals with super-long striped tails ran with them for a while. Every time Olivia tried to talk to them, they hissed out of their long sharp snouts. Up alongside a small creek bed thousands of butterflies pooled together on the bare ground, launching into the sky like confetti. Large boulders shone from decades of polishing by the spring runoff. The trees were much larger too. It felt different on the mountain, as if she stepped from the desert and into a dream. Olivia thought she saw a large, spotted cat leap from a tree and disappear into the thicket.

"Jaguar," she whispered in Hoolie's ear.

The creek bed flattened out as they climbed the mountain. Soon they could see over the treetops.

"Let's take a break." Olivia jumped off Hoolie. "I'm sure we're safe here." She scanned the horizon looking for any signs of trouble. Nothing was moving. Terrilyne, Chubascos, and her double would have probably twinned back to the tetracomb by now. She smiled at the thought of Flinch realizing that she had escaped once again. He probably drove his bike into a cactus. On top of that, she stole his gun so it would disintegrate in the neutrino wind. He must be out of his mind.

The breeze felt good. The air was cooler at this elevation. She looked up. She couldn't see the compound or the top of the mountain anymore, but she knew it was up there. Along with her aunt and uncle. At least she hoped so. She was basing everything on what her uncle yelled at her back in Florida. He may have been completely wrong. Maybe Wardenclyffe decided to take them somewhere else because he had yelled "Sky Island." She also had no idea how many thugs were waiting for her up there. Or what kind of security system they had. She and Terrilyne only had a plan for sneaking past the faino peplas. From now on, it was just her and Hoolie. The plan had run out.

Three hours of hiking later, Olivia's thighs were burning from the effort of going uphill. Her ankles stung from the thorns that had snuck through her socks. Her mouth was dry and dusty. Three hours of nothing but brush and rocks and cactus. Odd little lizards. Birds she had never seen before. Then she arrived at a stark white line. The line extended as far as she could see to the left and to the right. Everything from that line up the mountain was covered in snow. A little bit of water trickled out from beneath, mixing the dirt into a gooey mud. Hoolie sniffed the snow cautiously. He had never seen such a thing.

With a single step, Olivia crossed into a world of white. She was high enough up the mountain that the temperature never climbed above sixty-eight degrees, so the snow never melted. Her feet crunched into the snow. A clear track. Hoolie eased a paw onto the white and withdrew it as if he had stepped on something hot. The fur stood up on his neck.

"It's all right, Hoolie. It's just snow." Olivia laughed. She pushed him from behind. He wouldn't budge.

"You wouldn't survive in Wisconsin," she said and started walking to see if he would follow her. All he did was sit down and watch. A snowball arced through the air and landed on Hoolie's head. He jumped back. Olivia bent down and scooped up some more snow. It wasn't cold. It felt more like mud than the snow she remembered. She launched another snowball. Hoolie dodged it then rushed full speed toward Olivia. In one smooth tackle, they tumbled and rolled in the snow. Olivia swore she could see a smile on the bear's mouth.

"Night's coming soon," Olivia announced, lying on her back in the snow. The sun was dropping below the mountain. She could almost see it getting darker by the second. "Are you gonna be all right walking on the big old scary snow?" She tickled Hoolie's stomach.

"Let's see if we can find somewhere to sleep for the night." As evening grew, the only noise was the crunching of their feet. It was so loud she couldn't imagine why Flinch couldn't hear it too.

Olivia and Hoolie walked in silence for an hour. Ahead, she saw a rounded outcropping of rosy stone the size of a small house. An oval hole was carved through the stone like a potter had molded a lump of red clay into a smooth pot and laid it on its side. "A cave," Olivia said as she climbed up and inside the opening. "This will be perfect for sleeping."

The cave was high enough to stand up. Hoolie lunged up next to her. Inside, the cave branched off in five directions: east, west, north, south, and straight up. The walls and ceiling were as smooth as glass. Tiny holes punctured the ceiling. Olivia stuck her fingers into the holes. They were as precise as if they were drilled by a diamond drill. There were so many it seemed like the entire cave was more hole than stone.

A deep, calm pool of water filled a circular depression in the very middle, where all five of the passages converged. A drusy layer of quartz crystal lined the bowl of the pool.

"Water!" Olivia yelled out. "Hoolie, it's water!" She couldn't explain how liquid water could exist surrounded by so much snow. Hoolie lowered his head and lapped up as much as he could. Olivia scooped up handful after handful with loud slurps. As the waves of their drinking subsided, the clarity of the pool returned. Starlight from all of the tiny holes in the ceiling reflected perfectly in the calm water. More stars poured in through holes in the five passageways, overlapping and creating new constellations and galaxies in the pool. A vast pool of endless stars spinning with their engines of fire. It was a star map.

"The tafoni," Olivia whispered. "This must be the tafoni that Terrilyne told us about! The center of the universe." She leaped to her feet again and rushed from entrance to entrance. Each hole seemed perfectly placed to overlook a vast landscape. Designs were etched into the interior walls. Spirals spinning into each other. Trajectories and angles. Recreations of the star map. Measurements and magical words.

"Terrilyne would love this place."

Olivia sat down and hung her legs out one of the cave openings. The white snow spread out in every direction. The Hohokam valley was visible from here. She could see every detail. Lights were on in the Yazzi's home. The tetracomb fizzed and spun in its canyon. The giant purple, gray, and green cactus cast long shadows across the desert. Moki let out a gigantic yawn from his moon rock. The entire world of the Hohokam was laid out in front of her. From high above in the cave opening, Olivia floated over the tiny world. Its little inhabitants, the antelope and coyotes, the jaguar, the Hohokam, were just beyond the reach of her fingertips. She looked up. The starry sky seemed even closer than the valley, like she could drink from it just as she had drunk from the cave pool.

Olivia thought of the Hohokam's crops shriveling, the trees turning brown, the fish in the lakes crowding into the last, hot, muddy puddles. She thought of the fires burning the horizon, the charred bones they left behind. She thought of all those families leaving their homes in the north and moving to where water wasn't permanently frozen. She would give anything to be able to reach down and lift them to safety, to lift them all to a place rich with rain and rivers. Sitting in the tafoni, this perch high in the sky, she felt responsible for the entire world. To how life used to be, how it is supposed to be.

Olivia took the Pearl out of her backpack. Blue light flooded out of the tafoni and beamed into the night. Its chimes echoed over the snow. Once she ended the drought, she vowed to never open it again. It had caused too much pain and hurt too many people. She may be the Guardian, but that doesn't mean she has to open it. She might even just put it back in Junonia where she found it. It had been protected there for who knows how long.

She opened the Pearl and quickly worked the switches she was familiar with. Even after all this time, she knew precious little about how it worked.

Rain. She had to make it rain again.

She knew the Earth was burning because of her.

18

Virosa

The first rosy edge of the sun slipped over the eastern island summit and washed into the valley before fluttering lightly on Olivia's eyelids in the center of the tafoni. She moaned and turned her head, but the sun snuck into a crack between her arm and Hoolie's fur. There was no fighting it. Morning had arrived.

Hoolie would have none of it. Bears love to sleep more than anything other than eating. Olivia stretched and stood up. Her stomach growled. She hadn't thought about bringing food. Something moved outside. She snuck quietly to the edge of the hole and peaked out. Thousands of bright green beetles were clinging to the tafoni. Thousands more shone like emeralds on the white snow. They looked exactly like her chrysina charm.

"So you *are* real." She petted one gently with one finger. The charm around her neck felt warm. Something wiggled inside. A click. A tiny wheel spun. Its wings snapped open revealing a secret cavity. Hundreds of tiny, red sparks tumbled out into the snow, ringing like tiny bells. Slowly, the beetles awoke and scuttled toward the sparks. One by one, each beetle picked up a spark, spread its wings, and buzzed off toward the trees. Soon, all of the beetles and sparks were gone. The wings on her charm snapped shut again.

"Huh," Olivia said, "that was odd."

She heard the snow crunch.

A large orange jaguar crept toward her in the snow. He spotted her sitting in the tafoni. Olivia didn't dare move. She could hear Hoolie snoring behind her. The jaguar watched her with burning cinnabar eyes. Another jaguar walked from around the back and stood next to the first. Their sharp claws dug into the snow. The snow was packed down in a circle where they had been pacing all night.

"Hoolie," Olivia whispered and slowly took a step back. "Wake up." The words hissed through her teeth. She couldn't breathe.

The jaguars turned back into the shadows of the mountain.

Olivia breathed a sigh of relief. The big cats were gone. She'd had no idea they were so close all night. And now she didn't know why they'd left.

"Get up, lazy." She booted Hoolie in the backside. The bear released an enormous yawn.

"We'd better get going. You better keep your eyes out for those jaguars."

They started walking up the mountain again.

"We have to be close now. Be careful when we walk around corners."

The climbing was much steeper than before. Olivia's stiff legs felt like they were going to fall off. They felt like they were going to fall off. At the top of a cliff, she looked up. The Wardenclyffe compound was clearly visible near the mountain peak. It looked like a mountain chalet made of thick stone and wooden beams. There didn't appear to be any lookout towers or barbed wire fences.

Olivia's heart dropped. The compound was suspended over a very deep crevice, like a moth caught in a spider web. Several thick cables ran from the building's corners and anchored it into the mountain. It didn't seem possible that the cables were strong enough to hold up such a large building. A thin bridge swung across the chasm. The bridge was the only way across.

"Look out!" Olivia pushed Hoolie back. A helicopter appeared over the mountain peak and approached the compound. It circled around the area, flying right over her head, before it hovered over the compound. Slowly, it lowered onto a landing pad that Olivia couldn't see.

"That was one of the helicopters that tried to shoot us in the river."

She had to find a way to sneak into the building. She could shinny down a cable. She was good at shinnying. The thought of hanging over that deep crevice made her sick. Besides, how would she get into the building once she made it there? There weren't any doors where the cables attached to the foundation.

Maybe she could glide from the rocks above like a flying squirrel or a parachutist. There was no sign of Flinch or any other guard, but she was sure that flying into the compound would get too much attention. She couldn't think of a way to get inside other than the bridge.

A large shed was nestled in a grove of ancient juniper trees nearby. Olivia hid behind its thick stone walls. A gasoline tank sat next to the shed. Something was humming nearby, an air conditioner maybe. The end of the bridge was right there, just a few steps away. But there was no more cover between her and the building. She couldn't go any closer without the chance of being seen. She sat down and waited for evening. Some people rode up on dirt bikes. They parked them in the shed and left. Darkness was slowly falling. Olivia waited for a long time to make sure the men had truly left.

Gently, she stood on Hoolie's back and lifted her eyes to a window in the garage. No one was inside. The dirt bikes were lined up next to an ATV and some tools.

"It's dark enough now. Let's go see what we can find." Olivia snuck around the back corner and slipped through an old wooden door. Inside, she picked through an old cabinet.

"Nothing but shovels and rakes," she mumbled. An old work bench along the back was covered with a jumble of items. A greasy baseball cap hung on a nail. She put the hat on, taking care to tuck her hair inside.

She heard footsteps and voices approaching.

"I can't believe we have to go back out there."

"They get to sit inside doing nuthin'."

"We already searched the entire mountain. She's gone. I saw her disappear. She didn't fall off or jump off or fly away. She vanished."

"Well, it sure isn't my fault, Carl. I wasn't there, but now I have to go clean up your mess." The man swung open the garage door. Wind poured into the garage.

"I'll bet the bikes need gas."

"I mean, she just vanished into thin air. Poof. How did she do that?"

"I think you need to spend more time sleeping and less time partying."

"So what are you saying? You calling me a liar?"

"I'm just saying, that's all."

"Why don't you go tell Flinch that he didn't really catch her? You go tell him he is crazy."

"I don't have to tell anybody anything."

"Yessir, I'd pay to see that."

Olivia held her breath from behind the barrel of shovels. She could feel spider webs brushing against her neck as the men filled the gas tanks and lifted helmets from the handlebars. It was that precise moment that Olivia realized it wasn't a spider web. It was an actual spider. Frantically, she swatted at her neck. Her hand knocked into the barrel which sounded more like a gong as it rang loudly throughout the garage.

"Who's that?" Carl looked around. "Hold on, someone's in here." They walked toward the corner.

"Well, look at this." They stood in front of the barrel. "We just saved ourselves a lot of trouble," Carl said, reaching toward her. A dark shadow exploded behind the two men. They flew across the garage, knocking their heads against the bench. Hoolie stood over them searching for any sign of movement.

"Ha!" Olivia shouted. "Bring them over here. Help me." She grabbed their legs and started pulling. They were too heavy for her to budge by herself. But Hoolie flung them into the corner like they were pillows. Ten minutes later, she was wearing one of their flannel shirts and both men were leaned up against the wall covered with two rolls of duct tape.

"That should hold them," she said as she put pieces of tape over their mouths. "Hoolie, you have to wait out back. I'll come get you once I find Aunt and Uncle."

Hoolie showed no sign of moving. He didn't spend his last few months carrying and protecting the Guardian only to hide when things got rough.

"Listen, you are way too big. I have to sneak in there. If anyone sees us we will be trapped. Besides, they have guns." The more she talked, the crazier the whole idea started to sound. She rooted around in the toolbox and then grabbed the keys to the ATV. "I don't want you doing anything stupid. This isn't like Chuck's house in Texas. I will be all right. Just be ready to run."

Olivia pushed Hoolie behind the shed. "Now go *hide*." One big shove sent the bear into a snowy gully filled with junipers. She took a deep breath. This was it. She had no idea what she was walking into or even if she would make it inside the building. But enough was enough. She stormed around the corner and started walking toward the bridge. She didn't try to hide or sneak. She took long steps as if she were in a hurry. It was the only thing she could think of. Pretend she belonged there, like she was doing her job. Pretend like nothing unusual was going on. Hopefully, with the flannel shirt, baseball cap, and her confident attitude, she would pass as something unremarkable.

Olivia stepped onto the bridge. It swung gently as she moved across the chasm. She had never been on a swinging bridge before. Ragged, oily ravens roosted on the rocks along the cliff. She could feel them all watching her. Through the corner of her eye, she saw the blackness beneath her. A hollow breeze swirled, delivering the sound of howling animals fighting far below. It took everything she had not to look down or check the windows of the building to see if anyone was watching. She pretended she was walking up the sidewalk to her house and she could smell warm cookies baking inside.

A huge wooden door loomed over the other end of the bridge. Her heart skipped a beat. What if it was locked? She reached out, turned the old iron knob, and leaned into the heavy door. It barely budged, bouncing her backwards. She leaned into the door again, throwing her entire weight against it. Slowly, it swung open.

Olivia peeked into a grand foyer with a three-story staircase. White sheets draped against all the walls and billowed gently as the breezes from the chasm rushed into the old building. A giant chandelier made of hundreds of elk antlers hung from the ceiling. The tiny lights at the tip of each antler blurred yellow through a sheet of plastic that had been wrapped around it and taped at the top. A metal scaffold climbed up to a window high above the floor. Old dust lingered in the air. Musty cobwebs swayed. Voices floated from distant rooms. Sorrowful ghosts.

Footsteps clopped on the hard floor heading in her direction. Olivia ducked into a side room and carefully shut the door. Luckily she was alone. Large maps were tacked to the walls. Someone had drawn hundreds of thin lines across them and circled some of the locations where the lines converged. Discarded maps of the world covered the floor in thick layers. One wall was covered with photos of people with notes enumerated below. There was a picture of her surrounded by her mom, dad, aunt, uncle, and a blurry picture of Gnat playing a video game. Olivia recognized a photo of Nikola Tesla that Uncle had shown her from one of his books. Even the ceiling accepted the overflow of notes and the failed attempt at drawing magnetic convergence on a map of Florida. She tore down her picture from the wall and tossed it into the corner.

The footsteps disappeared down a hallway.

Olivia slipped back out into the foyer. She looked up the stairs that twisted around to the very top of the building. That would be the place she would imprison someone. In a moldy attic. Or a tower. Every step on the stairs creaked and groaned under her feet. She placed her feet on the outer edges of each stair but she couldn't find a quiet path. Every step seemed to creak louder than the last.

On the third floor, she started on the far end of the hall. With each door she opened, she expected a man with a gun to be waiting for her. But most of the bedrooms were empty and smelled like stale popcorn. There were piles of dirty clothes sitting in the middle of the floors. She burst into one room to find a man snoring under the covers. Quickly, she shut the door. "Who's there? Leave me alone. My shift isn't for four hours," an angry voice called out to her. A shoe or a book hit the door from the other side. Olivia scurried down the hall. One last room remained.

Slowly, she opened the door. The familiar stillness of an empty room greeted her.

Aunt and Uncle were not on the third floor.

A computer and phone sat on a small desk in the corner.

Olivia rushed over to the desk and quietly picked up the phone. She dialed her dad's number and held her breath. The out-of-service tone blasted through the phone.

"No, Dad," she sighed, pushing the button to hang up. She dialed again, hoping, hoping with all of her heart that she had dialed the wrong number before. She dialed again. Again. Finally she let the phone sit dumbly in its cradle. Olivia's legs shook. She wanted to collapse on the floor.

Olivia looked out the window. The entire compound was visible from the third floor. A red helicopter sat on a landing pad. Several out-buildings were built on the corners surrounded by various tanks of water, heating oil, and helicopter fuel. Thick cables ran from the edges of the compound platform up to anchors in the rocky cliffs. The final peak of the mountain loomed over her like a painting.

"It's beautiful, isn't it?" A voice boomed from the doorway. Olivia whipped around. An older man stood in the shadow of the doorway surrounded by two men and a woman. The blood drained form Olivia's face. She grabbed for the window and shoved the sill. It didn't budge. The man chuckled.

"Allow me to introduce myself," the man said, taking a step forward into the light. "My name is Karel Virosa. Welcome to Sky Island."

His arm outstretched and seemed to encompass the whole room. He wore a bright blue silk shirt only half-buttoned underneath a black sport coat. A thick gold chain with a medallion hung around his neck. His gray hair was neatly trimmed. He smelled like he had just come from the barber. Clean and spicy. He had the air about him that at some point in his past he was a refined gentleman. He extended his hand for a handshake. Three of his fingers had gold rings with large smooth gems embedded in them. Olivia didn't move a muscle. Virosa left his hand hanging in midair for an uncomfortably long time before he bowed gently toward her.

"Of course, you have already met Flinch," Virosa said, glancing menacingly toward him, "several times, unfortunately." The comment seemed to hurt Flinch like a knife.

"And Carl, who is going to be pulling duct tape from his hair for weeks. And this is Rieger," he said, gesturing toward the woman, "whom you humiliated in the canyon."

Olivia held a tiny smile back from her face. Virosa had the hint of an accent in his voice, but she couldn't tell what kind. She was never very good with accents.

"You surprised me." Virosa stood at the window with his hands behind his back as he stared up at the mountain peak. "Guardians throughout history have been runners and hiders, living in shadows, cowering like weak, hungry mice. You, on the other hand, are on the national news every night." He chuckled. "There are over one hundred websites dedicated to sightings of the Bear Girl. Stealing food. Breaking into homes. Disrupting county fairs. And now, now you show up here, right into my welcoming arms." Virosa turned toward Olivia and stared directly at her. One of his greenish eyes had a large brown spot in it, giving him a slightly crazed look. "You might be the worst Guardian in the history of the world."

Virosa continued. "Did you know that kids all over the country are wandering around, lost in the woods, looking for bears to ride?"

"N . . . no," Olivia stammered. She saw Flinch smirking by the door.

"And did you know this drought you created has already burned millions of acres of forest and that tens of thousands of families are homeless?"

"I'm going to fix it."

"Oh, you *are,* are you?" Virosa laughed. "Then why haven't you already? You have the sphere."

"No," Olivia said, staring at her feet, "I lost it."

Virosa nodded at Flinch, Carl, and Rieger. They grabbed her shoulders and pulled the backpack off. Carl unzipped the bag and dumped it. Doug's thermos thunked to the floor followed by a snowstorm of empty snack wrappers. A pile of sand trickled out.

"This is unbelievable," Flinch screamed at the top of his lungs and slammed the empty backpack onto the ground. "Just give me five minutes with her, Karel. Just five minutes."

Virosa held up his hand to shush him. "Olivia, dear," he whispered close to her ear. The smell of aftershave stung her nose. "Where is the sphere?"

"I told you I lost it."

"Give me the sphere and I will let you and your aunt and uncle go free."

"I . . . I can't." Olivia's heart raced. So Aunt and Uncle *are* here.

"That's it. All you have to do is hand it over. No more troubles. No more bullets. No more hungry days. No more running."

"I am never giving the Pearl to the stinking Cult of Wardenclyffe!" Olivia shouted and tried to squirm from Rieger's grip. "Never."

A loud crash of thunder rocked the mountainside. The compound swayed slightly in the wind.

"Cult? Is that what you think? A cult?" Virosa laughed. "All right, we will do this your way. Carl, Rieger, get five other men and find the bear as soon as the storm ends. What's his name? . . . Hoolie. He can't be far. Find him and shoot him. We don't need any more trouble."

"No!" Olivia pulled at Rieger's hair and lunged free. Flinch snatched her around the waist just as she reached the door. "Hoolie! Run!" Tears were streaming down her face. In her heart, she knew Hoolie wouldn't run away. He wouldn't leave her.

"Don't cry, Little Thing." Flinch ran his finger up her cheek, catching a tear. He held the tear up to the light. "Your ol' buddy Flinch doesn't like it when you cry. We'll keep Hoolie as a rug in the living room."

"Come," Virosa said, heading down the stairs. "I'm hungry. Let's eat dinner."

Flinch led Olivia along. He leaned into her ear. "Tell me how you did it."

"Let go of me."

"Come on. How did you disappear from my bike?"

"Because you smelled so bad."

Flinch pushed her forward. She could hear Carl and Rieger snickering behind them.

"This isn't about the old man and his superstitions anymore," Flinch said, grabbing her arm tighter. "I'll get my paycheck one way or another. This is between you and me."

The windows rattled from the storm. The thundercloud was just outside the glass. Oddly, the storm was all lightning. There wasn't any rain. Olivia had never been inside a thundercloud. It was frightening.

"I've never actually met a Guardian before," Virosa proclaimed as he threw open the double glass doors leading to the dining room. "I've read all about them, of course, and their cowardly ways. All just stories from ages ago. A Guardian hasn't actually been captured in over five hundred years."

Virosa dramatically sat down at the head of a long table. A large candelabra stood in the middle of the table although there weren't any candles. Windows covered one wall from floor to ceiling. The other three walls were covered with more white sheets. A pile of tools and paint cans were stacked in the corner. Flashes of lightning filled the dining room with frightening regularity.

"Have a seat, Olivia," Virosa said, gesturing toward an empty chair at the table. Rieger, Carl, and Flinch sat down around her. Several other people entered the room and sat down too. None of them seemed very friendly. Violin music played through some speakers.

Several well-dressed men and women filed out of the kitchen holding silver platters with lids. A platter was set before each diner except for Olivia.

"This smells stupendous," Virosa announced, eyeing Olivia for signs of weakness. "Tell me where the sphere is and you can have some."

With great flair, the lids were removed revealing grilled ham and cheese sandwiches and tomato soup.

A look of disappointment crossed Virosa's face and his shoulders dropped. The others at the table wolfed down their food like a pack of angry raccoons, burping and growling. Virosa cut through his sandwich with a steak knife and ate with a fork.

"You understand, of course," Virosa said between bites, "that you can have a delicious ham and cheese sandwich if you just tell me." Even as he said it, it was obvious to him that a sandwich wasn't enough of a bribe. He had specifically asked for the most delicious gourmet meal.

"Bah. Let's be done with this pretense." He threw down his fork, which clattered against the plate. "You and I both know I'm going to get the sphere. As long as I have you, it's just a matter of time. The Guardian and the sphere always come together somehow. This," he pointed around the room with his steak knife, "is just a small, insignificant outpost for Wardenclyffe. I was sent here over six weeks ago in case you made it this far. Six weeks of substandard food, substandard company, and substandard climate control!" He slammed his fist on the table.

"You should try eating what I've been eating," Olivia replied. She tried to ignore the smell of toasted cheese that filled the room. Her stomach growled.

"Ha! I suppose you are right. Regardless, all of the regional provosts of Wardenclyffe are on their way here. I called them as soon as you appeared on the border yesterday. They should start arriving tonight. To be perfectly honest, I would prefer to have the sphere for their arrival."

Olivia raised an eyebrow and folded her arms.

"You and I are not so different, Olivia. You think of me as some kind of evil monster. But think of your own behavior. You changed the climate, creating an environmental disaster. You stole food all across the country. You destroyed a house and a county fair in Texas. You hurt good, decent American citizens. Why did you do it? Who do you think you are? I'll tell you who you are. You are the Guardian. You are one in a long line of Guardians throughout time. You were right to steal from those peasants because you are better than they. I admire you for that. You knew what you had to do and you did it. You and I are part of history, Olivia, part of something great. We are not like these . . . these base brutes." He pointed around the table with his knife.

"Hey!" Carl snapped. "Watch your mouth."

"Shut up, brute. Shut up!" Virosa's face turned purple. A vein pulsed on his forehead. He flung his platter against the wall. Tomato soup splattered and dripped down to the floor. "You . . . you animals think this is a joke. You stupid little animals. If you did your jobs right the first time, the second time, or the third time, we wouldn't be sitting here in this moldy dump in the middle of nowhere eating filthy grilled cheese and canned soup."

The room fell completely silent.

"I'm not paying you animals to think. I'm paying you to do your jobs. Do you think I'm getting my money's worth? DO YOU?"

Carl looked down at the table. Flinch was staring at the wall.

"I don't like being taken advantage of. I don't like paying you every week and getting tepid results." Virosa's entire body arched with tense anger. He took a deep breath. "Now look what you've done. You've scared our guest. The storm is passing. Why don't you go get some rifles and start hunting? I could use a new rug for my room."

As Rieger, Carl, and three others got up to leave, Olivia grabbed the candelabra and flung it as hard as she could. The base of it clunked off Carl's head and crashed to the floor. Flinch yowled with laughter, pounding the table with his fists. Carl whirled around and grabbed the candelabra in his fist as he came toward Olivia. Virosa jumped to his feet and pointed him toward the door.

"Woo hoo, Carl," Flinch laughed. "You just got jacked by a ten-year-old girl."

Carl grimaced and pointed the candelabra straight at Flinch. Then he left to catch up with the others.

"Hey, Carl, you still have a piece of duct tape in your hair," Flinch yelled after him. Then he laughed so hard he had to lay his head on the table.

Olivia jumped onto the table and leaped halfway across the room. She hit the door running full speed toward the front of the house.

"Get her! Get her! Get her!" she could hear Virosa screaming behind her. "Unbelievable!"

Luckily the other thugs had gone toward the back of the house. Within seconds, Olivia was pulling on the heavy front door. A blast of frozen wind rushed through. She looked back to see Flinch and the others barreling down the hallway toward her. As she slipped through the door, she leaped up and grabbed one of the sheets that covered the walls. The gigantic sheet came down, folding and piling in a mound, blocking the doorway behind her.

The bridge swung wildly as she ran across the chasm. The wet boards slipped beneath her feet, sending her stumbling. She could hear Flinch cursing and sneezing as he struggled with the dusty sheet. A siren blared throughout the compound.

"Hoolie! Where are you?" she called out into the dusk. She ran around the garage. "Hoolie!" The bear stepped out from the junipers. "Come on, down here." Olivia scrambled into the rocky gully.

She could hear the men up by the garage. "Spread out. She ain't gone far."

"You have to get out of here, Hoolie. They are going to kill you." She could feel the muscles tense in his back. "I don't want you to fight now. You can fight later. I'm going to be all right. They won't hurt me unless I give them the Pearl. Aunt and Uncle are here. You need to go and get help. We need help!" Olivia wrapped her arms around Hoolie's neck. The tears in her eyes washed away in the rain. "Go! Go!"

The bear disappeared back into the junipers. Olivia slipped back up to the other side of the garage and raced across the bridge and into the house without being seen. She searched the entire second floor for Aunt and Uncle before Virosa found her again. He snatched her by the arm and pulled her down the stairs. The soaking wet thugs returned once the siren had been turned off.

"Because you can't be trusted," Virosa said, "and because my animals can't keep you contained, I will have to keep you locked up. It's a shame really. You and I have so much to discuss. Soon, however, you will reconsider your position and we will have all the time in the world."

Olivia stomped on his foot.

Virosa clenched his jaw and grabbed her by the hair. "I can see why Flinch likes you so much. Now, for the love of humanity, bring me the hide of that bear," he bellowed. "Don't forget the night-vision goggles. I bought those things five years ago and now is a good time for you to actually use them." Several thugs rushed off.

Olivia could hear the sound of a helicopter approaching.

"Ah, the first provost is arriving. I can't wait to present you to the council."

"Are they all incompetent or is it just you?"

"Something for you to think about," Virosa snarled. "Your little friend Doug and your brother Gnat are missing." He smiled a big arrogant smile. "I'll bet you didn't know that, did you? It was reported on the news. The Bear Girl's brother and boyfriend. Missing again. I would hate for something to happen to them."

The rage flowed up through Olivia. "No, they aren't!" she screamed and lunged toward his face. He was far too strong for her and he tightened his grip until tears came to her eyes.

"They say, once a child is missing for one day, the chances of finding him are only one in ten thousand." A steely sparkle flashed across Virosa's eyes. "Gnat and Doug have been missing for three."

Flinch opened a panel in the floor. A ladder led down into the darkness. "Get down there." Flinch pushed her down the hole and slammed the opening shut.

Virosa and Flinch walked off, laughing down the hall.

Olivia clung to the ladder and pounded her fist against the locked lid.

Olivia slumped down the ladder. A flash of lightning from the weakening storm flickered through the space at the bottom of the ladder. Her heart skipped a wild beat. Did the ladder descend into empty space, hanging from the floor above into nothingness? Another distant flash surrounded her with light. Olivia gently stepped down each rung of the ladder. She was waiting for that final step where her foot dangled into midair. Then, she realized that she couldn't feel any wind. She didn't hear any sounds. It wasn't a ladder into midair, it was a single room made completely from glass hanging from beneath the compound platform. There was only one escape and that was the lid in the ceiling. Olivia put her foot down on the transparent floor. It seemed solid enough. Another lightning flash illuminated the room again. She realized that she wasn't alone. A shadowy lump rose in the corner of the small room.

Two sets of very old hands reached out and grabbed Olivia close. It was Aunt and Uncle.

19

Sun Gazing

Doug sat on the stage with a tall plate of gritty pancakes in front of him. The thought of taking another bite made him slightly nauseous. He was exhausted. The Diadora had kept him up all night asking him questions and teaching him the rules of being a Diadora. For example, he wasn't to speak singly to any normal Junonian. He wasn't to touch surface animals, including Cheeto. Surface animals were filthy for some reason. He must always listen to Tagelus, whatever that meant. There were *a lot* of rules. Way more rules than Mrs. Vitaly had back at Silver Boils School. And a lot of the rules made absolutely no sense. *Never look a gompho in the eyes. Salty currents mean stay put. The Walleri live in darkness.*

Doug nodded at everything they said, even the parts he didn't understand. He had to learn as much as possible.

The Diadora even taught him some Junonian history. They measured large spans of time by dunes, each dune representing a rise in sea levels. It didn't sound very precise to Doug, but he decided it worked for them.

Many dunes ago, the Walleri, Junonians, and the Dark Eyes lived in peace with each other. The Junonians even spent the winter months living on the surface. When the last ocean receded, the population of Dark Eyes exploded. They started eating all of the Walleri's food. The Dark Eyes and Walleri were at a stalemate, each being equally powerful. Because Dark Eye flesh was poisonous to them, the Walleri started hunting Junonians. Since then, there has been nothing but warfare. Junonians are so physically weak that they must survive by cunning.

The Diadora were particularly interested in Walleri culture. "When a young Walleri reaches your age, they seclude into the wilderness for one year. They must travel north to where the snow does not melt and steal a flint blade from a giant Kappik. The Kappik only eat the hearts of their kill: reindeer, polar bears, Dark Eyes. They consider their knife as their soul and they will not give it up willingly. If the young Walleri returns home, he returns fearlessly. A killer of killers. Nothing will stop a Walleri from its prey."

The whole story sent chills down Doug's neck. There was so much brutal eating. He made a mental note of the Kappik. The thought of ferocious monsters ravaging the Arctic landscape was horrifying, but he had to know. Was it real? When Walleri reached his own age, they stood face to face with Kappik and came home to tell about it. What has he ever done to compare with that?

In the meantime, Doug was starting to understand the layout of Junonia. The Diadora almost exclusively used a network of hidden passages and secret doorways to travel throughout the city. Every intersection and door was marked with tiny carved symbols. The only two he could figure out were a sun symbol that pointed the way to the surface and three wavy lines that pointed the way down toward the aquifer. Unfortunately, he only rarely saw a sun or wavy line symbols. It was very disorienting to navigate in the darkness, especially in a vertical city.

Doug scanned the Hall of Nations. Hundreds of Junonians expertly used their sticks to shovel mouthfuls of pancakes doused with fruity mash. In the midst of the feast, Gnat was jumping on top of the table and waving his arms over his head. A half-eaten pancake flopped in one of his hands.

"Doug! Doug! Over here!" Gnat yelled. "Look over here."

Doug gave no indication that he saw Gnat. He calmly looked over the dining hall. Gnat was inexhaustible with his efforts to get Doug's attention. For what seemed like the entire meal, he was jumping up and down. The Diadora sitting next to Doug seemed to be studying his reaction. Finally Gnat slammed his utensil onto the floor and stormed out. Cheeto jumped up on the vacated seat, gobbled the last of his pancakes, and followed him.

With one simultaneous motion, all of the Diadora stood up to leave. Doug scrambled to his feet. He imitated their turn toward the right and filed out in line through the tall, thin door. They rushed up a narrow staircase that wound darkly around the city. Little lights seemed to grow directly and organically from the rock. The Diadora emerged in a place Doug hadn't seen yet, the Chapel of Light. A large lens hung from the ceiling. A shaft of sunlight beamed from the ceiling and focused through the lens, illuminating the terraced pools of light that formed along the sides of the chapel. On a small altar, the Pearl sat wide open, quietly humming.

"This is the Pearl of Tagelus," the Diadora announced. "It protects every entrance of Junonia from invasion. It protects the wisdom in our hearts from invasion. It was discovered thousands of years ago, in a quiet, silty pool deep in the lower aquifer. The Pearl was immediately recognized as a source of great power. Tagelus flows through the Pearl, like sunlight through a lens. The Diadora itself was formed to study and use it to protect the Junonian nation."

"How exactly does it work?" Doug asked.

"It forms a bubble that is impenetrable. Stronger than rock."

"Then how did we get back into Junonia after the harvest? How do you come and go?" Doug peered inside the Pearl. His eyes widened at the wondrous mechanisms.

"It is very complicated. We will begin that lesson later. Now it is time to foretell."

Each of the Diadora stood over the terraced pools. The water inside each shallow pool was perfectly still and burned with the unbearably bright light of the sun. They lowered their heads as if in prayer, stared into the light, and one by one, entered into a trance. They stood perfectly still except occasionally to touch a clear finger into the water, sending out circular ripples of light. The walls and ceiling pulsed with reflections.

Doug walked over to an unoccupied pool. He looked down. "Yow!" he yelled out. Instantly, he felt guilty for breaking the silence. "Yow," he whispered and rubbed his eyes. It was painful to look into the blaring water. Half of his vision blacked out with spots. Tears washed from his eyes. He looked around. None of the Diadora seemed to have noticed his outburst.

Hours passed. Doug paced back and forth. He read all of the symbols that were carved into the walls. If only he could understand what they meant. He saw stars in patterns and swirls. He saw a figure riding a gigantic armless squid. He saw teeth embedded in the walls. Lots of teeth. He counted the pearls that were stuck in the door frame. One hundred forty-four. He stole glances inside the Pearl of Tagelus. He needed to figure out how it worked. The secret to their return to modern time was right there. He fought the urge to just grab it and run. He needed the Diadora to teach him more about how it worked.

He wandered back to the pool of light and closed his eyes. Slowly, slowly he opened his eyelids, just the thinnest crack. A blast of white flooded into his brain. It was so bright he could *hear* it inside his head like a vibration. But he didn't look away, he clenched his hands. "I am Diadora. I am Diadora," he whispered to himself. The white shifted to yellow, then orange, and finally to red. The color of blood. And then the visions came. First it was just fleeting. Watery flashes of blue. Then the blue flashes started taking shape. Like a sack opened in a field and hundreds of blue birds took to the sky. They flew into the clouds then turned white. Doug heard a familiar twinkle of bells. They were the white birds that lived in Junonia! They flew higher until he could only see the countless specks of light against the tiny bells tied to their feet. With a sudden turn, they dove like lightning directly into his eyes.

And then Doug could see everything the birds could see, all at the same time. In a series of flashes, he could see the surface world as they flew. The mammoths pulled small trees from the sand and jammed them into their grinding jaws. The scimitar cat tended to her brood of kittens. A large group of people cooked something over a bonfire. They wore ragged skins and furs, unlike the armor-clad Walleri or monastic Junonians. Among them, a boy was smashing one rock into another. Larry! Larry was with the Dark Eyes. He seemed so small and weak. Helpless, really, as he smashed his rock over and over onto the bigger rock. Similar bonfires dotted the land all the way to the horizon.

In the distance toward the sea, a dark fog obscured the land like ink.

No matter how many birds flew over the spot, he couldn't see into the murkiness. *The Walleri live in darkness.* At least that rule made sense now. But Doug could see all of Junonia. In a singular blur of hundreds of bird-eyes, he saw all of the tunnels and caves, the elaborate city architecture, the cool pool of water at the bottom. The stunning blue water turned into a giant eye. The giant eye stared up at him from far below. Doug stood on the edge of the Chapel of Light and dove like an arrow. Down, down, the city flashed by. Just as he hit the water he never felt more sure, more confident that this was the place he belonged. He *was* Diadora.

Countless hands held him, pulled him closer. Doug shook awake. He was surrounded by the Diadora. They seemed very happy.

"As we said, Tagelus is strong within you. What did you see?"

"I saw . . . everything. The white birds showed me."

"No one so young has ever flown with the bells. We were right to bring you here."

"We are Diadora," Doug said.

"We are Diadora," they answered. "And certainly you witnessed the growing numbers of Dark Eyes. They overtake the land like a flood. The equilibrium is disrupted. Now we all understand what you and the Dark Eye child saw yesterday on the surface. We know you disapproved. But now you understand."

"I . . . I don't know what you mean."

"The Dark Eyes eat our food too. As their numbers grow, our food dwindles. We must join with the Walleri. We need their strength, their viciousness, or we will not survive."

"But what about Anachis?"

"The other Junonians must never know of this treaty. They are the food of the Walleri and they will not understand. These are grim times. The small sacrifices lead to survival."

Doug nodded his head.

"Come, we rest. Then you can teach us about the future."

"And you can teach me about how the Pearl works?"

"Of course. We can teach you what we know. There is still much for us to learn."

Junonia was filled with an eerie silence. The tiny white birds were gone. All of the Junonians were out harvesting jumjams or up on the tombolo sifting the sand for whatever it was they were searching. Doug wandered alone down to Anachis's apartment. Cheeto woke up from a nap and leaped into his arms. His whole body wriggled with excitement as he licked Doug's face. Doug had already broken one of the Diadora's rules by touching a land animal. Gnat's backpack was lying on the floor against the back wall next to his own pack, but there was no sign of Gnat. He rifled through the pockets to find a pencil and small scrap of paper.

Gnat: Stay in Junonia. Do not go to the surface. Will explain later.

Doug walked down the city stairs toward the pool of water at the bottom. It was so quiet and peaceful. He was too exhausted to sleep. He wandered in a half-dream.

Doug wondered where the Gnat was right now. The little guy really wasn't equipped for getting along in the world without supervision. Sure, he was annoying and stubborn. But he was just a kid. What if he was up on the surface harvesting and a scimitar chased him? Gnat would be caught instantly. He could barely walk normally, much less run. What if the Walleri trapped a group of Junonians again and Gnat was among them? Doug would never forgive himself if something bad happened.

And what about Larry? Stupid, mean Larry up on the surface smashing rocks? Lost in time, never to play football again or throw Doug's homework out the bus window. How in the world did he convince the Dark Eyes to let him join them? Did he even know that Doug was his only hope of returning home? Doug couldn't decide if he cared or not. He knew that he should care, that he was *supposed* to care.

The situation with the Diadora had spun out of control. Everything was so . . . complicated. The Diadora really seemed to listen to him, really respected his theories and opinions. In many ways, they *needed* him too. They needed his infusion of new knowledge in order to survive. They didn't judge him or mock him behind his back. And because the Diadora needed him, the Junonians needed him. The whole city needed him.

He couldn't just sit around though, eating pancakes and staring into bright pools of water while Anachis and the others were about to be butchered and eaten. He couldn't just wait for whatever was going to happen. That is why he had been pretending to be a Diadora. As soon as the real Diadora had tried to convince him of that fact, he knew it was an opportunity. It was the only way to discover the secrets of the Pearl. All he had to do was play along a little longer and the Diadora would teach him how to use it. Then he could save Anachis and return to his own time.

The stairs kept descending into the water at the bottom of the city, falling into deeper and more translucent blues. Doug laid his hand on the water. Then he had an idea. He untied his shoes and flung his dirty socks to the side. He climbed up onto the first terrace that hugged the side of the pool, stood on the railing, and executed a perfectly elegant belly flop. "Weeeehoo!" Doug yelled, coming up for air. His voice echoed throughout the city. The shockingly cold water sloshed in the pool like a giant bathtub.

All of his worries and problems washed away. He swam a lazy lap.

"All right. It is time to see where these stairs go," Doug sputtered to no one. Taking a deep breath, he bent at the waist and jackknifed down through the water. He never liked opening his eyes under water without a mask. Usually he just squeezed his eyes as tightly as they would shut and flailed around when he swam. But this time, he had no choice. At the bottom of his dive, when his ears started throb, he opened his eyes. A gigantic eyeball stared back at him, only inches away. The diameter of the eye was longer than Doug was tall.

With a frenzied blast of bubbles and kicking, Doug pushed toward the surface. He coughed out a gallon of water. "Help! Help!" he yelled out. No one was around to hear him. The stairway seemed to be a mile away. Something huge rose up under his flailing legs and lifted him out of the water. A loud rumbling groan reverberated from the gigantic body in the water.

Doug's mind raced. "Whale? Squid?" Then his panic cleared. "The Anaspidean!"

The body rising underneath him was so large it filled almost the entire pool. Doug half-swam, half-stumbled into the alcove in the wall. The very same alcove that he, Gnat, Larry, and Cheeto hid under while the icicles had crashed around them just a few days ago. The Anaspidean's eye came to rest right next to Doug. He could see a reflection of himself in its enormous cornea. They stared at each other for a few moments, before the gigantic creature flashed a series of colors across its body and let out another loud groan.

"You . . . you are like a cuttlefish."

The Anaspidean let out an exasperated noise.

"You don't like that?" Doug carefully touched his vast skin. "You don't like being called a cuttlefish?"

Something rumbled deep inside, like a purr.

"I have to go," Doug said, vigorously rubbing the Anaspidean. "I need to go to the Walleri camp. I'll come swim with you again when I get back. *If* I come back." Doug tried to leave the alcove, but he couldn't squeeze past.

"Uh . . . excuse me." He wedged his arms and pushed as hard as he could. The Anaspidean slid deeper into the water.

Suddenly, a large glass fusiform carriage surfaced from deep below and pressed against the alcove. A strange bronze metal reinforced the glass joints. A portal in its side opened. The door was the exact same shape as the alcove and it pressed tightly against the wall.

"What? You want me to get in there? Fat chance."

The Anaspidean let out a series of high-pitched chirps and sloshed the carriage toward Doug again.

"I can't. I have to find the Walleri camp."

The Anaspidean showed no sign of budging.

"All right. Just for a minute." Doug climbed into the glass carriage. The fabrication of the carriage was exquisite. Even the floor was glass. It wasn't apparent how the metal was attached to all of that glass or how the carriage even stayed together. But the curving shapes of the panes somehow fit together perfectly. The pool of water took on a whole new dimension. Like Gnat's snorkel mask, he could see all of the detail below the surface. The clear water was filled with tiny pulsating creatures that he couldn't see when he was swimming. Clear jelly creatures floated, covered in endless rows of vibrating rainbows. And the pool was deep. Far deeper than he had imagined. The architecture of the city continued on into the depths.

The shape of carriage warped around him and the portal closed over his head. "Hey!" Doug pounded his fists against the glass.

With one smooth movement, the Anaspidean dove downward. Attached by a short chain, the carriage resisted for a brief second on the surface before being pulled under water. Doug was chained to an ancient and gigantic animal. Down they plunged, deeper and deeper into the aquifer. The Anaspidean finally evened out and turned into a cave opening. Its lateral wings flared like waves, propelling them faster and faster. Its skin glowed pale green, illuminating the limestone walls as they sped by only inches away. Pale, blind creatures clawed and prodded the rock. Multi-colored clouds of clione slugs flew by, their tiny wings beating furiously in the currents. Every shade of blue water flashed and swirled. Vast caverns opened up in the darkness then quickly pinched into narrow passages. The carriage stumbled along in the Anaspidean's wake, crashing into the tunnel walls and shaking Doug inside. Desperately he hung on to the handle on the bench.

"Hey! Slow down. Where are you taking me?" Doug's voice never made it out of the carriage.

Then, an explosion of sun crashed through the water. Millions of tiny silver fish flashed in the light. A large undulating rope, part-snake, part-shark, flashed its teeth before deciding the Anaspidean was too large to mess with and zipped away into the deep. A tiger ray the size of a flying saucer flew by. They were in the ocean. Doug had read about secret freshwater springs that opened offshore called blue holes, where fish of every sort congregate. With a buoyant thrust, the carriage surfaced. Waves tossed Doug violently. The portal opened up. Water crashed into the carriage.

Doug stuck his head out. "I'm not getting out here! Take me back!" He tried to close the portal door. Another wave flooded the carriage. Doug churned in a somersault. When he surfaced again, he realized he had tumbled out of the carriage. He was floating in the ocean. He spun around. There was no sign of the carriage or the Anaspidean.

Sharks. Sharks. Sharks.

The word repeated itself over and over in Doug's head. Not just run-of-the-mill sharks either, but prehistoric sharks the size of semi-trucks with teeth like butcher knives. Insatiable and angry. As he rose up with each passing wave, he saw the shore. It wasn't a sandy beach like the shore back home. The waves crashed onto a rocky shelf with thunderous white foam. Landing there seemed a foolish thing to do, but the thought of crazy sharks compelled him to start swimming. He tried to swim without splashing, without flailing about like a wounded fish. Images of a shark rising beneath him filled his thoughts. He fought against the fear. The swim seemed to take forever, but eventually he approached the rocky shelf. He scanned the crashing waves to find the least imposing place to land. With one last push, a wave deposited him onto the rocks with a thud, tumbling him over and scraping his knees. He leapt to his feet and scooted away from the next wave. Thin rivers of blood ran down his shins.

Doug suddenly remembered that his shoes were sitting on the steps back in Junonia. He was barefoot and lost. The rocky shelf was filled with thousands of small interlacing holes, like jumbled honeycomb. Holes within holes. It was also sharp. He stepped gingerly toward the grasses above the tide line. Small crabs scattered into the rocky holes ahead of every step he took. He looked back over the ocean. He saw a few algae balloons in the distance. No Anaspidean. No sharks. Toward land he saw no roads or beach shops. Just miles and miles of rocky shore. Just the same angry Florida sun and no shade. He wasn't sure what to do. When lost, he knew the rule about staying in one place. But that rule didn't say anything about being lost in *time*. Besides, no one but the Anaspidean knew he was gone and it was the reason he was lost in the first place. So he had to move. If he kept his back to the ocean, he might luck out and find Junonia again. He stepped onto the grass. He was surprised and disappointed to find the ground was still predominantly sharp, holey limestone with only an occasional patch of dry grass. Spindly pine tree sprouted from the holes that had accumulated enough soil to support trees. The going was slow and painful as Doug had to cautiously pick where he put his feet. Even so, the sound of the ocean soon disappeared and only the blazing sun served as a landmark.

20

Oolitic

A thin finger of smoke wound its way through the scrubby pines. Doug thought it smelled familiar, but he couldn't quite decide what it was. He followed it as he would a river. He figured it may have been the smartest thing to do or the dumbest, but at least it was a plan. At least it was better than just wandering hopelessly on the sharp limestone and waiting for night and its voracious teeth.

Mosquitoes clung to the dried blood on Doug's shins. Every step on the razor-sharp limestone sent fire up his legs. He had to be very careful to position his feet so they didn't drop down into a hole. His ankles hurt. His neck felt like the worst sunburn he'd ever had. His lips were dry and swollen. And he was always pulling ticks from his skin. Red land crabs the size of volleyballs would sometimes rise from deep in the honeycombed rock and watch him. He walked so awkwardly, they felt no fear by his passing. Still, they would each raise one large claw toward him, salutes of intimidation.

The limestone was slowly giving way to sand and soil. Small, scrubby trees grew in the harsh ground. The smoke thickened and grew sticky. Finally Doug heard voices. Strange voices that rose and fell in an almost musical way. A hushed language he couldn't quite make out. He peeked around a palmetto. Ten or so Walleri were talking excitedly with several people. Dark Eyes. They all looked big and dangerous.

The Walleri camp, Doug realized, and he ducked back behind the palmetto. He took a deep breath and peeked out.

The Dark Eyes pointed dramatically to a familiar figure. Larry stood near the group and leaned against a tall pole with an owl carved into the top. He looked bored. Doug pulled a few berries from the palmetto. He carefully launched one and watched it sail high over Larry's head. He threw another. It bounced off the armor of one of the Walleri warriors with a clang. They all stopped talking and looked around for a moment before continuing their conversation. Doug knew he couldn't miss again or they would know something was wrong. He threw a third berry so it tumbled along the ground. It rolled up to Larry's foot. Larry looked toward the palmetto. Doug stuck his face out so Larry could see him. He put a finger to his lips and gestured for Larry to come. Doug walked farther back into the woods. Larry soon followed him.

"Corcoran! You ever hear of shoes?" Larry laughed.

"Shhhhhh. Keep it down Larry."

"You look like raw hamburger."

"Huh?"

"Like hamburger. All bloody and bruised. You look like raw hamburger. Coach used to say that after practice."

"O . . . kay."

"I could really go for a hamburger right about now. No wait! A *cheese*burger."

Doug cleared his throat.

"With a toasted bun and triple mayo," Larry continued.

"Triple mayo?"

"Yeah. And a giant basket of curly fries."

"Triple mayo," Doug mumbled and shook his head. "I need your help."

"How'd you get here anyway? No one with half a brain would walk on those rocks."

"I . . . I walked from the beach."

"Walked from the beach? If you don't want to tell me how you actually got here, just say so."

"I'm serious. I walked from the beach."

"That's no man's land out there. No one will walk on that."

"I didn't have any choice."

"Well, you sure are a long way from home."

"You aren't kidding. And so are you."

"Why are you lurking around here?"

"I'm here to help Anachis and the others escape."

"The Junonians? You are a little late, as usual. There are only four left."

"I will help those four then."

"You better watch out. These Walleri fellows are rough."

"What is going on here anyway? I thought the Walleri and Dark Eyes were enemies."

"Ha! They are joining forces to invade Junonia. They love me because I'm the only one who has been down there. I'm a living map. They say it's my destiny."

"Invade Junonia? That's impossible. The Walleri and the Junonians have a truce because the Dark Eyes are taking over the world. I saw it myself."

"You sure are slow in the head," Larry said and punched Doug in the shoulder. "Everyone up here is getting ready. Thousands of people are making weapons. I saw a whole herd of elephants with armor on."

"Mammoths."

"Huh?"

"They weren't elephants. They were mammoths. Columbian mammoths to be exact."

"You saying I don't know what an elephant looks like? Big, hairy ones too. They are getting ready to invade any day now."

"Well, we've got to stop it," Doug said.

"No way, Corcoran. You think you are so smart."

"But the Junonians haven't hurt anybody. They should just be left alone."

"Haven't hurt anybody? You just said you saw them joining the Walleri to destroy the Dark Eyes."

"But not for war. Not to kill anybody."

"Sure. I'll bet they are sooooo innocent," Larry mocked. "And quit calling my friends 'Dark Eyes.' They are *people*. People just like you and me. You gotta look out for your own. What do we care if those underground wimps lose their cave?"

"Can you at least tell me how to get back? I have to get Gnat out of there before the war starts."

"Suit yourself. Just past the camp, you should be able to circle around the swamp. You'll see a ridge just beyond a field. Just look out for the herd of gomphos. They like the grass there or something, and they are pretty ornery. Follow the ridge for about an hour and you should see Junonia, I think."

"Thanks, Larry."

"Listen, Corcoran. You don't have to be so book-smart all of the time. Sometimes, you have to be street-smart. Get out of Junonia before it starts. This isn't you and me just messing around. You and Gnat can come live with us." The look of concern in Larry's eyes surprised Doug.

"It never felt like just messing around to me," Doug said, shifting uncomfortably. "Thanks for your help. I can't let anything happen to Gnat."

"Well, if you care about him, come stay with us. You both will be safe," Larry answered. "Look, I have to go. Get outta here before it gets dark."

"See ya."

"See ya. And you might want to buy yourself some sneakers. It really isn't too bright walking around out here in bare feet." Larry grinned and gave a salute before hurrying back to the Walleri camp.

Doug skirted the edge of the camp, making sure not to step on any twigs. All along the perimeter of the camp there were more poles with owls carved into the top. The Walleri huts were circular and set halfway down into the bedrock. They were made out of a very hard, smooth material, like ceramic. The matte black surface of each hut was elaborately decorated with spiraling scrolls and constellations of dots that were glazed exquisitely into the ceramic. The color of the spirals shifted as he walked by. Red to yellow, green to blue. Iridescence. Doug couldn't help but touch the beautiful huts. It was cool on his skin. He pressed his sweating cheeks and forehead for some relief from the sweltering afternoon.

"Insulated somehow," he mused quietly.

Small groups of Walleri ambled by. Not all of them wore the intricate armor that Doug was familiar with. But it was clear that they valued craftsmanship and beauty in everything they did. Even their weapons. The flensing spears were one accessory that every Walleri carried.

In the center of the camp, he saw a silver cage swinging from a large frame. Inside were four Junonians. Anachis was still alive.

Right in plain sight, Doug thought. He sighed and returned to the outskirts of the camp. "I won't make it three steps before they catch me. Think Doug, think."

His only real hope was the truce between the Dark Eyes and the Walleri. He could sneak in as a friend. But he would have to look more like a Dark Eye and less like a kid from the twenty-first century. Doug pulled his shirt over his head and tucked one end into his shorts. Then he smeared mud and dirt into his hair and all over his body. He already looked pretty messed up from the blood and bruises. And then it hit him.

"Gomphos! Never look a gompho in the eyes. I know what they are now. Gomphotheres."

Doug rushed off toward the field that Larry had told him about. He wasn't sure what looking them in the eyes would do, but he had a hunch. Before long, he was standing on the edge of the field staring at a herd of over thirty gomphotheres. They looked like short, ugly elephants with a giant toothy shovel for a lower jaw, an impossibly enormous mouth, and four sharp tusks instead of two. They seemed jumpy and nervous.

This is stupid, Doug thought. They may have been short elephants, but they were still the size of buses and their mouths were frightening. It didn't take long for Doug to realize how smelly they were on top of it. He held his breath whenever the warm breeze blew toward him from across the herd. The gomphos wandered through the field eating the fresh grass.

Doug waited patiently. Finally a large one approached his hiding place.

This is *really* stupid, Doug told himself and took a deep breath. What happened next only took a second, but it felt like a lifetime. With one big dramatic move, he leaped out in front of the gompho.

"Hoopity blah!" he screamed at the top of his lungs.

The gompho jumped straight up and crashed to the ground with a thundering jolt. And then Doug did *it*. He looked directly into its eyes. Pupils dilated. Hair raised. The gompho reared up on its hind legs and let out an ear-piercing bellow. Its four sharp tusks towered overhead and it snapped its shovel mouth. All of the other gomphos stood up on their hind legs and looked at Doug with a mix of fear and elemental anger. Doug had not anticipated this. He had hoped that looking at a gompho in the eyes would simply make a racket that would distract the Walleri. Instead it unleashed a chaos of a size he never imagined.

In a blur, Doug turned and started running back toward the Walleri camp. A huge thundering dust cloud rose toward the sky behind him. Inside the cloud thirty gomphos who were out of their minds stampeded in the hopes of stomping him to death. Doug was never a fast runner. He was one of the slowest runners in class. But now, barefoot, bloodied, shirtless, covered in mud and exhausted, he ran like the wind. Still, the gomphos were gaining ground on him, advancing like an exploding avalanche. The ground shook beneath his feet. The pressure wave in front of them seemed to push Doug even faster. Within seconds, he reached the outskirts of the Walleri camp. Doug no longer felt any fear of the Walleri and their gruesome flensing spears. He bolted right past a group of five Walleri guards. The guards let out a wailing, high-pitched scream that pierced the entire camp.

"Doug!" Anachis called out as he ran past the cage holding the Junonians.

Doug was too focused to answer. The gomphos pummeled through the camp, crushing ceramic huts to dust like a tornado and earthquake combined. The wailing Walleris scattered. Doug passed by a hut then made and unexpected turn behind it. He ran perpendicular to his previous path until he left the outskirts of the camp and was back on the sharp, holey limestone. Instantly, the pain shot up his legs. He was forced to slow down to a walk. The gomphos turned to follow him like tumbling boulders in a landslide. A few of them lost their footing and crashed to the ground. Doug was a sitting duck. But only ten yards away, they all skidded to a complete stop. The crowd of gomphos stood motionless for a minute as the dust settled.

"The limestone," Doug huffed with a smile on his face. "You won't step on the limestone!"

A wall of gompho faces stared dumbly at him. Doug made sure not to look them in their eyes again. Their demeanor slowly mellowed. Before long, they were spread out over the entire Walleri camp, rolling in the dust and looking for something to eat.

Doug stepped back off the sharp limestone and started walking toward Anachis. The damage to the Walleri camp was almost total. A few walls still stood, but most of the buildings were reduced to rubble. There were no Walleri in sight.

"Easy . . . easy," he whispered as he passed the first gompho. This time, he made sure not to look in its eyes. The gompho ignored him completely, as if it hadn't stampeded and tried to crush him only a few moments before. The smell was overwhelming.

By some miracle, the cage holding Anachis lay tumbled on the ground but no one was hurt. Doug rushed up. A wave of exhilaration flowed across his body. Maybe for the first time in his life, he had decided to do something on his own, something dangerous and noble. He had stood up to the Diadora and Larry in order to do the right thing. He had looked a herd of gomphos in the eye and survived.

"Anachis, it's me Doug," he said as he fumbled with the latch.

Anachis reached his hand through the bars and grasped Doug's hand. All four Junonians said, "We know who you are. We know who you are."

"I'm so glad you're still alive."

"Never look a gompho in the eyes," they said, smiling.

"I guess not."

"Gomphos won't walk on oolitic."

Within moments, they all scurried out of the camp, past the swamp, and were well on their way to Junonia.

21

Marimo

A giant armadillo, the size of a minivan, was digging furiously. A blizzard of sand blew into the air behind its thick, clublike tail. It was so intent on its work that it had no idea that four Junonians and one small boy from the future were walking past it.

"Sugar tubers," Anachis announced to Doug. "That's all they eat. Sugar tubers and worms."

"Sounds good right about now," Doug answered as he put his dirty shirt back on.

"We would not advise coming between a glyptodont and a sugar tuber patch."

"I'll even be fine with pancakes when we get back."

A breeze rushed through the grass. The afternoon storms were kicking up. One of the giant clear balloons lofted through the sky, caught by the storm winds.

"There!" Doug blurted out and pointed. "What is that? I've never read about anything like it."

"That is a marimo seed. They grow on the deep water ledge offshore."

"A marimo?"

"It is an underwater alga. Big, round, green, and furry. Very few of us have ever seen a fully grown marimo. The only way to see them is to ride in an Anaspidean carriage and they only listen to Diadora."

"But why are they flying?"

"When they are mature, the marimo sends up a long stalk to the surface. They bloom in long clusters of upside-down flowers that are pollinated by pelagic dragons. The seed-head produces hundreds of these seeds. The winds pick them up and drop them everywhere. The ones that land in fresh water will germinate and eventually follow the currents back to the sea."

"Like a reverse salmon."

"We do not understand. What is salmon?"

"It's a fish that lives in the ocean but swims up rivers to lay its eggs."

"We see."

"And bears like to eat salmon."

"Why did you come out here Doug? Why did you come save us?"

"Let's just say we are even now." Doug smiled.

"No one has ever escaped a Walleri dinner cage before."

"The Diadora tell me that no one ever tried."

"That is true. We better keep moving or we will all be right back in there."

"I'm sure the Diadora are aware of your escape now. They aren't going to be too happy about it."

"Why would you say that?"

Doug walked quietly for a few minutes. "There is something I have to tell you, something you should know. I saw what happened when you were trapped. The dire wolves herded you toward Junonia where the Walleri were waiting. You didn't have a chance."

"That is true. If you saw, you were lucky to have escaped."

Doug stopped walking and turned toward them. "It wasn't a mistake that you were captured. The Diadora made a truce with the Walleri. You were the price for protection against the Dark Eyes."

"Impossible," the Junonians argued. "The Diadora would never hurt anyone. They are in touch with Tagelus. They foretell."

"They *sold* you for food. To be *eaten.*"

"Why? Why would they do that?"

"They believe it was for the greater good," Doug continued. "I know this . . . because I am Diadora."

"You are Diadora?" This news made the Junonians appear nervous.

"Well, that is what they say. I don't want to be, but they keep saying it. They tell me that Tagelus flows through me. I pretended to agree until I could escape and rescue you. They wouldn't let me go if I had asked."

"This . . . this cannot be."

"I saw it all through the eyes of the white birds. The only thing I couldn't really see was the Walleri camp. It was covered in darkness."

"You flew with the bells? Then you truly are Diadora. There is no pretending."

"Whatever. The point I was trying to make was that the danger isn't over. I don't know how the Diadora are going to react to your return."

The Junonians grew more agitated. "Perhaps, we should return to the Walleri."

"What!? Are you crazy?"

"It is what the Diadora wish."

"No! The Dark Eyes and Walleri are preparing for war with Junonia right now. We have to get back and warn them before it is too late."

"We will no longer be welcome. We broke the will of the Diadora."

"But I *am* the Diadora. You said so yourself. You haven't done anything wrong."

Anachis and the Junonians collapsed on the ground in exhaustion and huddled together. "We give up. We give up."

"You can't. I came all this way. You can't just die." Doug sat down next to them.

"This is all very confusing, Doug. We mean, your eminence. We aren't even supposed to talk with you."

"I broke a lot of rules today too."

"We've never experienced this discord in Junonia before. We always speak with a single voice."

"I've noticed that," Doug said, rolling his eyes. "Why don't you ever speak for yourselves?"

"Peace is maintained."

Doug lay back in the grass and stared up at the mosaic of clouds and marimo seeds passing overhead. He was still having a hard time accepting how different everything was. The land was different. The animals were different. Even the air felt different. It was like he was an astronaut living on a distant planet. The only thing in the whole world that remained the same was the sky. The wide, beautiful sky. This reminded Doug that he wanted to memorize the different cloud formations and the conditions under which they form. Cumulous. Stratus. Cirrus. And then their altitudes. And then a whole bunch of other cloud types. The weird ones. He couldn't remember them all without a little more work. It would be good to understand weather patterns. It was something that his dad wouldn't be too happy about if he were alive. Clouds were for dreamers. His dad had wanted him to be thinking about a career plan.

"That's it. I'm done," Doug blurted out.

"We do not understand," the Junonians answered.

"I'm done. I'm done with all of it. I used to sit in class, sit on the bus, and let other kids push me around. Larry Mutch and his friends picked on me every day. They stole my books and threw them out the bus windows. They tripped me down the entire hallway. They laughed at my answers in class even though I was right. They hit me on the back of the head every time I earned an A. They made fun of my little ears, my haircut, and my shoes because they weren't expensive enough. And when my mom finally bought me expensive shoes, they made fun of them for being too shiny and white."

"When I told my teacher, she told me to stay away from them. But she didn't hear me say we were on the same bus. When I told my bus driver, he told me to sit down and shut up. My mom complained to the school and their parents but it only made things worse. My dad just said, 'The truth is not always easy.' What was that supposed to mean?

"I thought the best thing to do was to listen to the bus driver. Just sit down and shut up. It made my teachers happy. It made the bus driver happy. Larry and his friends were happy because no one was stopping them. And it even made my mother happy because she didn't want me to be in pain. Only my dad wasn't happy. He just kept saying, 'The truth isn't always easy.'

"And then my dad got sick. He got cancer and no doctor knew what to do. In less than a year, he was gone. I stopped caring about school. I stopped caring about Larry. I just accepted that every day, I would be teased and hit. I didn't want there to be any more pain in the world than there already was, so I didn't complain. My dad's voice was just another painful reminder so I let his words disappear.

"Here in Junonia, with Gnat and Cheeto counting on me, and you, my friends needing my help, I started to hear Dad's voice again. And now I'm finally understanding what he was trying to tell me all of this time."

"What? What was he trying to tell you?"

"The right thing to do isn't always what everyone wants you to do. Sometimes, all of the voices you normally trust are wrong. Sometimes, you have to listen to your own voice."

"What does your voice say?"

"I'm a nerd. If Larry and Richard and Cuke and Mr. Ott don't like it, even if my dad didn't like it, they can blow it out their enormous ears. I *like* documenting tortoise burrows. I *like* memorizing scientific names and reading books. They are only mad because I'm better at some things than they are. And if the Diadora thinks I'm just going to let my friends die, they have another think coming."

"You . . . you are right."

Doug was shocked. For the first time, Anachis had spoken alone without the other Junonians joining in. He had spoken as an individual.

"You are my friend and I will do everything I can to help you return to your time. I promise you will not die here like I said before," Anachis said.

As if a spell were broken, the other Junonians started speaking for themselves too.

"I do not want to be eaten by the Walleri."

"How could the Diadora betray me and my family?"

"I miss Junonia."

"I hate pancakes."

"You guys are saying 'I' now instead of 'we' all of the time," Doug said.

"Yes, and I like it," Anachis said. "My voice sounds smaller, but it feels bigger."

"Your young Dark Eye, Gnat, gave Anachis his name," one of the Junonians said. "What is my name?"

"Name me too," another Junonian said.

"I'm no good at it. You should think of your own names."

"I am Talus."

"I am Sonorella."

"You don't have to decide right now." Doug laughed.

"I am Scimitar Hunter," the last Junonian said.

"Hey, I like that one. Flip me a pancake," Doug said, holding out his hand.

"I . . . I don't have a pancake."

"No, I mean slap my hand. Gimme five, you know, like this." Doug grabbed Scimitar Hunter's hand and swung it onto his own. "You try. Make it smack."

"Flip me a pancake," he repeated and slapped Doug's hand.

"Nice."

For the next few minutes, the Junonians slapped hands and laughed.

A loud wailing growl sung out. Everyone spun around. Only fifty yards away, a gigantic dire wolf stared intently at them with burnt orange eyes. Its body was thick and muscular, solid. Its wiry white coat bristled as it pawed the ground. The wolf lifted its head toward the sky and released a howl. In the distance, several wolves answered. A savage wind tore across the countryside, charged with lightning, magic, and revenge.

Dark storm clouds pulsed with electricity.

"The dires are hunting," Anachis whispered, slowly standing up.

"Come on," Doug blurted, "let's go."

"It is already too late. We were foolish for letting our guard down."

"There are no Walleri," Talus said. "There will be no capture this time."

"They sent the dires to finish us off."

"We are too far from safety. We will never make it," Sonorella said.

Doug could hear more large wolves sprinting across the land. Their heavy bodies sent tremors into the ground with every footfall. They were spiraling in, closer and closer.

"We have to go, now!" Scimitar Hunter turned and ran.

"Wait!" Anachis called out. "We must run as one."

But it was too late. A dire wolf lunged for his leg and flung Scimitar Hunter to the ground. Another dire launched into the air and came crashing down on him with an audible snap. The sound of their jaws tearing flesh made Doug sick to his stomach. His skin went cold with the thought of that happening to him.

"Come," Anachis whispered. "We must go now."

"I . . . I can't run as fast as you," Doug said. "I don't even have shoes."

"We must stay together. You run and we will stay with you."

Doug took off. The Junonians fell into stride with him. All three of them were close enough that he could reach out and touch them all. Their legs moved in unison with his own.

"Go as fast as you can, Doug," Anachis encouraged.

"They pursue," Talus announced.

Doug could hear the wolves fan out behind them. He could hear their snarling breath. Their sense of hungry urgency.

"Turn now," Anachis shouted.

Doug took a hard left. The others stepped left with him. A pouncing wolf crashed to the ground behind them.

"Now!"

Doug veered to the right. Another wolf slammed into a pile right where they had been running. The wolf immediately jumped to its feet and resumed the chase.

"I . . . I can't . . . keep this up," Doug called out.

"Duck!" A dire wolf soared directly over their lowered heads. Its hind paw scraped against Doug's ear. The wolves were having no trouble keeping up with them. He had to do something.

"Marimo," Doug called out.

"What?" Anachis asked.

"We . . . need . . . a marimo."

"I don't understand."

Doug didn't have enough energy to explain. He jolted to the right. A wolf stumbled into a palmetto behind them. He kept one eye on the sky and zigzagged over the sand. It seemed like the zigzagging worked because the wolves were losing ground.

Finally, one of the giant clear marimo seeds started dropping in a down draft. Doug had to time things just right. Then he realized why the dire wolves had dropped back. Two wolves stood in front of them, right where the marimo should land.

"It's a trap!" Talus yelled.

"Turn," Anachis ordered.

"No," Doug answered.

"Turn!" Anachis yelled louder.

"No . . . stay with me." Doug ran straight. A collision was inevitable. The dire wolves hunkered for the attack. The wolves behind them drew closer.

"Jump . . . NOW!" Doug commanded. With one smooth motion, all four of them leaped into the air with all of their strength. Surprised, the two dire wolves jumped up to meet them. But they were too late. Doug and the Junonians landed directly on the side of the marimo seed as it caught on the wind and launched upward.

"Hang on." Doug didn't have to say anything. The Junonians were already clutching the seed with all of their strength. Their combined weight kept the marimo seed from spinning, so they were hanging on to the bottom with their legs dangling. A stronger wind caught and sent the seed soaring. The earth dropped away and within seconds they were in the clouds. The ground disappeared. The sky blurred from view. All they could see was gray. Cold, featureless, gray.

That is when Doug noticed something was pulling him down. He could barely hang on to the marimo.

"Dire!" Anachis yelled. One of the wolves had latched onto Doug's shirt.

Doug looked down. The wolf's enormous mouth was only inches away from his side. Its angry eyes were locked onto his own. Its feet were digging furiously in the air trying to gain a foothold. Doug kicked with his legs and landed his foot on its tender belly. Kicking only seemed to infuriate the wolf. It shook its head back and forth. A growl rumbled from deep within.

"Get it off. Get it off!" Doug screamed. "I can't hold on."

But the Junonians were helpless. All they could do was hang on to the marimo and watch Doug struggle. They floated quietly through the eerie gray cloud. A loud rip finally tore through the silence. The dire wolf fell and disappeared into the gray with one-third of Doug's shirt still in its jaws. The marimo seed and its stowaways floated off into the interior of ancient Florida.

22

The King of Junonia

His stomach full, Doug had never slept so hard and long in his life. The soft floor of Anachis's apartment was irresistibly cozy. He would have kept sleeping too if Gnat and Cheeto hadn't landed square on his stomach.

"Wake up, Slovenly," Gnat encouraged.

"Come on, Gnat, I can't move a muscle," Doug moaned. Cheeto responded by licking Doug on the mouth.

"Ack. Bleah."

"But you have to get up. Everyone is waiting for you."

"Who is everyone?"

"*Every*one."

Doug struggled to his feet. A brand new shirt was folded on the floor. Orange, the color that the Diadora wear. He held up his old shirt. Torn, bloodied, and covered with dirt.

"I suppose I don't have much choice," Doug said as he slid the new shirt on.

"You've already missed breakfast," Gnat admonished. "Guess what I did."

"Huh?"

"While you were gone. Guess what I did. You'll never guess."

"I dunno."

"I helped collect quartzite nuggets." Gnat struggled to pronounce quartzite.

"Wow. That's extreme," Doug said, rolling his eyes.

"They said I did awesome for a first timer."

"What do they do with quartzite?"

"How should I know?"

"I'm just asking."

"And I'm just telling you that I did awesome."

"What time is it?" Doug asked, stretching his arms up toward the ceiling.

"Who knows what time is it? I don't even know what year it is."

"I wonder if they will make a snack for me since I missed breakfast." Doug opened the operculum door. The shimmering light of Junonia flooded the room. A loud cheer erupted. He stepped outside. Hundreds of Junonians lined the stairs, balconies, and verandas of the city. Hundreds of voices rang out.

"He is finally awake."

"There he is!"

"Doug! Over here! It's Sonorella."

Flocks of tiny white birds swirled in the great circular column of space that ran up the entire spine of the city. Drips of prismatic light fell from the ceiling. It truly was beautiful.

Doug quickly realized that the vocal chaos in the city was due to the Junonians speaking individually instead of as a whole group. Once Anachis, Talus, and Sonorella learned to speak as individuals, it spread like wildfire through the city. Everyone was speaking for themselves, *thinking* for themselves. A buzz of excitement filled the air.

"Why? What is all of this for?" Doug asked the crowd.

"It is for you," Anachis smiled. "You have done what no other Juno-nian has ever done. You walked into a Walleri camp and rescued one of your brothers."

"They think you are some kind of juggernaut," Gnat added.

"And more importantly, you have taught us to think for ourselves."

"We have already had many beautiful thoughts."

"The Diadora no longer control us."

"The Diadora!" Doug said. "I need to talk to those guys."

"They didn't eat breakfast either," Gnat said.

"No one knows where they are," Anachis agreed.

"Listen, everyone," Doug yelled. The crowd fell silent. "I appreciate this, I really do. But we're in grave danger. The Walleri and the Dark Eyes have formed an alliance and are on their way to invade Junonia. At this very moment they are preparing to attack. We have to defend ourselves."

"What should we do, Doug?" Talus asked.

"I don't know. Don't you have an army?" Doug answered.

"We should attack them first," someone yelled out.

"We don't have the kind of weapons to attack them on the surface."

"We should form our defense at the entrance," another said.

"No! We attack on the tombolo so they are trapped."

"But then we are trapped as well."

"We should destroy their villages when they leave."

"Doug has already destroyed one Walleri camp."

An argument ensued. None of the Junonians could agree on the best course of action. They each had their own ideas. Cheeto barked at two Junonians who were shoving each other.

"Quiet!" Gnat screamed at the top of his lungs. No one stopped yelling.

"All right," Doug said. "All right! Everyone, calm down." Slowly the crowd quieted. "I am going to fly with the bells so I can see where the Walleri and Dark Eyes are. Anachis is in charge of getting our defenses ready. We have an advantage on the tombolo. We know it better than they do. At least we have the Crogan Horses down here." Everyone seemed agreeable to that plan. Doug wasn't sure if it was because it was a good plan or because they would think anything coming out of his mouth was brilliant.

"I am going with you," Gnat announced.

"No way," Doug argued. "You have to stay here where I know you are safe."

"I'm not a baby."

"No. You aren't a baby. You are my best assassin. I need you here to . . . cover . . . my . . . flank."

This seemed to stump Gnat. He thought about it for a minute. Doug turned and ran up the stairs toward the Hall of Nations.

"I'm not a baby," Gnat repeated and stumbled after him followed closely by Cheeto. Gnat could hear the Junonians starting to argue again once Doug was out of earshot.

Doug snuck through the side door of the Hall of Nations and into the secret, dark tunnels. He could hear the faint chirping of canary snails. There was just enough dull, orange light to see where he was going. He was starting to get familiar with the directions in the dark tangle of routes, what stairs to leap up, what hidden doorways to slip through. He felt a wind rush past his face. He turned and followed the wind until he came to a stop in the gill room. Hundreds of translucent red gills breathed in and out. In the middle of the room stood all of the Diadora.

"Hurry up," Doug said out of breath. "We have to get ready for an attack."

"There is nothing to worry about," the Diadora said.

"Yes. Yes, there is. Hurry. The Walleri have double-crossed you and are planning to attack Junonia with the Dark Eyes. I saw it myself."

"We know."

"You know? Then what are you? . . ."

"We are on our way to shut down the Pearl and open the gates."

"You are leaving Junonia helpless? But everyone will be killed."

"No one will be killed in battle. The Junonians will be farmed as food and only harvested in a way that sustains the population. It's our only chance at survival. It is time to stop hiding underground, in the shadows. It is time to stop living in fear."

A Walleri warrior stepped out of the darkness. His intricate armor caught and enhanced what little light shone in the room. The flensing spear reached all the way to the ceiling and seemed to sing as the breeze passed over its floppy blade.

"Look out! A Walleri!" Doug yelled.

The Diadora didn't move. They looked calmly at Doug.

"You . . . you knew. You let one inside Junonia," Doug said. He realized just how tall and intimidating a Walleri was up close. His birdlike face was stiff and sharp. This one locked his eyes on him.

"Come with us. It is too late for the rest," the Diadora said.

Doug didn't move a muscle.

"This is the one that destroyed our town." The Walleri spoke with a syncopated, nasal music behind his words. Doug had a hard time understanding it, but he had no trouble recognizing the anger in his voice.

"Consider your choice, Doug," the Diadora warned. "Despite your treasonous actions, we still want you to join us."

Doug shuffled backwards. "*My* treasonous actions? You have destroyed everything."

"What have you done with your life that you think you can fight this? You can't stop what is happening. You couldn't even face a scimitar by yourself. We are giving you and Gnat a chance to stay alive. Come with us. There is still much for you to teach us. Tagelus flows in you."

Doug considered what they were saying. They were right. His only hope of making it home was to use the Pearl. If he didn't stay with it and the Diadora, he and Gnat would be hopelessly stuck here on the losing end of a war. He considered Larry's words about looking after himself and Gnat, about protecting his own.

"I am going to go get Gnat. Where can I meet you?"

"We will wait in the Chapel of Light for you."

"All right. I'll be right there." He hoped they believed him.

Doug headed out of the gill room. Behind him he heard the Diadora say, "Do not let him escape."

In a sudden rush, the Walleri entered the tunnel behind Doug. He could hear the Walleri's armor clinking in the dark. Doug sprinted down a long tunnel. He picked random directions to turn. Sometimes he turned left. Sometimes right. Sometimes he ran straight. He climbed ladders. He slid down ramps. Still, whenever he stopped to listen, he could hear the Walleri tracking him. The short, narrow passageways gave Doug an advantage, but the Walleri was relentless, methodically hunting him in the dark.

Doug came to a familiar tunnel. It was completely black. Not even the tiniest hint of light penetrated the darkness. He paused. Clinking quietly, the Walleri considered an intersection. He was close. Doug could almost picture him investigating all of the options before turning down the right path. Doug heard a faint whistle coming from the other end of the tunnel. There were no more turns, no more escape routes. He would have to make his stand here.

The Walleri crept closer. Doug held his breath and stepped back against the tunnel wall. The clinking of the Walleri armor stopped. Doug tried to focus his eyes in the dark, looking for any sign that the Walleri was close. An eerie silence filled the darkness. He could be gone or he could be inches away. There was no way to tell.

Doug bolted down the tunnel just as the Walleri lunged with the flensing spear behind him. He ran as quietly as possible and didn't dare look back. The Walleri armor made a racket as the enraged warrior blasted full speed toward him. But Doug couldn't worry about that now. It took all of his focus to listen above the noise of clinking armor. He was nearing the end of the tunnel. He slowed down. Listening. Listening.

A faint whistle.

Doug jumped full speed through the end of the tunnel and skidded halfway off the rotating stair. Two seconds behind him, he could hear the Walleri jump out into the open tunnel, letting out a high-pitched wail as he fell into the fathomless black.

Doug climbed to his feet. Now he had a new problem. It was completely dark and he couldn't see the tunnel entrance so he could jump off the stairs. He had to do something soon. If he couldn't find the tunnel, he would have to walk all the way to the surface again and find his way back.

"Acorn Chucker? Are you out there, Acorn Chucker?" A voice rang out.

"Gnat? Is that you?"

"Who else would it be?"

"Keep talking so I can get off this thing."

"I figured out how to get past level thirty of Vampire Hunter," Gnat yelled and paused. "Doug, did you hear me? I said I figured out how to get past level thirty of Vampire Hunter."

A loud thud hit the wall.

"Ow!" Doug yelled. "I missed."

"Did you hear me?"

"I heard you! Geez. Just keep talking."

"You have to use the wooden stake, not the inferno torpedoes or the silver photons. Just the wooden stake like at the beginning. Don't you see? You forget that you have it."

Another thud.

"That *really* hurt. Keep talking. I'm going to try again."

It was completely silent.

"Gnat. I said keep talking. I can't keep doing this. Gnat?"

Silence.

"I can't believe this."

A kaleidoscope of lights suddenly flashed out into the darkness. The lights bounced up and down. It was Gnat holding out his flashing rubber ball.

"Doug! Follow the disco pearl. Follow the dis . . .co pearrrrrl!"

Seconds later, Doug tumbled into the tunnel, sending them both rolling backwards. Cheeto jumped onto both of them.

Doug let out a loud breath. "Sometimes I swear you are a genius, Gnat."

"I know. You forget you have it because by then you have over ten weapons and you have to select all the way back. If you don't hide behind the modified bus while you are choosing your weapon, you won't have time."

"That's not what I was . . . Oh, forget it."

"Doug, you really are disconnected."

Doug hit his foot on something in the dark. He reached down. It was a Walleri flensing spear. The warrior must have dropped it as he fell out the doorway. Doug picked it up. It was much heavier than he expected. It took two hands for him to even lift it. He could feel the paper-thin blade vibrating on the end of the shaft like a musical instrument.

"Whoa, a Walleri spear."

"Weapons upgrade. Cool."

"Hurry. We have to stop the Diadora."

They rushed along the dark tunnels. Gnat kept his rubber ball lit so it was a little easier. Doug struggled manipulating the heavy spear through some of the passageways. His arms burned with the effort.

Ten minutes later, they burst into the Chapel of Light. The Diadora jumped. Two of them had their hands inside of the Pearl.

"Keep your grubby paws off that," Gnat called out. Cheeto snarled.

"Doug! We are happy that you are here," the Diadora said.

"Get out. You are no longer welcome here." Doug took a menacing step forward. He pointed the flensing spear at them. The blade sang like the wind. "We killed your Walleri friend. I know what you have been doing and it's over."

"Listen to us. It is for the best. Junonia will survive. The Junonians will live on even in prison."

"Get out. And please stop talking all at the same time. It really is annoying."

"Very well. Your Tagelus is strong, but you are only delaying the inevitable."

"Maybe, but we will deal with it as it comes."

"There is one thing you need to know. Junonia is not just a city. It is a living being. If you are going to kick us out, you are solely responsible for its survival. This war is about much, much more than the lives of a few Junonians."

"I don't believe you. Not anymore. Not ever. Get out." Doug shoved the nearest Diadora. They smiled menacingly, as if they hadn't told him everything. Then they filed out through the side door marked with a small sun.

"That's how Olivia and I left last time," Gnat whispered.

The door slammed shut behind them.

Doug walked to the balcony overlooking all of Junonia. The view was stunning, a one-thousand-foot drop straight down, circled by spiraling architecture. Droplets of light fell into the abyss until they sparked like stars in the darkness. He could hear hundreds of arguing neighbors screaming at each other, the result of their newfound individuality. The Pearl was his responsibility and he still had absolutely no idea how it worked. They were lost in time. The deep thunder of the Walleri and Dark Eye armies attempting to break through their defense reverberated throughout the earth.

Junonia was in chaos.

And Doug Corcoran was their king.

23

The Provosts of Wardenclyffe

"No, no, no, no, no," Aunt repeated over and over, holding Olivia and rocking back and forth in the complete darkness of the Arizona night.

Olivia was sobbing quietly into her shoulder.

"You shouldn't be caught up in this," Uncle complained, pacing back and forth. "This is all my fault. I should have kept my big mouth shut."

"I came to find you," Olivia cried.

"Gnat? Where is Gnat?" Aunt was wheezing. "Is he all right?"

"Gnat and Cheeto are living with Doug." Olivia chose not to divulge what Virosa just told her about him being missing. Besides, she didn't even know if it was true. "He is fine. Mrs. Corcoran has a giant television and all the video games ever made."

"You feel so skinny," Aunt said.

"You do too," Olivia replied.

"How in the world did you find us?" Uncle said.

"We ran." It was so dark that Olivia couldn't see either of them. Uncle's voice floated invisibly around the room.

"Who is 'we'?"

"Hoolie and I."

"Who is Hoolie?"

"My bear. He's Thunder's son."

"You ran with a *bear?* All the way from Florida?"

"Yeah. And I was hurt really badly and he saved me. And we ate grubs. And that isn't even the half of it."

"No, no, no," Aunt whimpered.

"But how did you find us? We don't even know where we are except they call it Sky Island."

"I'm not really sure. Hoolie knew where we were going. Doug did some research on the Internet. Then we went through the cave of spinning colors and met the Hohokam and Moki the giant lizard who eats mustangs. They live across the valley and they build crystals for the tetracomb so they can travel in time but they had a truce with Wardenclyffe so I had to go to Hovenweep so I could sneak in past the faino peplas."

"All right. Slow down." Uncle ran his hand through his hair. "Couldn't you just fly here on a helicopter like normal people?"

"Well . . . no. Normal people don't have helicopters. And did you know that Dark Eyes can't see into the Hohokam valley because of the neutrino bubble?"

"I can see that you have a lot of stories to tell us. I don't understand half of what you are saying." At least Uncle wasn't whimpering.

In the complete darkness, she could feel the gentle swaying of the compound as it hung in the wind. At that moment the enormity of what she had lived through hit Olivia. She sat down on the glass floor with her back against the wall. There was no way to sit comfortably. Aunt clung to her awkwardly.

"What about," Uncle paused, "the Pearl? I assume Virosa doesn't have it or else we would all be dead."

"I hid it for now. It's only a matter of time before they find it though."

"It must be close. I can feel my strength returning."

"We have to get out of here."

"I've examined every centimeter of this room. The door up there is the only way out."

"Then that is how we will leave," Olivia said.

Aunt was quietly weeping. "We tried so many times. It gets so hot in here during the day."

"We have to figure something out. Eventually Hoolie will return and try to rescue me. I couldn't live if something happened to him."

"We'll do anything to get you out of here safely," Uncle said. "*Anything.*"

"Oh, there is something else you don't know. I caused a drought. All the water is frozen up north. There isn't any more rain because of me. There are fires everywhere."

"I see." Uncle didn't know what else to say.

Aunt was silent.

"This is way outside of my expertise," Uncle conceded. "But it seems to me that we should focus on escape first and the drought second."

"And your house is gone."

"What?" Aunt screeched.

"Your house is completely gone. Even Uncle's opal rock."

Aunt started whimpering again. Uncle punched the wall.

"Harold, no! It's glass."

"Just let me get my hands on one of them. Just one of them." Uncle stomped. "Give me that Flinch."

"Let me take care of Flinch and Virosa," Olivia warned. She could tell that Uncle's spirit was broken. He didn't really believe he could do anything about their situation, much less fight Flinch. "Hoolie and I can handle them. When we get out of here, you and Aunt cross the bridge, and go into the garage on the other side. Get on the ATV and head down the mountain." Olivia pulled a small key from her pocket and handed it to Uncle. "I took these from the ATV. Just keep going east until you meet some people across the valley. Tell them you know me."

"We are not going to leave you alone here. Not now. Not now that we are finally together again," Uncle said.

"You must," Olivia said. "If just one of us gets away, we can get help. Oh, and be careful at the bottom of the mountain. It's um. . . . floating."

A silence filled the glass room. Olivia fell in and out of sleep in-between telling stories of her adventures. During the quiet moments of complete darkness, she could hear the singing of the Pearl inside of her, humming and chiming, calling out to her.

A faint glow spread across the horizon. Its rosy light illuminated Aunt and Uncle enough for Olivia to finally see them as they slept. It looked like they had aged fifty years. Their eyes were dark and sunken. Their skin was as thin as onion skin. They looked frail, like starved deer. The look of defeat filled their faces.

"You, you are so old," she said. Calmly, they both awoke.

"We *are* old, Olivia," Uncle explained, his eyes filled with tears. "We had been living near the third pole, near the Pearl, for so long that once we were separated from it, we have aged incredibly fast."

"Making up for lost time," Aunt added.

"How old are you," Olivia asked, "really?"

"Older than everyone else."

"Oh, Harold. Quit with the games. I'm one hundred and fifty-one."

"Just a spring chicken," Uncle added.

"We had just about given up sitting here," Aunt said, "but you fell into our lives again like an angel."

"Not exactly what you signed up for when you came to get us in Wisconsin, huh?"

"Your eyes," Aunt noticed, "have changed color."

"How did that happen?" Uncle asked.

"Terrilyne says I have the eyes of a baby bear."

Uncle put his hand on Olivia's cheek. "You have seen so much," he said. "No one should have to endure that."

Olivia noticed Uncle's hands shook slightly, like tiny vibrating animals. Olivia's heart was slowly sinking. It took everything she and Hoolie had to get here. How were her impossibly old aunt and uncle going to escape from a hanging mountain compound populated with gun-toting criminals? She doubted that Uncle could even drive the ATV down the rocky mountain.

The morning light was creeping into the gorge beneath the glass prison. It made her dizzy to look down into the ragged crevasse. Her stomach looped. Her hands froze. Even in full light she couldn't see the bottom. Birds zipped back and forth beneath them. Instead of feeling like she was flying free, Olivia felt completely exposed and helpless. She closed her eyes to fight back the nausea.

Something plunked against the glass wall like a little pebble. Again she heard it. Olivia crawled over to the wall because it made her too nervous to stand up. More plunks. This time she saw what was hitting the glass. Green chrysina beetles were flinging themselves against the prison walls. Time and again, a bright green beetle would fly full speed into the glass before bouncing off and tumbling end-over-end into the gorge below.

"Well, would you look at that," Uncle said. "They are hitting the exact same spot in the glass."

Faster they flew, one after another. Olivia pressed her hand to the glass. She couldn't feel a thing as each beetle slammed off. The glass showed no signs of breaking. She watched them fall like green hailstones onto the dark rocks below.

"They aren't doing anything," Olivia said.

"They are giving their lives to save the Guardian," Uncle whispered and placed his hand on her shoulder.

The sound of helicopters coming and going vibrated through the compound. One dark blue helicopter veered up the gorge from the valley floor and settled somewhere above them.

"The Wardenclyffe provosts are arriving," Olivia announced. "We've got to get out of here. Soon they will be coming for me."

Aunt shuddered. She showed Olivia the long scar on her arm. "Please be careful. Those men are evil. Flinch did this when he was trying to get your uncle to talk," she said with a worried look in her eyes.

Before long, they heard footsteps. The door in the ceiling opened. Aunt clung desperately to Olivia.

"Little thing?" Flinch's voice called down. "Git up here, Little Thing. It is time to have some fun."

"It's all right," Olivia whispered. "Just be ready to go. You'll know when the time is right." She peeled herself away from Aunt and Uncle.

"You leave her alone, you little punk," Uncle screamed up the ladder.

"Shut up, old coot," Flinch laughed. "Don't you forget, we don't need you any more now that we have Little One."

"Why don't you come down here then?"

"I will, coot. Just wait your turn. I'll make sure to bring your walker." Flinch and Rieger grabbed Olivia's arms as soon as she neared the entrance and pulled her up. They didn't see her jam a wadded-up shoelace into the door frame latch as she passed through the door. Olivia could hear both Aunt and Uncle crying. Flinch spit down the open door and slammed it shut again.

"We're going to have a party Little One, and you're the star. All of the provosts are here to see you."

"I'll bet they are scared of me just like you are," Olivia said with a sneer.

"Now listen," Flinch grabbed her hair shoving her forward, "this is a big deal. Don't you make me look bad."

"I'll be a perfect little angel."

Olivia could see several helicopters parked out on the mountainside. There was only room for one to land inside the compound. Rieger walked in front as Flinch pushed her along. The halls were filled with people rushing back and forth. Olivia noticed that Rieger kept one hand on her gun at all times.

Flinch and Rieger escorted Olivia back into the main dining room. The white sheets had been removed from the walls and the paint cans were gone. When she entered, every chair around the table pushed back as their occupants stood up. Olivia did a quick count. Fifteen provosts including Virosa. Each provost seemed to represent some foreign country. Men, women. Every race. An outburst of applause and angry disappointment flashed through the room.

"What is this, Virosa?" one man screamed. "A mere girl?"

"Who are you to say the Guardian cannot be a girl?" a woman wearing a colorful sari scolded.

"How do we know?"

"You brought us all the way here for this?"

Virosa boomed over the room. "You were all aware of the increased reports of telluric activity in Florida. Telluric convergence is a well-known indicator the sphere has resurfaced. The sphere is known as the Pearl of Tagelus in the local parlance." The provosts rumbled with approval. "The convergence eventually centered on the home of Harold Milligan, one of the more prominent searchers in the southern United States. My team of professional insurgents quickly acquired him." Virosa gestured proudly toward Flinch and Rieger.

"Then where is this Milligan now?" The angry man slammed his fist on the table.

Virosa ignored him. "We have him in custody. I am ashamed to admit that we were in error, however. Harold Milligan is an old fool. A well-connected fool perhaps, but a fool nonetheless. His niece, Olivia Brophie, is the true Guardian," he said, putting his arm around Olivia. She squirmed away from his grasp.

"Does she have the mark?" Several of the provosts rushed up to Olivia and pushed her head back. "She doesn't have the mark."

"Ah, yes, the mark. Previously, we had investigated Olivia and ruled her out as the Guardian because she did not possess the sacred mark. Despite that fact, we maintained surveillance on her because she possessed all of the other indicators of being the Guardian. She was drawn across the country to the area of convergence. Filthy animals were attracted to her. She showed a remarkable ability to elude contact."

"This is nothing new. History is filled with similar dead-ends and false leads," a woman said.

"What Wardenclyffe provost has not dreamed of capturing the Guardian, seeing shadows where there are none?"

"Hardly a decade goes by when someone doesn't think they have captured the Guardian!"

"We should just kill the girl."

"She has no mark, for goodness sake!"

"What difference does it make now? She knows too much for us to simply let her go."

"This is true. You have forced us to kill an innocent child, Virosa."

"Don't you see? The mark *is* the myth!" Virosa seemed to swell larger than life. His voice filled the room. "Who among us has ever seen a Guardian in real life? Who can say? You, Kunzo? You, Januar? How about you, Syifa? History is filled with false leads and dead-ends, yet none of you never *ever* questioned the sanctity of the mark!" Virosa's jaw clenched triumphantly.

An old man wearing a homburg hat stood up from the table. The room went silent. Slowly, he wobbled toward Olivia with a cane. His passage across the large room seemed to take forever. He removed his glasses. "Pray tell, Virosa, if what you say is true, then where is the sphere?"

"We do not . . . we have not exactly located it yet, Mr. Wah," Virosa answered.

The room burst into shouts.

"But I assure you," Virosa's voice carried over the din, "I *assure* you that we are very close. The telluric convergence shifted from Florida to southeast Arizona in the past week. Not coincidently, Olivia arrived in this area at that time. I know . . . I know we had ruled out telluric activity as a viable method for locating the sphere decades ago. I continued to monitor it only as a precaution. As it turns out, convergent telluric pattern analysis is our *only* effective tool. It is a rough tool, however, susceptible to disruption by even the weakest of electromagnetic conductivity. We cannot pinpoint the exact position due to the neutrino force field that protects this valley."

Mr. Wah leaned close to Olivia. "Why don't you tell us where it is, little girl?"

"I . . . I don't know what you are talking about . . . what any of you are talking about. Where is my Mommy?" Olivia whimpered and pretended to bawl into her arm.

"This is ridiculous."

"I can't believe I flew all the way from the Ukraine for this, this fiasco."

"This is just a little girl. I'll be surprised if you aren't on the news for child abduction, Virosa." All the provosts in the room laughed.

Flinch dug his fingers into Olivia's arm. Her tears were suddenly very real.

"I do not ask you to take my word for it," Virosa yelled defiantly. "We no longer need the Guardian, and I assure you that she is indeed the Guardian, because all we have to do is disable the neutrino field and we can locate the sphere ourselves."

"Preposterous!"

"We cannot allow you to expose Wardenclyffe to the outside world, Virosa. This is one of our best safe-houses."

"Your entire theory is premised on this innocent girl being the Guardian."

"Even as we speak, my men are removing all indication of our presence here," Virosa argued. "All the authorities will find is this vacant, creaking old house. Maybe a cupboard filled with cans of disgusting, stale tomato soup. Once we have the sphere, we will have no need to hide. We will have no need for anything."

Carl entered the room carrying a belt with several hand grenades.

"All we need to do is destroy the neutrino generator on the eastern side of the valley," Virosa announced. Olivia knew that he was talking about the tetracomb. "We will fly over this morning and drop these grenades. I assure you that we will have the sphere in our possession by noon."

Olivia strained against Flinch's grasp. "Don't you dare," she snapped through her teeth.

"Ah, so our innocent little butterfly awakes." Virosa smiled slyly at her.

Olivia was taken aback at the nickname her father always called her. The room immediately noticed her change of demeanor.

"Perhaps we should allow Virosa this one dalliance," Mr. Wah said. "It is, after all, one of his outposts."

"This isn't Vijayanagara, or Culebrita, or Faneuil Hall," Syifa added. "The risk is small."

Some of the others nodded their heads.

Virosa pounced on the turn of sentiment. "We can afford this . . . this chance if you wish to call it that. Think back in history to all of those near-misses, those fleeting moments when our noble goal was within our grasp and it slipped away for another millennium. The common element in each of those moments was the failure to act caused by a provost who hesitated too long, afraid that the sphere was merely a myth and he would look a fool. Or a council," Virosa swept his arm across the room, "locked up in politics and indecision. If I am wrong, we lose a vile, inaccessible, hermit's shack that we so eloquently named the Sky Island. But if I am right, and I know I am, we will possess the very thing we have been searching for our whole lives. *We* will be the ones who write history. *We* will control the weather, the riches of the world, the people who would defy us. *We* will be the leaders of the future. No more eloquence. No more talk. No more conspiracies. No more plotting."

The room was completely silent.

"Now, who is with me?" Virosa boomed.

The provosts jumped to their feet and roared with approval.

Virosa leaned forward into Olivia's face. "This is your last chance."

Flinch gave her a rough shake.

"You can give me the sphere now or I can destroy your savage little friends over there."

Olivia crossed her arms and stared straight ahead.

"Very well. It doesn't matter to me. I'll have no use for you in a few minutes."

An alarm sounded.

"What? What is it now?" Virosa yelled.

Flinch shoved Olivia into Carl and Rieger's arms. He grabbed a walkie talkie from his belt. "Andre, what is going on up there?"

A voice crackled in the speaker. "Intruders on the eastern slope. Thousands of them. I . . . I don't know where they came from. I can't tell if they are armed or not."

Flinch turned to the provosts. "We need all of your guards and every available gun." People were running everywhere. Something in the kitchen crashed to the floor.

"There's something else," Andre crackled.

"What? What?" Flinch screamed.

"There is a bear with them."

"We have plenty of firepower. Let's go," Flinch commanded.

"Carl, Rieger, complete the mission and destroy that neutrino generator," Virosa yelled over the noise. He wheeled around with gigantic eyes. "Where? Where is the girl?" His voice rose to an uncomfortable volume. His scream reverberated throughout the compound.

24

Acrophobia

Olivia had never held a hand-grenade. She had only touched a gun once before and that was two days ago. She knew better than to mess with things like that. But when Flinch had shoved her into Carl's arms, it was so easy to pull the grenade from his belt. At first, it seemed like a brilliant idea to steal it. Now it sat in her hands, heavier than a stone. She didn't know how to use it except what she had seen in cartoons. A pin should be removed. And then you have five seconds to throw it. Or was it three seconds? Or does it explode in three seconds? Would it explode in her hands? Her mind raced as she ran down a side hallway. She could hear Virosa screaming over the sound of alarms somewhere behind her.

She screeched to a halt. The entire front hallway was filled with Wardenclyffe guards preparing to go fight the Hohokam. They all turned to face her. An awkward moment passed that felt like five minutes.

"Here! Here she is!" someone in the group yelled.

Olivia turned on her heels and rushed down a hallway toward the back of the compound followed by the mob of guards. A bullet winged into the door jamb behind her. She caught a quick glimpse of Carl and Rieger rushing at her from the other direction. She burst out the back door and leaped down the short stairs onto the helipad and compound yard. She jumped and dodged around the power stations and transformers on the deck. It was all suddenly clear to her. She could blow up the helicopter with her grenade and save the tetracomb. She pulled at the pin. It didn't budge. She stopped running and pulled the pin with all of her strength. It slid out with a jolt.

A bullet bit into the ground next to her feet.

"Stop, Olivia!" a woman shouted. Olivia turned around to see Rieger with her guns pointed at her.

"Geez," Carl shouted, "that grenade is live."

Olivia's heel hit a landing light and she stumbled backwards. The grenade launched from her hand and rolled across the helipad, coming to a rest underneath a large tank in the corner.

"The fuel!" Rieger screamed, diving to the ground. Olivia rolled off the edge of the helipad and covered her head.

The explosion blew over her head like roaring dragon, fizzing the air. Her head rang and throbbed. Rieger and Carl were pushed back toward the building. The glass windows on the entire back wall shattered and rained down to the ground. She peeked over her shoulder to see a gigantic fireball roiling toward the sky.

Suddenly, the entire compound platform jolted. The supporting cables on the corner that ran up toward the cliff snapped free from their anchors and snapped into the air. One by one the cables whipped out into the gorge and hung loosely against the cliff. The extra weight stretched the remaining cables. A loud groan rumbled and vibrated. A smaller explosion rocked the platform. The second corner snapped and the platform tilted violently. Several barrels dropped over the edge and slammed onto the rocks far below. One of the barrels exploded and sent an acrid ball of smoke erupting back toward the platform. Olivia hung on to a strut as debris rolled and slid past her. She could see the provosts and their guards rushing across the bridge as they evacuated. The helicopter broke free from its tether and slid toward her shooting sparks as the metal gouged the concrete. She dug her sneakers into the ground and scrambled on all fours toward the house. The helicopter just barely missed hitting her before it tilted over the edge and disappeared with a shrieking crash into the gorge. Carl and Rieger were gone. The back door swung open and she pulled herself into the building.

She leaned against the back wall. The entire house swung back and forth, screaming a deafening noise. The walls and ceilings cracked open. Plaster dust smoked the air. Her heart raced and jumped in her chest. Tears poured from her eyes. The whole world spun.

"Aunt! Uncle!" she shouted and jumped to her feet. She half-crawled up the hallway that she had raced along only moments before. Junk was tumbling down around her. Cans of corn thumped and rolled by like small boulders. She ducked as a phone vaulted over her head and dropped out the back. She looked back and the door opened up to the gorge below. The entire compound was falling apart and crashing down. Every few moments another cable snapped and jolted the building, sending her sliding backward. Finally, she scrambled to the entrance to the glass prison. She flung open the door. The lock was still jammed with her shoelace. "Aunt! Uncle! Come on!"

There was no response. She stuck her head down. No one was there. Olivia sighed in relief. They had escaped. Hopefully they had made it down the mountain. She could hear the provost's helicopters taking off from beyond the garage.

She had to get off the compound. She rushed through the foyer, opened the front door, and almost stepped off the edge. The bridge swung loosely against the cliff wall. There was no way to escape. Virosa spotted her from the window of his helicopter. He stared straight into her eyes and tapped his watch. He gave a cavalier shrug, smiled, and motioned the pilot down toward the valley.

With a jarring lurch, a huge slab of the compound broke away and tumbled down into the chasm. Olivia watched the debris crashing against the rocks until it disappeared from view. The sight of it knotted her stomach. The compound was now almost completely vertical. She was standing on the walls and leaning her hands against the floor. The elk-antler chandelier lay crumpled on the foyer wall. If she didn't somehow get over to the cliff, she would be no different from those crumbling chunks of concrete and the twisted metal lying at the bottom. She looked over to the remaining cables. If she climbed along the edge of the building, she could reach where they attached. Did she dare shinny out across the chasm?

"Hoonaw kookam! Olivia!" A voice called out to her.

She looked up. There on the cliff, stood two figures and a bear.

"Terri! Chubascos! Hoolie!"

"Hi, Sis," Terrilyne waved.

"What are you doing over there?" Chubascos laughed.

Hoolie looked like he was smiling. A huge weight lifted from Olivia's shoulders. Seeing the three of them made her feel like everything was going to be all right. Another piece of the compound crumbled off, shaking Olivia to her knees.

"How am I going to get off this thing?" Olivia yelled. She didn't want them to see the tears in her eyes.

"Hold on," Terrilyne yelled. She and Chubascos disappeared from sight. Hoolie didn't budge. After a few minutes, they returned with a long rope from the garage. Terrilyne placed one end of the rope in Hoolie's mouth. Then the kids scrambled across the thick cables like two spiders. They were fearless. Olivia couldn't believe what she was seeing. Without a thought, they left the safety of the cliff and joined her on the rickety remains of the crumbling compound.

"Looks like we got here just in time," Terrilyne cried as she held Olivia tight. "I missed you."

"It's . . . it's only been two days," Olivia sniffed.

"Two and a *half* days," Terrilyne corrected.

"Come on, let's go," Chubascos said. He tied the rope around Olivia's waist.

"I can't," Olivia said. "It's too far down. I can't balance like you two." Her legs suddenly felt like rubber bands.

"It isn't any worse than climbing the old ladders back at home," Terrilyne responded. "You used to be scared of that too."

"You guys go. I'll stay here."

"There are a thousand Hohokam ancestors fighting Wardenclyffe in the valley right now," Chubascos added, "but you faced them all by yourself. Climbing across is nothing for someone as brave as you."

Olivia shuffled her feet, nodded, and swiped her nose with her arm. Chubascos went first. Olivia was to be next with Terrilyne to follow.

"It's really no different than if the cables were lying on the ground, you know," Terrilyne said. "They aren't any thinner just because they are hanging high above those sharp rocks down there."

Chubascos, out on the cable, shot her a look that was half-scolding, half-laughing.

Olivia shuffled one foot out onto the thick cable. Suddenly, she felt just how much the crumbling compound was swinging in the air. "I . . . I can't do it."

"Let's go, Sis. You are thinking too much," Terrilyne said. "Just look straight ahead and walk. No big deal."

"I can't. I said I *can't*."

Chubascos strolled halfway across and spun around and strolled back as if he were on a sidewalk. "Walk toward me. Look in my eyes."

Olivia lifted her eyes to meet his. They were soft and brown. Welcoming. Calm. She felt her cheeks burn. Chubascos held out his hands. Any other time, she would have laughed in his face. But without thinking, she placed her shivering hands in his. She felt his fingers close around her like a warm sunflower closing around a bumblebee.

"I cannot believe," he spoke low, "that you walked right into Moki's cave." He slowly stepped backwards, pulling her gently forward. "And not just once. You did it at Hovenweep. No Hohokam would ever do such a thing. I have never met . . . anyone like you." She could tell that he meant every word. He wasn't pretending. His eyes flared, almost imperceptibly, but she saw them bright like colorful trout beneath a mountain creek. Before she knew it, she was walking across the cable toward his calm voice and eyes.

"Um, Olivia?" Chubascos asked.

"What?"

"You can stop looking at me. We're on solid ground now."

"Gross." Terrilyne looked at both of them skeptically.

"Oh . . . OH!" Olivia yanked her hands away from his and pretended her shoes needed tying. Only one shoe had a lace because one was still jammed in the glass prison's door.

Hoolie rushed over and nuzzled against Olivia. She grabbed his ears and pulled him close.

Olivia looked back as another chunk of the compound broke free and crashed down the chasm. The cable they just walked across snapped free of its anchor. Nothing recognizable was left of the building. They had escaped just in time.

Then Olivia remembered something. "Doug's thermos! I promised to return it."

"It's down at the bottom now," Terrilyne said.

"Oh shoot." They heard gunfire from the valley.

"We don't have time to worry about it," Chubascos interrupted with a fierce look in his eyes.

"What are we going to do about it, Chubby? We don't have any guns," Terrilyne said.

"I'm not going to wait up here like a scared little lizard," he argued.

"The Pearl. We need to get the Pearl," Olivia said. "I can make a force field."

"Come on, hurry and show us," Chubascos said. They started running across the snow. Olivia retraced her steps down the mountainside.

"Did you guys see my aunt and uncle?" she asked.

"What do they look like?" Terrilyne responded.

"Old. And riding a red ATV," Olivia answered. "You know, old Dark Eyes."

"No. We didn't see any ATVs. There are a bunch of Dark Eyes down there though."

If there was one thing that Olivia was good at after weeks of crossing America, it was running. She casually strode past Chubascos, not even breathing heavily. He looked at her shocked. No one beats him in a race. He leaned into his momentum and caught up to her. Olivia let the slope of the mountain take her weight. Like a breeze, she accelerated past Chubascos again. Faster and faster they raced.

"Guys," Terrilyne huffed, "wait up."

But neither of them stopped. They soon left her far behind.

Olivia thought of a deer, slender and bright, leaping over fences, lighter than smoke. Chubascos was struggling but would never give up. Never.

Suddenly, they both skidded to a stop. Snow ploughed forward under their shoes. Terrilyne came chugging up behind them. "What? What is it?" she asked, not able to see what they were looking at.

"The tafoni," Chubascos whispered. "I'm sure of it."

"The tafoni," Terrilyne repeated. "Wow. *The* tafoni!"

"I slept in there," Olivia said.

"You slept in the tafoni?"

"I had to sleep somewhere. I couldn't sleep in the snow, could I? There are jaguars around here too."

"The stories say that jaguars guard the tafoni from intruders."

"Come on, the Pearl is inside."

Chubascos and Terrilyne didn't move.

"Come on. It's all right," Olivia encouraged. "I already slept in there. Hoolie too. We have to get the Pearl. It's all right."

"Only the family elders are supposed to go inside the tafoni," Terrilyne warned, pulling on Olivia's arm.

"But you will be elders to future generations."

This seemed to be a satisfactory argument.

They entered the tunnel into the rock. Chubascos and Terrilyne looked around, pointing at different petroglyphs and chattering to each other. Olivia knelt by the quiet pool in the center. She reached down in the cool water almost up to her shoulders. When she stood up again, the Pearl was safely in her arms, dripping with water. The blue light flooded the interior of the tafoni, spilling out into the sun outside. The petroglyphs lit up with shimmering life. Tiny details in the etchings were enhanced. Histories. Legends. Instructions.

A shadow swooped through the rock, knocking Chubascos to the ground.

"Whoa, what was that?"

Another shadow blew through from another hole. Olivia and Terrilyne covered their heads.

"It's Crokley!" Olivia shouted. They ran outside and looked up. Thousands of ravens swirled in a dark tornado above the tafoni. There were so many that the sound of their wings sounded like a train.

"Which one is he?" Terrilyne yelled.

"That one!" Olivia said, pointing into the center of the spinning cloud.

"What difference does it make?" Chubascos said. "We need to get going." He started running down the mountainside toward the battle.

"Wait, Chubascos. Those men have guns. How will you fight?" Terrilyne yelled after him. Olivia jumped onto Hoolie's back and pulled Terrilyne up behind her.

"Hurry up, Hoolie. We have to catch him." Hoolie barreled down the slope, crashing through brush. In seconds, they had already descended past the snow line. A plume of dust kicked up behind them. The ravens looped up high into the sky then plummeted down toward the valley like a screeching, dark wind. Something was running behind Hoolie.

Terrilyne pulled on Olivia's shirt.

"What is it?" Olivia called out. "Just hang on. I know it looks dangerous but Hoolie knows what he is doing."

"It's not that. J . . . jaguars," Terrilyne stammered. "Behind us."

Three jaguars were matching Hoolie stride for stride. Olivia could feel his skin twitch.

"Don't worry. They're with us," Olivia shouted.

Over a ridge, the full battlefield came into view. Hoolie skidded to a stop. The jaguars fell into a line next to him and nervously clawed the dirt. The ravens circled in the sky. Thousands of Hohokam swarmed the hillside, men and women alike. Some of them had guns, but most of them just ran headlong toward the enemy. Wardenclyffe thugs huddled in groups and fired guns into the crowd. Several dirt bikes zipped in and out leaving behind bodies of wounded. Three helicopters hung overhead shooting bullets in every direction.

"There are so many," Olivia said.

"They are all the ancestors," Terrilyne replied.

"Look, they are disappearing like ghosts."

"They are twinning in and out."

"Buy why? Why are they all fighting?"

"Because you are the Guardian and the Hohokam have sworn throughout all time to protect the Guardian and the Pearl. We are members of an ancient league called . . ."

"The Fellowship," Olivia interrupted, her heart leaping in her chest.

"You are in the Fellowship! It's real!"

"Yes, of course," Terrilyne laughed slyly. "I didn't tell you that?"

"But how did they know? How did they find out?"

"I had to tell them when you didn't come home."

"Look, there's Chubascos." They watched him scurry near the edge of the battle and hide behind a giant cactus. A dirt bike rushed by. With one smooth jump, Chubascos knocked the driver from the bike and sent them both tumbling. The bike catapulted and smacked into a rock. The biker and Chubascos stood up and faced each other. In slow motion, the biker raised his arm and punched him across the face. Chubascos crumpled to the ground. The biker stood over his body and kicked at his side.

"Chubascos!" Terrilyne screamed, tears exploding from her eyes.

"No!" Olivia shivered frantically. "No!" A rage uncoiled in her chest, burning and heavy. She felt it fill her blood and rush through her body. Terrilyne's crying faded away. The sound of bullets and helicopters disappeared. She didn't hear her own angry command for Hoolie to charge. She didn't hear the ravens cry out. She didn't hear her own scream descending down the hillside like an unstoppable boulder. In seconds, Hoolie swatted and tossed the biker like a rag doll. A jaguar landed on him with a terrible thud. Terrilyne slipped off Hoolie's back. Olivia looked back and could see her cradling Chubascos' head and weeping.

Bullets winged over Olivia's head as soon as she and Hoolie were noticed. The thunderous noise spooked the jaguars and they retreated back up the ridge. A Wardenclyffe thug ran past screaming in agony, completely covered from head to toe with thousands of jumping cholla spines.

Hoolie dismantled a small group of thugs. They barely knew what hit them. Hoolie had been waiting for this moment for a long time. Pressing her legs into his side to steady herself, Olivia opened the Pearl. The humming of the Pearl filled her ears. Deep inside, her fingers found what she was looking for. She could feel the energy well up in her hands. A blue force field bubble enveloped her and Hoolie. They barreled through the largest crowd of Wardenclyffe fighters, knocking them all stunned to the ground. She held the Pearl high above her head, a violent star. Thick, green arcs of electricity shot outward from the energy ball. She focused the bolts by tilting the Pearl one way or the other. One lightning bolt shot directly toward the metal of a helicopter. The engine fluttered and smoked before exploding into the ground. A cheer rose from the Hohokam warriors and they surged forward.

Olivia looked up. She could see Virosa in another helicopter redfaced and screaming as he pointed dramatically in Olivia's direction. He was punching the wall of the helicopter with all of his strength. Olivia clenched her jaw. Before she could aim the green electricity, the tornado of ravens altered their path and threw their weight full-speed into the helicopter. At first, their lifeless bodies dropped to the ground with countless thuds. But nothing stopped their plunging flight. The thick of the flock cracked into the windshield and jammed through an open window. Olivia could see them clawing at the pilot inside. Virosa flailed wildly. The helicopter veered away and disappeared over the ridge. The cloud of ravens followed.

The remaining Wardenclyffe thugs panicked and scattered back up the Western Island. The last helicopter sped off above the clouds. A loud roar erupted from the Hohokam. Olivia closed up the Pearl. The battle was over.

"Hoonaw kookam!" Terrilyne called out. Olivia whipped around. Chubascos was standing sheepishly next to her, blood pouring from his nose. Olivia rushed up to them.

"Now we've both been injured." Chubascos smiled.

"By idiots." Terrilyne laughed.

In the distance, Olivia could see the Yazzi and Ganado families rushing toward them covered in blood, tears, and smiles. From the other direction, an ATV puttered down the mountainside, driven by Uncle with Aunt clinging on with all of her strength.

25

A New Horizon

"To the liberators of the tafoni," Dr. Yazzi spoke from the balcony overlooking the tetracomb, "the restorers of the Western Island to the Hohokam Nation, the Guardian of the Pearl of Tagelus, and the two most beautiful daughters a father could hope to have. On behalf of the seven hundred generations, we are here to honor the fallen dead and the heroism of Terrilyne Yazzi and Olivia Brophie."

The crowd of Hohokam roared with excitement. Terrilyne jumped up and down at a frantic pace. She leaned into Olivia. "And don't forget the only kids ever to go to Hovenweep!"

Olivia smiled and adjusted her new backpack. The Pearl quietly hummed inside. She wondered where Hoolie was in the dark of the valley. People were patting her on the head and shouting 'Thank you!" and "What's next?" Uncle put his arm around Aunt and smiled wider than she had ever seen. Chubascos was showing off his broken nose to his friends. John Whistle met her eyes across the crowd. Without expression, he stared at her.

"And never let it be said that the Hohokam do not learn lessons from the wise amongst us," Dr. Yazzi continued. "Our fear of the outside world has restrained us for so long that it took a fierce and remarkable child to illuminate our darkness. The world is filled with dangers, yes. But it is also capable of great beauty, sincerity, and kindness. Although we are not ready to lower our shield and expose our valley, from this point forward, Hohokam youth will be allowed to apply for sabbatical and venture forth to the world for the duration of one year. There, we hope they will learn new ways that will not only strengthen our traditions, but infuse our culture with new life."

A mix of cheers and boos filled the air.

"It is said of the olden days, that Moon placed her hands on the ground and pulled away the sand to find the creek that runs through our valley. The piles of sand became the beautiful mountain islands. But Moon was so enthralled with the silver ribbon of light flowing from the ground that she jumped into the water and would not leave. She would no longer plant corn. She would no longer hunt. She would no longer repair ladders. She would only soak in the bright, clear waters. Little by little, Moon's skin turned to crystal. She grew heavy and clear. For generations, Moon soaked. One day, the people could barely see her in the water because she was so clear. Only the faintest whisper of her heart remained. Before she completely disappeared, it was decided to throw her into the starry heavens where she could be seen by all people against the dark sky. Let us not be afraid to leave the water my friends, no matter how comforting the water is.

"As for tonight, this sacred blessing of a night, I look at my family, my friends. I look at our ancestors, the wise original generation. I look across our valley to the moon laying her crystal hands on the Western Island and my heart is filled with a wholeness it has never known. Let us celebrate our return to a whole people!"

The crowd erupted with pure joy. Tiny bits of glowing confetti fluttered down from the surrounding cliffs until their hair was completely covered. Everyone crowded around Olivia and Terrilyne. Olivia no longer felt like an intruder. Terrilyne pulled her over to the buffet table.

"Prickly pear popsicles again?" Terrilyne scrunched up her nose. "This is seriously annoying."

Olivia carefully picked some confetti off her popsicle. "There are flowers frozen inside. We could make a fortune with these."

"Well, I would give you all of them for a single rocket pop."

A man in a hooded sweatshirt patted Olivia on her back. "Thank you for your heroism, . . . Little Thing."

Flinch!

The man spun Olivia around and locked his arm across her chest. He held a long knife point to her neck.

Terrilyne screamed.

"Let her go, Dark Eye," Chubascos yelled.

"Stay back. All of you stay back or Little Thing gets it right in an artery." Flinch pulled Olivia backwards. "This juicy, tender artery right here." The light from the tetracomb flashed across his snarling face. She could feel the tip of the blade pressing into her skin. It was a homemade knife. Long and silver. Irregularly jagged as it was made by an amateur, but sharp enough. Sharp enough.

Three more hooded figures made their way to the front. They pulled guns from underneath their coats and pushed the crowd backwards.

"Did you really think this was over?" Virosa raised his face into the light, toward Olivia. A fresh burn left a slashing, bloody mark across his face. "Did you really think a flock of ravens would stop my destiny?"

"Get your stinking hands off her!" John Whistle lunged toward

Flinch with lightning speed. He landed a heavy punch on Flinch's jaw. A shot rang out. John collapsed onto the ground in a heap and didn't move. The crowd screamed.

"Anyone else? Anyone else want to get shot?" Rieger announced and swung her gun through the air. The crowd pressed closer and closer. She blasted a few bullets into the sand by their feet for emphasis.

"You cannot shoot us all," Dr. Yazzi said.

"We will not let you harm her," Uncle said.

"Spare me your sentiments," Virosa growled. "This little charmer single-handedly destroyed my outpost and killed twenty people, including the provosts of the Yucatan peninsula and central Asia. All you have to do is hand over the sphere and you can all get back to your little hippie festival. I won't hold my financial losses against you."

Everyone was yelling. The angry words flew back and forth and filled the air with tangible noise.

Twenty people. She, Olivia Brophie, *killed* twenty people. Six months ago she was worried about summer vacation and finding a way to pay for ballet lessons. And now she had ended the life of twenty people, even if they were evil and deserved it. She was a murderer. A mass murderer. Who knows how many other people had died on her behalf during the battle? Even John Whistle who hated her three days ago had given his life trying to save her. *Why?* Olivia saw John's body through a blur of tears. She looked over at Terrilyne, the fear blooming on her face. She saw Aunt and Uncle scolding Virosa and Flinch. She looked at the Ganados. Chubascos was so beautiful the way his concern for her exploded from his eyes. She could tell Dr. Yazzi was about to rush toward Flinch. Her eyes kept shooting back at John Whistle's lifeless body. She knew what to do.

"Let them have it."

A silence fell across the crowd. All eyes turned to her. Even Virosa didn't believe what he heard.

"Let them have it," she repeated. "It's all right."

"Listen to the girl," Virosa yelled out.

"No one wants to hear you," Olivia snapped. "Just take it and leave."

Flinch slipped his knife through Olivia's backpack straps and flung the bag to Virosa before returning the blade to Olivia's neck. Virosa unzipped the bag. The swirling blue light of the Pearl beamed into the night. His hands visibly shook as he fumbled with the zipper and shut the bag again.

"Oh my," his voice wavered. "Oh my." Virosa almost fainted before he regained his composure. "Wise choice. Now let us go peaceably. Once we are outside your territory, we will release the Guardian."

Virosa, Carl, and Rieger started working their way past the crowd, swinging their guns in sweeping arcs to keep the Hohokam away.

"It'll be all right everybody. Don't worry," Olivia yelled through her sobs.

"Now it is just you and me, Little Thing," Flinch whispered in her ear. "I'm going to finish our business." Olivia could feel the knife pushing hard against her neck. With all of her strength, she bent her knees and pushed her entire weight backwards. Flinch stumbled back several steps never letting go of her. Purple light spun around them. They were inside the tetracomb.

In an instant, Flinch and Olivia twinned to the alpine meadow, the same meadow that Dr. Yazzi showed her on her very first trip through the tetracomb. It was nighttime and thick drifts of fog rolled by. Through the fog Olivia could see some of the dark outlines of wild horses sleeping. There would be no rescue from Hoolie or the Hohokam this time. There *couldn't* be. They were back in the distant past. She and Flinch were alone.

"Wha . . . What is going on?" Flinch's voice wavered. He grew weak with the shock of twinning and Olivia scrambled off into the fog. She could hear him calling wildly.

"What is this place? How did you? . . . how did we? . . . "

Olivia wove her way past sleeping horses. They appeared through the fog like apparitions. She moved silently so they didn't wake. Huge, vertical shafts of rock stood over the meadow like gigantic tombstones.

Flinch slowly recovered his senses. He let out a loud growl that woke some of the horses. They huffed nervously.

"Where are you, Little Thing?" Flinch called out. "Take me home from this place and I will let you live."

Through breaks in the fog, Olivia could see him zigzagging across the meadow. The sliver of moon sparked against the edge of his home-made silver knife, then he would disappear in the fog again. She could hear him. Stumbling and cussing. Clumsy like a Dark Eye.

"Little Thing, . . . ohhhhhh, Little Thiiiiing. I know you didn't go far." Flinch scrambled with an urgent, angry gait.

Olivia stepped silently around the stallions. Their breathing, warmed by embers deep in their chests, turned to mist when it left their nostrils and mixed into the night. It was almost as if the horses themselves were manufacturing the fog. Flinch surprised her one time, only a few steps away, slashing his knife blindly through the air. But Olivia stood still as only she and bears knew how and he moved on, chasing other ghosts. They circled each other in the meadow. As every minute passed Flinch grew angrier and more afraid.

A breeze picked up the fog and swept it over the mountain peaks. The moon was suddenly free from its foggy curtain. Olivia hid behind a silver mare.

"Ya, YA!" Flinch called out as he jumped up and down. The wild horses scattered and ran off down the mountain slope. Olivia was wide open. "There you are, Little Thing. There you are."

He leaped across the meadow like a madman. Olivia sprinted behind a large rock, but the meadow ended in a plunging gorge. Sharp, black rock dropped away endlessly below her. She was trapped. Olivia stumbled onto the ground as he stood over her. For some reason, she noticed all of the details around her now. How beautiful the world was. She remembered how the dew felt in fresh grass. How even the tiniest of breezes could awaken something within. Every tiny wildflower was shut into tiny bells or purses until morning, waiting for sunrise to open their petals like lighthouses for bees. What a sight they had been in the full sun, swaying in the colorful light!

"See this?" Flinch rolled up a sleeve. His arm had a line of scars that looked like tallies. There were so many Olivia couldn't count them. "I keep track of the poor unfortunates that I have killed." He dragged his knife across his arm. A crimson streak of blood appeared as though it came from the blade itself, and trickled down his hand onto the grass. Flinch inhaled loudly. "That one is special, maybe more special than my first. That one is for you, Little Thing. I will never forget you."

Flinch's eyes were blank and dark, erasing what little light existed from the night sky. "There is no more running. There are no more magic tricks. It is too bad you will never see your mother and father again. I will

personally tell them the news. I promise."

"You . . . you know where they are?"

"Of course!" Flinch's laughter rung out.

"Where? What happened?"

"I suppose I can tell you, since you will be dead. It was quite ingenious really, a masterpiece." Flinch suddenly looked pale, almost sickly. "What's happening!?" he called out, spinning wildly around. He lashed out into the night with his knife. "Who's there?" The knife fell through his hand and hit the ground. He looked at his hand. It was blurring, turning to dust, and blowing away. He was settling out of existence in front of Olivia's eyes.

"Wait! Wait! Tell me? Where are they?" Olivia screamed.

With a whimpering screech, Flinch popped into a fizzing cascade of green sparks. He was gone.

"It's over," Olivia whispered. "It's over." She reached into her pocket. In her hand sat two perfectly formed crystals. Within seconds, she felt the pull of the neutrino wind twinning her back to the tetracomb.

***

A large white cargo van parked along a lonely dirt road in a nameless desert. Cardboard was duct-taped over the back windows. Near the van the entire Ganado and Yazzi families surrounded Olivia and the Milligans. One by one, Olivia hugged everyone. She was going to really miss the Hohokam valley. She knew that once they drove through the secret exit, they would easily be able to get back in. But even though she would be allowed back whenever she wished, she somehow knew it would be a long time. Part of her felt like she had let everyone down because she allowed

Virosa to take the Pearl. But no one seemed angry with her. When it came to the Pearl, everyone trusted her completely. Part of her was relieved that the running and hiding was over. She was sick of being the Guardian even though she could still hear its chiming in her heart.

Amythie Yazzi sobbed on her husband's shoulder. "You have her co-ordinates right? So we can visit her? You have her coordinates?"

"Yes, I'm sure of it," Dr. Yazzi consoled her.

"Bless you for taking care of Olivia." Aunt rubbed Amythie's back. "We are forever indebted to you. You will always be family."

Olivia ran out of hugs. Only two more people remained. Terrilyne and Chubascos stood shoulder to shoulder next to the van. Olivia took a step toward them. Tears ran down her face. Terrilyne was so nervous and excited, she was bouncing up and down. A gigantic smile crossed her face. Terrilyne and Chubascos stepped aside, revealing two suitcases sitting on the ground.

"What? . . . What?" Olivia asked.

Terrilyne couldn't stop jumping. "We . . . are . . . going . . . with you!" She let out a squeal that echoed across the desert.

Olivia ran and tackled both of them to the ground. They all landed into a pile of laughter.

"For one year," Dr. Yazzi said. "I suggested the new law, so it is only natural my daughter and nephew be first to go."

Uncle snatched up the two suitcases and crammed them into the back. After more hugs and tears, Olivia jumped into the van. She scrambled over the seat and landed on top of Hoolie, curled up in the back.

"It's going to be waaaay easier crossing America this time, Hoolie," she said, giving him a gigantic hug.

"I've never ridden in a car before," Terrilyne said, sliding onto the seat.

"I'm not afraid," Chubascos said.

"Gimme Squirt. I want to hold him." Aunt handed back a plastic container filled with water. Squirt flushed pink and let out a loud squeak.

"Everyone buckle up. We have a long drive ahead of us," Uncle announced and started the engine.

"First chance we get, we're stopping to get a rocket pop," Terrylyne said.

"Peeyuuuu. Your bear stinks," Chubascos said as the door slid shut.

"He ate too much fry bread, I guess," Olivia answered.

The white van drove off. Within seconds, someone rolled a window down, letting in the fresh desert air.

Here are some other books from Pineapple Press on related topics. For a complete catalog, visit our website at www.pineapplepress.com. Or write to Pineapple Press, P.O. Box 3889, Sarasota, Florida 34230-3889, or call (800) 746-3275.

Fiction

A Land Remembered, Student Edition by Patrick Smith. The sweeping story of three generations of MacIveys, who work their way up from a dirt-poor Cracker life to the wealth and standing of real estate tycoons. Volume 1 covers the first generation of MacIveys to arrive in Florida and Zech's coming of age. Volume 2 covers Zech's son, Solomon, and the exploitation of the land as his own generation prospers. Age 9 and up.

Blood Moon Rider by Zack C. Waters. When his Marine father is killed in WWII, young Harley Wallace is exiled to the Florida cattle ranch of his grandfather. The murder of a cowman and the disappearance of Grandfather Wallace lead Harley and his new friend Beth on a wild ride through the swamps and into the midst of a conspiracy of evil. Ages 9–14.

Escape to the Everglades by Edwina Raffa and Annelle Rigsby. Based on historical fact, this young adult novel tells the story of Will Cypress, a half-Seminole boy living among his mother's people during the Second Seminole War. He meets Chief Osceola and travels with him to St. Augustine. Ages 9–14.

Solomon by Marilyn Bishop Shaw. Eleven-year-old Solomon Freeman and his parents, Moses and Lela, survive the Civil War, gain their freedom, and gamble their dreams, risking their very existence on a homestead in the remote environs of north central Florida. Ages 9–14.

Kidnapped in Key West by Edwina Raffa and Annelle Rigsby. Twelve-year-old Eddie Malone is living in the Florida Keys in 1912 when suddenly his world is turned upside down. His father, a worker on Henry Flagler's Over-Sea Railroad, is thrown into jail for stealing the railroad payroll. Eddie is determined to prove his father's innocence. But then the real thieves kidnap Eddie. Can he escape? Will he ever get home? Will he be able to prove Pa's innocence? Ages 8–12.

The Treasure of Amelia Island by M.C. Finotti. These are the ruminations of Mary Kingsley, the youngest child of former slave Ana Jai Kingsley, as she recounts the life-changing events of December 1813. Her family lives in *La Florida,* a Spanish territory under siege by patriots who see no place for freed people of color in a new Florida. Against these mighty events, Mary decides to search for a legendary pirate treasure with her brothers. Ages 8–12.

The Spy Who Came In from the Sea by Peggy Nolan. In 1943 fourteen-year-old Frank Holleran sees an enemy spy land on Jacksonville Beach. First Frank needs to get people to believe him, and then he needs to stop the spy from carrying out his dangerous plans. Winner of the Sunshine State Young Reader's Award. Ages 8–12.

Esmeralda and the Enchanted Pond by Susan Jane Ryan. Esmeralda visits a mysterious pond with her dad. While she wants real, scientific explanations for the natural phenomena all around her, her dad offers imaginary, mystical answers. Much to her delight, he finally reveals the science behind the enchanted pond. Ages 8–11.

The Old Man and the C by Carole Tremblay. Meet Charlie, whose dream is to catch the biggest fish in the sea. He signs up for a fishing tournament, but what he catches is a big surprise. Unlike Hemingway's hero, Charlie turns his quest for a big fish into an amusing adventure that involves a bad case of the hiccups. Ages 6–10.

Nonfiction
Those Amazing Animals series. Written by various authors, each book in the series offers 20 questions and answers sure to engage children and teach them about animals such as alligators, owls, turtles, eagles, pelicans, butterflies, manatees, dolphins, flamingos, vultures, and lizards. Lots of color pictures and funny illustrations. Ages 5–9.

America's REAL First Thanksgiving by Robyn Gioia. When most Americans think of the first Thanksgiving, they think of the Pilgrims and the Indians in New England in 1621. But on September 8, 1565, the Spanish and the native Timucua celebrated with a feast of Thanksgiving in St. Augustine. Teacher's activity guide also available. Ages 9–14.

The Young Naturalist's Guide to Florida, Second Edition by Peggy Sias Lantz and Wendy A. Hale. Provides up-to-date information about Florida's wonderful natural places and the plants and creatures that live here, many of which are found nowhere else in the United States. Learn about careers in the environmental field and how to help protect Florida's beautiful places. Ages 10–14.

Florida Lighthouses for Kids by Elinor De Wire. Learn why some lighthouses are tall and some are short, why a cat parachuted off St. Augustine Lighthouse, and much more. Lots of color pictures. Age 9 and up.

Native Americans in Florida by Kevin M. McCarthy. Long before the first European explorers set foot on Florida soil, numerous Native American tribes hunted, honored their gods, and built burial mounds. This book explores the importance of preserving the past and how archaeologists do their work. The different types of Indian mounds and their uses are explained, as well as Indian languages and reservations. Age 10 and up.

African Americans in Florida by Maxine D. Jones and Kevin McCarthy. Profiles more than fifty African Americans during four centuries of Florida history in brief essays. Traces the role African Americans played in the discovery, exploration, and settlement of Florida as well as through the Civil War to the Civil Rights movement. Age 10 and up.

Legends of the Seminoles by Betty Mae Jumper with Peter Gallagher. For the first time, stories and legends handed down through generations by tribal elders have been set down for all to enjoy. Each tale is illustrated with an original color painting. All ages.

Hunted Like a Wolf: The Story of the Seminole War by Milton Meltzer. Award-winning young adult book that offers a look at the events, players, and political motives leading to the Second Seminole War. It explores the Seminoles' choices and sacrifices and the treachery of the U.S. during that harsh time. Age 12 and up.

Iguana Invasion!: Exotic Pets Gone Wild in Florida by Virginia Aronson and Allyn Szejko. Green iguanas, Burmese pythons, Nile monitor lizards, rhesus monkeys, and many more kinds of nonnative animals are rapidly increasing their populations in subtropical Florida. This full-color book provides scientific information, exciting wildlife stories, and identification photos for the most common exotic animals on the loose, most of them the offspring of abandoned pets. Age 12 and up.

The Gopher Tortoise: A Life History by Patricia Ashton and Ray Ashton Jr. Color photos and simple text illustrate the behavior and daily life of this endangered animal. Explains the critical role this tortoise and its burrow play in the upland ecosystem of Florida and the Southeast. Learn how scientists study them and try to protect them. Age 10 and up.